A Per
Plar

FERNANDO GRAJEDA

DEDICATION

This book is dedicated to all the warriors around the world who have fought against a terminal disease, and in turn have come to appreciate the great gift of living.

ACKNOWLEDGMENTS

I would like to thank my parents Fernando and Blanquita for their constant support in my many adventures including this book; my sisters Lucía and Gabriela for being my best friends and for believing in me; my cousin Lisa for always picking me up when I'm down; and finally, I would like to thank my friends Lesley and Chuck for supporting me and helping me make this dream come true.

INTRODUCTION

We may face unexpected events in our lives which may take us out of our comfort zone. These events may scare us and, it is very likely that we will blame God for it, whether we believe in Him or not. This is because we are just too close minded to realise that a disease, the breaking up with someone whom we have loved with all of our hearts, losing a loved one through an unexpected death, being sacked from a job we have been doing for years or to be sunk in financial debt, can be some of the many forms which God can use to talk directly to us.

We can choose to face these events with the right attitude by reflecting on why this may be happening in our lives and by giving it a purpose. We may choose to take this attitude and see the positive side of things from each situation we live or we can very easily give up and quit. It is also our choice to remain tied to the sad memories and negative situations which have left a mark in our lives, and therefore continue to live an unhappy and frustrated life. Even if we may not be conscious about it, God has a plan for each of us and He speaks to us through signs and events which we may not understand at the time or even worse, which we may decide to ignore.

This is the story of Andrés de la Vega, a young Guatemalan man who at the age of 18 decides to leave his home. He feels ashamed of his own family and believes that by leaving Guatemala he will be escaping from a reality he didn't want to live in. Helped by someone who harmed his father many years ago, he chooses to move to England with the hope of becoming someone successful. He studies his University degree and then turns into a high-flyer in the City of London.

Anyone who sees Andrés could think that he is a man who has everything anyone could have ever desired. He has a job in the City which makes him earn lots of money. He has been able to generate a fortune he could have never imagined in his wildest dreams. He travels to all of the financial capitals of the world. At the age of 28, he owns his own flat in Richmond —a very exclusive neighbourhood on the outside of London— and drives an Aston Martin. Such a professional like him, dresses with the most stylish and expensive suits in the world. He is a man who was everything under control and who lives by his own rules.

However, one day while staring at himself in the mirror, he realises that there is something wrong with his body. He observes a little lump in one of his testicles. He is terrified. He experiences a possible disease he never thought could happen to him. At this point, he becomes aware of his loneliness. No matters how much money he may have, he is alone and feeling empty. In the last ten years of his life he avoided any contact with his family. He fell in love with a girl, but the idea of sacrificing a professional move to New York City, made him end this relationship. He left her out of his life without notice.

Having to face his own mortality makes him feel vulnerable. In this moment the image of the one person who he felt strongly connected to, comes to his mind. It was his grandmother who passed away when he was 12 years old. Moved by the memory of this woman in his life, he feels the need to be close to her. Without thinking about it and with no agenda to stick to, he makes an irrational decision and decides to travel to the place he never thought he would go back to: Guatemala.

It is during this trip that Andrés gets to experience situations he had never been close to living. Without wanting it, he leaves his comfort zone which exposes him to many events, people, emotions and feelings which start making him question his priorities in life. During this adventure, Andrés learns the real important things which make him feel alive and makes a personal commitment to change, but will he have enough time to see it through?

This is a book that seeks to give the reader the tools to face any unexpected event which may put in danger one's earthly experience. It is a story that seeks to demonstrate that material wealth is not always the answer to true happiness, as our current hedonistic society tries to convince us of. Moreover, it is a story which tries to show how surrendering our lives to God and accepting things as they come: being positive or negative events that can occur; at the end it all happens for a reason.

I hope that this book helps the reader be grateful for the opportunity to live his or her life. To be grateful to experience a sunrise, for every time we can stare at the stars and for every hug we can give and receive from the people we love.

It is my only wish, that after reading this book, readers will be able to enjoy their lives to the maximum and that we can share an ideal based on the thought that together, as one unit, we can be a light in a world that has been shocked by an economic and social crisis in the last few years, a crisis which has left many people in despair and which also caused many to lose their faith in humanity and in their own spirituality.

Finally, I would like readers to become aware through this simply story of love, that God has "a perfect plan" for each of us.

CHAPTER I

An alarm clock starts sounding, simulating the sound of church bells ringing. It is only 4:30 in the morning. As usual, Andrés de la Vega only allows one tone to be heard and one minute after he is preparing himself to leave his flat in Richmond —located in West London— and heads towards the park where he runs 10 kilometres religiously every morning.

There is only one day in which he doesn't run, and that is on Sundays. Ever since he was a little boy, Sunday for him represented a day in which he allowed himself to break from the routine of the week. Even though he left Guatemala about ten years ago, he got stuck with the tradition of making Sunday the only day he could relax.

At 4:33am, Andrés puts on his running shoes and all the running accessories including his iPod and leaves the flat. After finishing his run, he returns home and takes a shower at exactly 5:30am. At 5:40am he suits up and goes out to work. Every day, he wears a black designer suit, white shirt and black tie, which make him look like a classy undertaker.

He has always believed that dressing like this every day reflects elegance, self-confidence and above all, power. He doesn't dress like this because he has no more suits or shirts. On the contrary, Andrés is a City boy, director at the age of 28 of a financial boutique firm in the heart of London's financial centre, with a six digit salary plus his annual bonus. It is for these reasons that he wears the same style of clothes day in and day out. Because he firmly believes that dressing in such way reflects how successful he is to others.

Andrés has 13 black suits —all Armani—, 25 white shirts and 10 Italian black ties. All of these are exactly the same. No one has ever seen Andrés wearing a different suit, tie or shirt which aren't black and white.

Back to his routine. At 5:50am, he catches the train to Waterloo at Richmond station. On the way to the station, he always buys a ham and cheese croissant and a skimmed milk latte at his favourite French organic shop.

During his journey from Richmond to Waterloo he never stops playing with his Blackberry for a single second. He reads the Financial Times, catches up with his emails and plans the strategy on how to make more money that day.

He arrives at Waterloo Station at 6:15am and walks for 20 minutes to his office located in Cheapside Street, very close to Bank Station, in the heart of the City of London. Even if he is able to ride the tube from Waterloo to Bank Station, ever since he got promoted to director two years ago, he still prefers to walk or take a taxi to get to his office. It doesn't matter if it is rainy or grey. He prefers to walk than to smell the beggars in the tube, or to hear the yells of a baby crying because he is hungry, or to listen to a student blasting his iPod with electronic music. Andrés considers himself at a higher level than the ordinary Londoner, and that is why he prefers to avoid these common encounters.

He always gets to his office before 6:35am. Taking the lift, he gets nervous as he gets closer to the reception of his firm, which is located on the tenth floor of the building. Upon arrival, he looks down to the floor to avoid any eye contact with people there.

Every time Andrés comes in, his colleagues feel uncomfortable. However, there is always the new guy who trying to make a good impression on him, generally yells out loud from his tiny desk: "good morning, Andrés", expecting to be the "chosen one" who will receive a response from him. As usual, all he gets is an ever deeper silence than the one there was before Andrés made his appearance at the office.

All the people working with Andrés are afraid of him. And some have even come to hate him. On one occasion, he forced Tom —an older colleague— to come to work during the day his wife was giving birth to his first child. It was a Friday morning and with the financial markets still closed, Tom arrived very excited to the office to share his joy with everyone. His mates bought coffee and croissants from a nearby shop to celebrate the good news. Andrés wasn't there when this celebration started. Once he got to the office floor and saw what has happening, he turned to Tom and asked him to meet him at his office immediately.

—Excuse me, Tom. What the hell is this ridiculous celebration for? —shouted Andrés washing away the sweat that was dropping down his face as a result of the anger he was feeling at that moment.

—Well… eehh… uhmmm —Tom got so nervous at Andrés' reaction that he even forgot for a second why they were holding this celebration —. It's just that… today is the day… that… I… will become a father for the first time! —he said with excitement and with tears in his eyes.

—Do you really think that the fact that you will be a father will have any impact on the profits that we need to make today? Do you think that this is a good enough reason to have a stupid celebration and to make your colleagues waste their time?

As Andrés was uttering the last word, he turned his back to Tom and put his right hand on his desk. The first thing his hand found was a golf ball. He picked it up and started playing around with it keeping his eyes fixed on the majestic Saint Paul's Cathedral which he could appreciate from his desk.

Tom was very confused by what he had just heard. After all the sacrifices he and all his colleagues had done to please Andrés through the years, he didn't allow them to have a simple celebration? "What a bastard", Tom thought. He just couldn't believe what was going on.

Tom left Andrés' office with reddened eyes as he was trying to control some tears from falling because of the anger he felt deep inside. His mates didn't even ask him what had happened, as his expression said it all. The rich slaves of the XXI century decided to put an end to their brief celebration and continued working on the money machine to please their masters.

No one could believe Andrés' attitude towards life. They couldn't understand how there could be someone as bitter and ambitious as he was. However, for Richard Stephens —Andrés' boss— it was these qualities which made Andrés generate more wealth for him and his company. And this was why Richard was the only one able to put up with him in this place.

CHAPTER II

To get to the financial and professional position that Andrés had achieved at such a young age and in such a competitive city as London, wasn't an easy task though. He was raised in a Guatemalan middle class family. His father, *don* Rafael, worked in a family owned accounting business that Andrés' grandfather founded in the 1950s. His mother, *doña* Margarita, was a devoted housewife who had always looked after her children, house and husband. His sister —Mariela— was four years older than him and they never had a close relationship. Ever since he was a kid, everyone at home feared him because of his lonesome and rebellious character.

He had always been independent and meticulous with his way of doing things. At home, whenever he had a tantrum attack, everyone tried not to get in his way as they feared his reaction. His parents never took the time to really understand him. The slightest whim the kid had, they simply tried to please it and ignore it as they feared his reaction if they didn't fall into his trap. The only woman who was able to touch his heart and who really broke that barrier he built with people around him was his loving grandmother Anita.

As a kid, Andrés used to spend all of summer holidays at his grandmother's house. This happened every year until she passed away. *Doña* Anita —*don* Rafael's mother— lived in a very old house on the outskirts of Guatemala City. This one storey Spanish colonial house was built around a square space. It included six bedrooms, one living room and an enormous dining room. In the middle of the house, there was a magnificent fountain which was surrounded by a garden full of sunflowers and jasmines. To *doña* Anita, the garden was the source of life and energy in her life. As a kid, and even as an adult, Andrés never understood why she used to say that flowers, trees or even a sunset were the real joys of life. Even if he saw her full of life and happiness, he could never understand how these simple things could make her feel so happy. She was a wise and simple woman.

Doña Anita was the only person who wasn't afraid of Andrés. She kind of related to him, as she also had a strong character. She was the only person who didn't consent his whims. During the three month period which she would get to share with her grandson, she taught him how to mow the lawn and how to take care of sunflowers and jasmines. Andrés —without realising it— felt free and felt himself when he was around his grandmother.

On the last day of his school holidays —when he was just 12 years old— he was running around the garden and at some point he got trapped with his loose shoe lace and fell down to the ground. He hit his knee, but he cried bitterly as if he had broken it. When *doña* Anita heard his sobs, she ran to see what had happened. What she got to see when approaching him broke her heart. She saw her grandson crying as if he had lost the person he loved the most. She then understood that Andrés wasn't crying because of the pain he was feeling, but because of the pain it meant to leave her once again. It really hurt him to be away from her and from that house in which he felt freedom to be whom he really was.

Once she knelt next to him, Andrés felt her presence so close to him that he hugged her as hard as he could. Even though they didn't talk while they shared this moment, she knew that he was saying "I will miss you, grandma". She was a bit surprised at Andrés' intense emotions, but she simply hugged him, kissed him and told him that everything was going to be OK. They both walked back into the house, and as they got in, his grandmother started playing an Edith Piaf record on her old record player and asked him to dance with her. As they were holding hands swinging smoothly from one side to another, doña Anita said:

—My dear Andrés, you are a very special and unique young boy.

Andrés didn't quite understand why she was saying this to him, but decided to listen to her closely with his eyes locked on hers. He had this weird and unexplainable feeling that this would be the last time he was going to be able to see those beautiful black eyes. She continued:

—Remember that you are the only one who can decide what will become of your life. Your father, your mother or even I, can't decide what's best for you. You are the only one who has that answer, Andrés. Never stop dreaming and working hard to achieve your dreams and be the man you want to be.

Andrés couldn't hold back and a tear rolled down his cheek. He hugged her stronger than ever. Doña Anita wrapped her arms around him and concluded this conversation by saying:

—I'll always be here with you, and I want you to know that I love you with all my heart.

The music stopped. Grandmother and grandson stopped dancing in the middle of the living room and a few minutes later, Andrés' parents arrived there to pick him up. Andrés said good bye to his grandma. He winked one of his eyes and then kissed and hugged her once again.

It could be that doña Anita and Andrés both knew what would happen later, so they lived this simple moment very intensely together. The next morning doña Anita didn't wake up. During her sleep she had a stroke and died without feeling any pain.

Andrés' life was never the same after that sad day. When he was 12, Andrés turned into an even lonelier kid, and as the years went by he turned into a more rebellious and bitter teenager. Five years after his grandmother's death when he was studying his last year of high school, he told his father that he was going to leave Guatemala to study abroad, no matter how or when, but he was determined to do so. His father, who always dreamed of having a close relationship with his son, simply said:

—Son, as a father I want you to succeed —he said fearing his son's reaction to his words —and even if it may be very difficult for me to afford the life you wish to live, I ask you not to let your dreams be taken away from you because of money obstacles.

As a result of this conversation, Andrés promised himself two things: the first one was that he would leave his country as soon as possible and the second one was that he didn't want to become a failure like his old man.

Soon after graduating from high school and turning 18, he knew it was time to start making things happen. One night, as the family sat down to eat dinner together, *don* Rafael, as it was usual for him, started to ask questions to everyone at the table in an attempt to start a casual conversation. Dona Margarita mentioned that she had heard from a friend that Andrés' uncle —*don* Rafael's brother— had bought a beach house in Miami. Once she slipped those words away, the atmosphere around the table turned extremely tense and *don* Rafael stood up and left the table as if someone had offended him.

Andrés' father reacted in this way, because he had a broken relationship with his brother Jose Roberto soon after their mother's death. As with most Latin American families there had been family issues with the inheritance left by *doña* Anita. *Don* Jose Roberto —a well-known lawyer in Guatemala City— had managed to deprive his brother from the assets he was entitled to. *Don* Jose Roberto sold the country house where she had spent her last years of her life and the place where Andrés used to spend his summer holidays. He used the profits from the sale to re-invest it in his law firm. In the meantime, *don* Rafael continued to live a simple life as an accountant at the small firm his father had founded.

When Andrés heard about the fact that his uncle had been able to purchase a house in Miami, he knew there was something he could do with it. "If my uncle, a real bastard, has so much money that he has been able to afford a beach house in Miami, perhaps he could lend me some money to study abroad?" He thought. He didn't mind what could happen if his Machiavellian plan could give the results he expected. It was clear to Andrés that he didn't want to end up like his father and if there was someone successful in his family, why not make use of him? He remembered a saying by Machiavelli which said that "the end justifies the means".

One afternoon, Andrés visited his uncle's law firm without anyone knowing about it, including his uncle. When he arrived at the office, located in a very exclusive area in Guatemala City, he told the receptionist that he was there to see *don* Roberto. She asked him who he was, and he proudly said, puffing out his chest and standing very straight and tall: "his nephew".

Don Jose Roberto wasn't expecting any visitors that afternoon but as he was busy he told his receptionist to let the visitor in, without exactly knowing who Andrés was. The moment that he stepped into his uncle's office, *don* Jose Roberto was on the phone, but as he saw his nephew turned into a man now, he dropped the phone, stood up from the chair and walked slowly to where Andrés was standing. It had been six years since they had seen each other, and *don* Jose Roberto who felt some sort of remorse, simply hugged him.

Andrés didn't know how to react to this gesture. He knew his uncle was a bastard and had screwed his father with their mother's inheritance, but to him, he was an opportunity to achieve his goal. Unwillingly, he put his arms around his uncle for a split of a second and then let go. However, *don* Jose Roberto couldn't separate himself from Andrés, and suddenly he whispered in his ear: "please, forgive me brother".

Andrés knew that these words put his uncle on the position he was hoping to get him to. He fully perceived his uncle's guilt towards his father. He didn't care. He knew that without needing to say a single word, his uncle was in the position he wanted him to be: he was entirely vulnerable now.

The young man sat down and without giving any opportunity for any idle chatter, he said:

—Uncle, you really screwed my dad when grandma died.

Don Jose Roberto was speechless to hear his nephew speak with so much conviction. He was trying to find words that would allow him to defend himself, but he just didn't know what to say back. He was aware he had been a real bastard. Andrés continued:

—You can't imagine the suffering that my mediocre father went through. You took away from him the only chance he had of having a bit of money. And he wasn't the only one who lost in it. My mother, my sister and myself suffered from it as well.

His uncle didn't know what to say. As a lawyer with more than 40 years of experience, no one had ever intimidated him as this 18 year old kid had. Andrés was showing so much conviction and self-confidence that even *don* Jose Roberto felt threatened by him. Without any possibility to say something back, Andrés continued:

—If you want to make up for what you did to us, I would like to make a deal with you.

Don Jose Roberto was so puzzled by all of what he was hearing that he didn't know what to make of it. He simply answered in a brittle voice:

—What? —he paused—. How can I help your father?

Andrés fixed his eyes on his uncle's before he could turn his face away and replied:

—This deal has nothing to do with my father. It has to do with me. Help me leave this shit country for good. Help me get out of here. Grandma always told me to fight for my dreams, and here I am asking you to make this come true. I want to leave behind this reality and this mediocre family of mine.

For a moment, *don* Jose Roberto didn't understand what his nephew was saying. He couldn't understand how Andrés was able to make him feel so guilty and one second later he was calling his family a "mediocre" one and was trying to reach a deal by asking him to help him leave the country.

Don Jose Roberto decided to ignore what had happened in the last five minutes and what he had whispered to Andrés' ears. He wanted to hide the uneasiness he had experienced with this 18 year old boy and got back to being himself again by turning into a bastard. He loosened the knot of his tie and unbuttoned the top of his shirt, and in a very calm voice he said:

—If your dream is to leave this country and leave your family behind, then I can help you. Do you now understand why I did what I did? Do you? —*don* Jose Robert said trying to feel good about himself.

Without hesitation Andrés answered:

—Yeah. I perfectly understand. I would have done the same if I had been you.

Don Jose Roberto, now feeling comfortable with the situation, tried to behave as if he was Andrés' pal, and asked him:

—Where do you see yourself living, my dear Andrés?

After hearing these fake words, Andrés got a bit annoyed and replied:

—Come on, man! We're not "buddies", OK? So don't try to come with this 'dear Andrés' bullshit, all right?

Don Jose Roberto simply smiled. He even felt proud to see that this kid was very smart and that that he didn't like the bullshit. Andrés continued:

—Anyway, coming back to the topic which is of relevance to us. I have considered going somewhere in Europe as most of the people here in Guatemala emigrate to the US, and the least I want is to go there and deal with the whole "illegal immigrant" prejudice they have over there. That's why I think that England, and especially London, is the place where I can study my university degree and hopefully become a successful professional.

As he finished saying this, *don* Jose Roberto was amazed by the determination of his nephew. He told Andrés that he was going to help him leave Guatemala under one condition only: if he was to be accepted in a university and was able to complete his studies, he wouldn't come back home. Andrés accepted this condition and promised to not come back if he was to be successful in London. His uncle also asked him not to say anything back at home until everything was set in stone.

Five months after that conversation, on a sunny August morning, Andrés was catching a flight to London. He was leaving behind his country, his family and a few broken hearts, especially that of his own father. *Don* Rafael got to know about the deal between his son and his brother. He felt betrayed by both of them, but it hurt him the most that his own son had done something like this to him. At the departure gate at the airport, Andrés didn't shed one single tear. And this broke his father's heart even more. The issues with the inheritance were nothing compared to the misery of seeing his son leave, without feeling any remorse. After saying goodbye at the airport, Andrés decided to leave all behind —family included— and to begin the path to success he had always desired.

CHAPTER III

During the first 18 years of his life, Andrés had only been able to travel to Miami in the United States. This trip happened when he was 13 years old, and it was soon after his grandmother had passed away. His parents thought that it would be a good idea for them to take their kids to Disney World in order to ease their pain after such a big loss in their lives. Andrés has no recollection of those days he travelled with his parents. The only thing he remembered was one occasion when he asked his father for some money to buy an ice-cream but he didn't get it.

This was the reason why the journey of nearly 16 hours to London with a stopover in New York City, was an important event for him. He felt liberated. He was anxious to take over the world. He neither regretted leaving his family nor his country. On the contrary, his excitement at this new adventure increased even more as the aircraft was leaving the Guatemalan air space. When the plane landed at JFK, in New York, he knew his life was about to take a turn he had never imagined.

As he was waiting at the gate for his flight to London, he was able to see people from all over the world. Something which he had never experienced in his life before. He was surprised to see a group of Jewish people wearing their traditional suits, with big hats and their curls falling over their ears. He also saw a group of Japanese tourists who were showing pictures from their travels to each other. During the two hours he had to wait for his flight, he was able to hear about twenty different languages. He noticed a few very elegant men wearing stylish suits —and even if he had no fashion knowledge whatsoever— he knew those were expensive suits. He wished to be one of those "elegant gentlemen" as he referred to them.

He was feeling a bit overwhelmed to see so many people from different places and to hear different languages being spoken close to where he was sitting and waiting. Andrés felt intimidated by all of this. His self-confidence was threatened for the first time. For around ten minutes, he feared what could happen with his life. He felt vulnerable as he started wondering what would happen to him in this new place he was going to be living at. "Who is going to be there for me in case I need some help? Who is going to be there to cook for me? Who is going to be there to take care of me?" He doubted himself for what he was doing. He doubted if leaving the comfort of living with his parents was the best decision for him. However, after ten minutes of letting fear consume him, he told himself: "I'm leaving home because my parents are not people I admire. This is my life, and I will live it under my own terms and conditions". Perhaps these were the last ten minutes Andrés actually experienced fear and uncertainty in his life. After these ten minutes, his life would be controlled by him and no one else.

Andrés finally landed to Heathrow Airport after 16 exhausting hours between aircrafts and airports. When he was coming out of the plane, he drew a cheeky smile on his face and felt ready to conquer the city. He had convinced himself that he was about to start a new life, and that it was time to forget his past. From that day on, he didn't permit himself to think about his parents or his sister. He only allowed himself to remember his grandmother and no one else.

After leaving the airport he took a cab and asked the driver to take him to his new home: the dormitories of his university which were close to the Strand in central London. Andrés made sure that he was going to get a single room, as he wasn't willing to waste any time interacting with people, and more importantly, he wasn't willing to share a space to live in with anyone. As the cab driver was approaching the dormitories, he said in a very strong Liverpoolian accent: "it's 35 quid, kid". Andrés didn't understand the words the cab driver was saying. Worse of all, he had no idea of the worth of the British pound compared to the US Dollar. Without thinking, he took a 20 dollar note and handed it to the driver. The cab driver got impatient, and with an angry tone he said:

—Are you an idiot or what? This doesn't even cover half of the trip.

Terrified and confused, Andrés considered the possibility of running away, but he couldn't because he had to carry both pieces of luggage he had with him. He froze for a second and suddenly he forgot the little English he thought he could speak. He then took his wallet out again and taking all the cash he had with him, threw 90 dollars to the driver. As Andrés was about to take his second luggage out of the cab, the driver took off. While he was driving away he managed to scream and laugh out loud at the same time:

—It is because of idiots like you that we become rich in this country!

That first encounter with a new reality he was about to live, made him promise himself one thing: this would be the first and last time that someone would make a fool of him.

Ever since he decided to leave, Andrés was clear of one thing and one thing only: he wanted to become a successful man and earn a lot of money. But back then he was a bit lost about how to make this happen. His father was never the best role model for him, and that's why he took another route and decided to study Economics and Finance. His logic told him that working with money would allow him to make more money. And he was right about it. From the first day at school, he became addicted to books, the library and to the world of finance. He was one of the few —or maybe the only one— who would not join his fellow classmates from university at the pub to drink some pints of beer. He would never miss a day of class because of a rough night at a club because he never went out. He was determined to study as hard as he could, to get good marks and to keep an updated view on what has happening in the world financial markets. To him, this was the ideal formula to achieve his goal: to get a job which could let him live the life of a "high-flyer".

The catharsis in Andrés' life took place during his second year of university when an English guy, who was about 30 years old and who was a former student at his university, came to give a speech about his experience working in the financial district of the City of London. His name was James Terrence. He was wearing a black Armani suit, a white shirt and a black tie. Every word that this young man was saying was charged with so much energy that the whole auditorium was magnetised by him. His posture and his self-confidence made all the students feel as if they were listening to Tony Blair himself. James was telling students that he worked as a Mergers & Acquisitions manager in one of the biggest investment banks in the UK. He openly shared with them, how his main driver and motivation of making money had allowed him to amass a large wealth in a short time. He told them that there were crazy hours involved, between 12 to 14 hours a day, that pressure could get out of control often and that the biggest risk of working in the financial sector was to acknowledge that your personal and social life could be non-existent. However, he told them that every February —when bonuses were given— all of these factors were forgotten. And to top it all, he ended his speech by sharing with these kids that his annual bonus could be of up to 300% of his base salary. Everyone in the auditorium felt energised by this young man.

Andrés left university that day feeling as if he had discovered the Holy Grail. He saw in James Terrence —from his way of speaking to his dressing style— the role model he had always wished to have in his life. However, all the students were not aware that this "successful" man was leading a miserable life. His girlfriend —to whom he was close to getting married— had left him because he never had any time to be with her. Even if his bank account was loaded with money, he wasn't living it with a meaning as he had no one to share it with.

The days and nights spent at the library continued, and now that he had a clearer view on the route he needed to take, he was giving an even greater effort in his studies. His professors respected him a lot, because he showed what a great student he was, and because they could all see how confident this young man was about his own future. However, his classmates really hated him because he was a loner and overall, because he was selfish. Andrés preferred to work on his school projects by himself, even if it was meant to be worked as a group. He considered that all the other students were there to have a good time, and that he wasn't in a position to get lower marks because of them. He simply wanted to have everything under control.

Even if he showed confidence to his professors and some classmates, on the inside Andrés was a shy and insecure person. And this shyness affected his relationships with girls. Since the very first day at uni, he had a crush on an Australian girl —Sophia. She was blond, tall, and slim with beautiful blue eyes as clear as water. Occasionally, they exchanged looks with each other, but Sophia, being aware that Andrés wasn't willing to start a casual conversation —let alone ask her out— lost her patience and started dating another guy in their class. This marked the end to Andrés' "love stories" as a university student. By the end of his third year at school, his best and only mates were his books and financial magazines.

His determination, persistence and long hours of study were fruitful though. During his last year at university, he had the opportunity to do an internship at a very prestigious financial boutique house in London which was located on Cheapside Street, very close to Bank Station and just a few metres from the magnificent Saint Paul's Cathedral.

During his first day as an intern, he met his boss and —soon to be mentor— in the finance world. His name was Richard Stephens. He was an Englishman of about 45 years old. He was a workaholic who was devoted to making money and recently divorced for the third time. He was a person who would only talk about business and football. Ever since they met, Andrés started to see in Richard a paternal figure —just as he wished to have looked up to his own father.

The internship lasted for three months, and by the end of it, he managed to impress Richard so much because of his devotion to work and his ambition for money, that he was offered a full time job as an analyst. He started earning more money than any of his classmates and just when he was 22 years old, he felt he was on the right path which would lead him to acquire great material wealth, just as he had planned for.

CHAPTER IV

It was during the first week of work as a full time employee at this financial house, that Richard invited Andrés to have lunch in one of the oldest pubs in London, located on Fleet Street, pretty close to their office. Although Andrés had been living in London for a few years now, he hardly had been at a pub before, something unimaginable for anyone living in this city.

As soon as they sat down, Richard, a typical Englishman, ordered two pints of lager, one for him and for one Andrés. This young Guatemalan guy, who was 22 years old by then, had never drank a drop of alcohol before. He had always feared losing control of what was going on around him if he had one too many. Even if he was a very methodical and rigorous person, he allowed himself to make an exception this time. The simple fact that he was face to face with his boss and mentor made him very nervous. He thought that drinking one beer was going to be able to relax him a little. In that specific and important moment of his professional life, he decided to make an exception to one of his own rules, and for the first time he let himself be influenced by the English culture and by alcohol.

After drinking two pints of beer, Andrés started to experience dizziness, something he had never experimented before, not even as a teenager or as a university student. During the whole meal, Richard would not stop talking, and so Andrés was trying his best to not lose sight of what his boss was saying. After the third pint, he was dizzy and not only because of the effect of alcohol but because of Richard's non-stop monologue which he wasn't able to fully comprehend.

Andrés decided to keep on sipping his beer to relax even more, given that he had never felt that relaxing feeling. However, once he finished drinking his fifth pint, Andrés just stopped being himself. He didn't know what was happening around him. He was feeling dizzy and sick. He felt as if he was invisible. He felt as if he was a mere spectator of what was going on around him, and not a participant.

Everything in the pub was moving in slow motion for him. His head was spinning and he was feeling sicker. He felt like vomiting. In the meantime, Richard now wanted to prove that he was an intellectual as well. By this time Andrés felt the need to run to the toilet. As he was standing up from the table, he heard Richard saying that a Greek philosopher once said that "men who have never drank, did not know what it was to be alive". Andrés, who was standing up pretended to be interested in the phrase his boss had just recited for him, but this fake moment lasted less than 30 seconds. He just couldn't help it and ran to the toilet as if there was no tomorrow. Andrés threw up like he had never done in his life.

Andrés would never forget this experience and was grateful with Richard —obviously he never said a word to him— because he had learned a golden lesson of not to letting himself be controlled by alcohol. Andrés felt bad because of the hangover he experienced later that day but felt even worse for having lost control of what was going on around him. Andrés, being as smart as he was, decided to have only one pint of beer whenever he had to dine out with clients or colleagues. He was now aware that drinking was a big part of the English business culture, but he was determined not to go beyond his own limits.

As he started to live the life of a "high-flyer", he opted to make the office his new home. He would always get there just before 6:35am and finished his working day right about midnight. During his first year as an analyst in this financial firm, he earned his boss' respect but also a profound hatred by his colleagues. They saw him as an opportunistic suck up and a despicable human being who would do anything to get promoted, even if that meant stepping over someone else.

During his second year at the firm, his team was performing a valuation of a company they wanted to sell to a group of American investors. However, Andrés inflated the valuation price of the company, as he considered that the current volatile situation of the financial markets could still provide room for a bigger margin even if the increased price made no sense. Rahul —an older Indian colleague of his — suggested Andrés not to do this, as this was a very important negotiation for the firm and they had to make sure they reported the fair value of the company; but Andrés couldn't be bothered. Being as ambitious and stubborn as he was, he told Rahul to go to hell many times. The negotiation lasted almost three months and it included very long days and working overnights and weekends. This also created physical and mental stress which wore the team out by the end of the process. At the end, the American investors decided not to go ahead with the purchase as they felt that there was something wrong about the price that was being quoted by Andrés and his team. This meant a loss of almost 100 million pounds for the firm.

When Richard learned the bad news, he called Andrés and Rahul to his office. Richard was sitting in his leather chair staring out the window towards Saint Paul's Cathedral. Without looking at them, he asked:

—Have you heard that we missed the opportunity to earn about 100 million pounds?

Andrés and Rahul remained silent. Richard continued:

—I have also heard from your colleagues that there's a rumour going on that you inflated the selling price and that this prevented the Americans from purchasing the company. Is that true?

Without thinking twice and with Richard still not facing them, Andrés was the first one to talk and said:

—Yes, Richard. There was a big mistake when valuing the company.

Rahul was shocked by Andrés' attitude. He never thought he would hear these words coming out of Andrés' mouth in such a humble tone.

—The person who did this mistake is standing here, next to me — said Andrés without looking at his colleague.

—Rahul was amazed by this and shouted out loud:

—You have got to be kidding me, Andrés. That is not true! You know this better than anyone!

In a very calm way, Andrés looked at Rahul and then walked towards Richard's chair and without any hesitation and feeling determined, he said:

Richard, you very well know that even if I have only been in this firm for two years, I have made you over 50 million pounds in profit, whereas this guy, who has been with you for more than six years, and who calls himself a financial analyst, is only good at the administrative part of the deals that I usually bring to this place. Who do you think is telling the truth?

As Andrés finished saying this, Richard turned his chair to face them both. Rahul was pretty upset at what Andrés had just said, and as usual, Andrés wasn't showing any type of remorse. He was so determined to convince Richard that he was right, he even believed that the words he had uttered were the truth and nothing but the truth.

Richard approached Rahul, and asked him in a sober tone:

—Andrés has a point here, Rahul. Perhaps you did try to inflate the selling price, with the expectation that the Americans would agree to it. If this would have happened then you would have taken credit for it and that would have allowed you to get some respect from your colleagues and myself. If this deal would have gone through, perhaps you could have asked me for a promotion given that you've been stuck for the last couple of years. Could all of these things be a good enough reason to do something like this, Rahul?

Rahul felt insulted and humiliated by this. During his six years of work at the firm, he had never been accused of such a thing. He wasn't as ambitious as Andrés but he was an ethical person who deserved some respect. It was true that he hadn't generated that much money for the firm, but he worked according to his own principles and above all, because he felt he had to set an example for his children. Feeling so much anger which almost turned into tears, Rahul nervously said:

—Excuse me, Richard, but you know better than anyone how I work. If you actually want to convince yourself that what Andrés is saying is true, then let your own conscience decide.

In that moment, Rahul turned his head towards Andrés and stared at him with a penetrating look filled with hate and told him:

—If you want to be glorious all the time and you don't accept your own mistakes, you're digging your own grave, boy. Maybe you will get far, but you will remain alone.

Andrés couldn't care less about what his colleague had said to him. Rahul left the office, and that afternoon he sent an email to Richard with his resignation as he decided to quit his job at the firm.

As it was expected, Andrés became Richard's protégé after this situation with Rahul. Even though he never talked about it, Andrés knew he could not afford to do anything as stupid as he had done by inflating the price of any company ever again. He didn't really care about Rahul quitting his job, but he was worried that if there was another mistake, Richard would not be able to forgive him. Richard was no fool.

The years kept passing by and Andrés' career at the firm grew exponentially. He knew how to play his cards with clients and with the executives at other banks. He managed to build a very important network of contacts for his personal interests and that of his firm all around the world. He was well known in London, New York and Hong Kong. He started to travel frequently to these and other cities around the world in search of new business opportunities as he was aiming to expand the presence of Richard's firm. In no time, and as expected, he became the star of the business.

When he turned 28 years, he became the General Manager of the firm. Even if it was a small company, Andrés got to a point in which the only person above him in the corporate ladder was Richard himself. At such short age, a kid coming from an underdeveloped country, who had never imagined all that he had achieved and accumulated, now had turned into a vital element for the success of this firm, not only in the British market but around the globe. He had gained a reputation that only few were able to achieve.

His reputation as one of the most successful "high-flyers" in the City of London expanded outside of the financial world. As a result, he became a regular guest at many social, artistic and cultural events of the elite English society. Still a shy man, he now used his social and economic position as his presentation card. He was always dressed with the most expensive suits, owned a flat in a very exclusive area in the outskirts of London and drove a beautiful grey Aston Martin, which made him look even more attractive to the girls. But this hadn't even always the case.

When Andrés was 25 years old, he was still a virgin. At that age, he was quite curious about how he was going to live his first sexual experience. A lonely guy, fully devoted to his job resulted in him leading a very poor emotional life. However, by using his financial and social status, he decided to be a bit more daring with girls. On one business trip to New York City, he managed to settle a deal with an American counterpart. He managed to generate almost 40 million pounds in profits in one single handed operation. This was, without a doubt, the greatest achievement of his career. That night he decided to go out and celebrate in the streets of Manhattan. He went out by himself. That night, in a little bar in Soho, he decided to get drunk for the second time of his life. He ordered a bottle of the most expensive whiskey and started to drink alone. One girl was sitting at the bar right opposite to where he was. She stared at him for a while, and liked what she was seeing, so she decided to approach this loner.

—How come a handsome guy like you is drinking alone? —asked the girl with a sexy voice.

—Well, I'm simply celebrating that I'm the best in what I do — replied an arrogant Andrés.

—And what is it that you do? —asked again very intrigued.

—Money! —shouted Andrés —. That is exactly what I do. Lots of money.

Andrés had a beautiful girl in front of him. She was an American woman with Greek blood. Her tan was stunning, her curly hair went all the way down her sexy hips and her penetrating green eyes made him fall for her in a split of a second. Her name was Mia.

After drinking the whole bottle of whiskey between the two of them, they headed to the Waldorf Astoria Hotel, where Andrés was staying. He was drunk for the second time of his life, but this time he was being able to control what was going on around him a bit more. He was very clear that there was no chance of ending up with his head down the toilet as it had happened a few years back while drinking with Richard.

Once they made it to the room, Andrés started to kiss Mia with so much passion that she was astounded by the strength and lust of this stranger. Andrés, who at times remembered his failed love story at university, permitted himself to be carried away by the moment and saw in Mia the most beautiful woman he had ever been with —just like a Greek goddess he thought to himself— and completely forgot about the sad and short lived memory of Sophia.

After kissing so passionately, Mia told him that she was going to the toilet and asked him to wait for her in the bedroom. Once he heard these words, he got extremely nervous. Suddenly he didn't feel drunk anymore as he started to prepare himself for the most unique and unforgettable moment of his life. He was about to lose his virginity.

Mia spent a few minutes getting ready and then headed to the bedroom completely naked. Andrés couldn't believe what his eyes were admiring. Even though he was an adult now, he had never been able to contemplate a woman's breasts, her naked hip, her legs and her perfectly shaped vagina. He had everything in front of him to satiate all of his desires and fantasies. That night in New York City, inside a room of one of the most renowned hotels in the world, Andrés was ready to experience —in an almost romantic manner— his first sexual experience. This was something he waited for a long time and which was missing from his "bucket list". This was something he had always dreamed of. This was the moment in which he was going to be able to become a woman's man.

He was so sexually aroused at the sight of this beautiful naked woman that without notice, he ejaculated with no penetration. As he was coming, he screamed releasing all the lust he was feeling, but felt like trash at the same time. Mia, who was very surprised for what had just happened, tried to comfort him telling him that this happened to a lot of guys. Little did she know, that this was going to be the first time for this man whom a few hours ago seemed so experimented. She wanted to see him with tenderness, but he felt contempt and disgust at her, and asked her to leave his hotel.

He paid her cab back to her house and hoped to never see her again. Everything seemed —before this incident happened— as if it was going to be an unforgettable night for this young man. And it was. For all the wrong reasons, though. The first attempt to lose his virginity had turned into a complete humiliation for him. A humiliation which made him fail as a man. He tried to trick himself into remembering the deal he had closed earlier in the day in order to forget what had happened. But this humiliation wasn't easy to ignore or forget.

He was determined to never ever go through this again. "How could this happen to a man like me?" he wondered over and over. That's why, during another business trip —this time to Amsterdam— he decided to pay a prostitute for sex. Andrés lost his virginity paying for it. He paid and felt like he had control of the situation as he had always done. After this, he started to have regular encounters with different girls. One night stands with women whom he would never call became part of his routine. He found that this was a very good way to enjoy the little free time he had, as he didn't have to commit to anyone. Andrés just wanted to satiate his sexual desires and nothing else.

However, when he was 28, a day he never expected or even hoped for, finally arrived. It was a cold February night, and Andrés was having dinner with some French clients and with Richard. As the meal ended and everyone was ready to leave, he spotted a beautiful girl sitting down in the restaurant bar. He was overwhelmed by her beauty, by the colour of her eyes and her perfectly drawn eyelashes. Her almost perfect features made her look like a fine-looking doll. Staring at her from his table, he assumed she was Nordic. She had her reddish hair clipped with a wooden stick and was wearing a green olive jacket and a brown scarf.

Once everyone left, he walked towards the bar to start a conversation with this girl, but she ignored him. Andrés felt like his ego had been hurt, and so decided that this was a challenge he was going to win. He was now used to get things done his way and his external self-confidence helped him most of the times.

As he was trying to start a conversation, he asked her:

—What is your name? —and before she even had a chance to respond, he said —My name is Andrés de la Vega.

She stared at him in surprise and simply replied:

—Marie.

Andrés being as arrogant as he was, said:

—I want to pay for your drink. What are you drinking?

She was in the middle of a conversation with her friend when all of this was happening. She finished her drink and told him:

—No, thanks, we are leaving soon.

—I just want you to know, that you will see me again —said a confident Andrés.

He stood up and walked towards the exit door.

As he was leaving, he asked the waiter —in a demanding way— to hand his business card to the girl as she left the restaurant. It was now impossible for Andrés to conceive that things didn't unfold as he wanted, not just at work, but with women as well!

Even though he was trying to fool himself, meeting Marie was something different from what he had experienced with any other girl. For some strange reason, he wasn't attracted to her solely because she had ignored him, but because there was something in this girl that he couldn't explain.

One day passed by, two days passed by and Andrés was stuck to his Blackberry day in and day out, waiting for her to write him an email. He was acting like a teenager even if he wasn't aware of it. After 72 hours thinking about this stranger, he finally received the email he was hoping for. The email said the following:

"Hi arrogant boy: let me tell you that no one had ever been so arrogant with me before. I told you I was not interested in talking to you and you just kept on trying. Leaving your business card to the waiter was a very original move! And it seems like it worked, right? Marie. X."

Once he read the email, Andrés felt some sort of happiness within him. It wasn't just a relief for his hurt ego, but he was feeling an emotion he had never experienced before. He didn't want to give it too much importance but he was curious as to why this specific girl made him feel this way. He replied to her email straight away and invited her for dinner at a very exclusive restaurant close to Mayfair, a place in which many of his friends worked and where he was well known. She accepted.

CHAPTER V

Marie was a 26 year old Norwegian girl, who was raised by a farming family in the south of the country. Her father worked all of his life as a farmer and her mother was a music teacher in the secondary school of their town. She had two older sisters, being her the youngest. Marie decided to study at the University of Oxford as that had been her long life dream. She worked hard to earn good enough marks in Norway which allowed her to be accepted in such a prestigious institution.

She was a girl with strong family values, but living most of the time in the countryside she felt the need to explore what the world had to offer, just like most teenagers in the world do. This was the reason why she decided to venture into leaving away her comfort zone.

After graduating from Oxford with a degree in Law, Marie was hired by a very prestigious law firm in London located between Embankment Station and the Westminster Parliament. Even though she had to put long hours to her job, she knew how to balance life and work, and at least twice a week she would block some time off her agenda to play the violin. This was something she did to feel connected to the memory of her childhood when she used to play with her mother. She also loved going to the National Gallery —her favourite museum— as there were many paintings by Van Gogh, a painter she really appreciated. Whenever she felt sad or lonely, Marie would pick up her iPod and head to the hall which was filled with Van Gogh paintings and would simply let the fantasy world of this painter take over her. She loved going there in search of peace. She would contemplate the paintings, the colours, the shapes and the texture of each canvas.

She would never get tired of appreciating the same paintings. Every time she went to the museum she got amazed by how these "simplistic" impressionist paintings were able to set a new trend in the world of art during the XIX and XX century. This was the reason why she admired Van Gogh and other impressionist painters so much. She was startled by their capability to go against the current and change the perception of art, even if they weren't able to enjoy it during their lifetime.

Before meeting Andrés that night at the restaurant bar, Marie's love life included a long distance relationship which lasted for almost three years with a Norwegian guy who cheated on her. When they broke up, Marie decided she was going to enjoy herself during her last year at uni and searching for a new relationship was the last thing she wanted. She decided to let life flow and to enjoy the ride as much as she could. She never had a sexual experience with any other guy, besides her ex-boyfriend, as she was convinced sex was something which needed to be performed with love and not just to satiate a temporary pleasure or desire.

The night she met Andrés she was having a few drinks with a friend from uni, because she needed to share with her the recent opportunity she had of moving to New York and work there. She had been considering it for a few days, but she felt she needed to talk to someone about it. At work she was told that she should seriously consider this opportunity as it would be a good opportunity for her and for the firm.

She only had two weeks to make a decision. Marie was a bit scared, as this would only get her farther away from her family, and she knew that this move would definitely require starting all over again. Nonetheless, she also knew that this was a once in a lifetime opportunity which she couldn't take lightly. Her friend from uni —Alison— who was English, listened to her thoroughly and told her that she would support her in any decision she'd take. Alison did tell her that it was a great opportunity which wouldn't come twice in her life. She also joked with her asking Marie to seriously consider the move, as that would mean she would have a place to stay when visiting the Big Apple. They both laughed.

Alison and Marie were in the middle of the conversation when Andrés approached them to try and chat with Marie. However, she wasn't in the mood to flirt with anyone considering that there was a serious topic going on in the table. When they left the restaurant, the waiter walked towards these girls and handed Andrés' business card to Marie as he had requested. She wasn't used to this type of details from guys, so she was very surprised —and a little nervous— for what just had happened. They started laughing, and Alison asked her to get in touch with him, but not straight away as that would make her look desperate. She told Marie:

—Maybe this is how you will give your farewell to London. The guy doesn't look too bad, so please do me a favour, and be a whore for the first time in your life and say good bye to this city in the best possible way —. They both laughed.

On their first date, Andrés took the lead and ordered for both of them. He ordered lobster and the best bottle of champagne in the house. For dessert he ordered a delicious Belgian chocolate cake. Marie was impressed by the way Andrés had taken charge of the situation while ordering the food and drinks. Two characteristics which were vital for her in regards to a man included that he had to be proactive and self-confident.

Marie was very surprised Andrés wasn't talking about himself. For the first time in Andrés' life, he was the one eager to listen to everything the other person had to say about herself. He just wanted to get to know her and so he was listening closely to every word that came out of her mouth. As the minutes kept passing by, Andrés was getting more nervous and he just didn't understand why this was happening. He was afraid this uneasiness could be reflected and that she would think he was a weak guy. But he couldn't help it. Marie, on the other hand, found him tender and knew that the arrogant and proud guy he pretended to be was actually just a facade.

While they enjoyed a glass of champagne, he asked her:

—Tell me, Marie, what is it that you miss the most from your country?

Without hesitation Marie replied:

—What I believe everyone living abroad misses the most... my family!

Even though Andrés was on his tenth anniversary of having left home, he didn't really agree to it as he was used to getting in touch with his family on Christmas day only. He pretended like he agreed with what she said, and told her he wasn't as attached to his family as most people.

The evening continued filled with laughs and stories —mostly from Marie— about her time as a student at Oxford, her life in London and about her favourite books.

Andrés turned into the spectator of the night. Each word that Marie said moved him in a way he had never experienced before. He was feeling closer to her as he got to know her more and more. Feeling a bit selfish that she had talked too much, she said:

—So Andrés, tell me more about you. I'm sure that you have many stories to share from your beautiful Guatemala —Andrés couldn't think of anything and remained silent and Marie continued—: you'd better say something or I will have to stay with what Miguel Angel Asturias wrote about your country.

Andrés couldn't believe that Marie, a Norwegian girl, knew about this Literature Nobel Prize winner from Guatemala, and that she had even read some of his books. He tried to come up with a smart answer, but he simply couldn't. He blushed, lifted his shoulders as he had nothing to tell her, and they both laughed.

This was the first time Andrés actually wanted to know everything about another person. In his mind, there was no sexual desire; this time it was all beyond a simple and casual sexual encounter. He wanted to dig deeper, to ask more personal questions, to get to the depths of her life, something he had never intended to do with anyone else. The very strong feelings she had aroused in him, made him remove all kind of shields and walls he had built around himself.

—Listen, Marie, people talk a lot about dreams, and for me it is a bit hard to understand it, but do you have any dreams?

She got a bit surprised by this question and replied:

—This is a very deep question to ask on a first date, don't you think?

Andrés felt like a complete imbecile. This answer felt as if he had crushed his head against a wall, and while he was trying to come up with a response, Marie continued with a big smile:

—Well, I'll tell you, but this has to stay between you and me, OK? —she then asked him to get closer to her, and whispering in his ear she said —: I believe my dream is the same as yours. I just want to be happy.

Having Marie so close to him, made him feel an emotion he hadn't felt before. He got even more nervous after that. His cheeks turned reddish. He thought that "the butterflies in the stomach" was a girly thing, but he was experiencing that precise feeling at that very moment.

At the age of 28, Andrés was feeling butterflies in his stomach. He was desperate to embrace her and give her a sweet kiss. He wanted to hold her in his arms. He was feeling like a teenage kid who falls in love for the first time in his life.

He slowly moved away from her as if waking up from a dream. Marie could perceive how nervous this guy was and simply smiled at him. Whenever she would smile, Andrés would feel at ease. He couldn't explain all that he was feeling.

Once dinner was over, he walked her to the Bond Street station, where she needed to take the tube to get home. Before they said good bye, Marie came closer to him once again, and kissed him on the cheek. This was without a doubt the best moment of the night for Andrés. She asked him to text her whenever he got home just to make sure he had arrived safe and sound. She said: "I had a great time, you arrogant boy" and winked at him. He stood there frozen for a couple of minutes as she walked away.

Two weeks after their first date, Marie took a decision about her future. She decided to stay in London for a longer period and was not going to take the opportunity to move to New York. Was this driven because she met Andrés? Only she knew. Andrés wasn't aware she had to make up her mind about something so important the moment they met.

Soon after she took the decision to continue living in London, she asked Andrés to meet up with her in Old Street, east London, on a Sunday morning. This was an area that he wasn't used to visit, as he believed that only "hippies and weird people" hanged out there. However, this time it was different. He left his prejudices aside and agreed to meet with her in east London. He couldn't care less where they were going as long as he got to see her. He was dying to be around her.

It was a cold morning in March. Marie took him to the Flower Market in Columbia Road, very close to Bricklane, a place Andrés had always refused to visit. However, this time something was different, because Marie was with him. They walked through the little alley filled with flower sellers, little cafes and shops. As they were walking, there was a young kid selling sunflowers. Maybe he was eight years old, and he was helping his parents on that morning. The kid spotted this couple walking and told Andrés:

—Why don't you get your girlfriend some sunflowers, mate? They're only five quid. Don't be cheap, mate.

Once Andrés heard the word "girlfriend" he freaked out. He was afraid of how Marie would react to it, but she simply smiled to the little boy. She told Andrés that those were her favourite flowers. He thought of his grandmother, because those were her favourite flowers too!

He took his wallet out and handed the kid a five pounds note. He grabbed a sunflower and gave it to Marie. She loved the gesture and without crossing a look between them, she grabbed his hand. Andrés felt how his fingers were touching hers. He started caressing her hand. Andrés couldn't have been a happier man. The simple act of holding hands was enough for these couple of lovers to smile and enjoy the beautiful sunny, yet cold morning, in London town.

The two lovers stayed in contact through text messages. A few weeks after their date in the Flower Market, Marie asked him to meet up with her at Portobello, very close to Notting Hill on a Saturday afternoon.

Marie who hadn't been dating for quite a while now, was very excited to enjoy with Andrés the little details that London had to offer. She was happy to go to the markets, parks, museums, theatres, restaurants. However, Marie started realising that Andrés would disappear all weekdays as he wasn't able to disconnect from work, even if he really wanted to. She wanted to convince herself this was because he really enjoyed what he was doing and that was why he worked so many long hours.

That Saturday afternoon, Andrés got to their meeting point 15 minutes earlier than expected. He started to feel nervous and anxious just by the thought that he was going to see her again after a couple of weeks of not being able to see each other. Marie arrived right on time. They both didn't know how to act, and so they kissed on each cheek. She led the way, and Andrés —who looked like a first timer tourist— had no idea of how to get to the market. As they were walking along Portobello Road, Andrés became courageous and reached for her hand once again. Marie didn't reject the gesture.

They walked along holding hands, taking in all the little vintage shops and cafes which were on their way. All of a sudden, Marie let go of his hand and started running like a little girl towards a bakery, which was her favourite. Andrés didn't do anything but smile at her innocence and followed her all the way to the store. He was happy to see Marie being so spontaneous and enjoying her freedom. Something he had never experienced himself.

They bought two carrot cakes and two coffees. Marie asked him to walk a little further down the street as she wanted to show him another place. Andrés had no clue where he was walking. They kept on going for a few metres until they made it to the entrance of Little Venice —a canal on the west side of London.

It was a cold afternoon and the sky was painted in an orange and blue tone. During their walk through Little Venice they decided to sit down on a bench next to the canal so that they could enjoy the beautiful view and the cakes they had just bought. Andrés couldn't believe what he was experiencing in that moment. He had a beautiful girl sitting by his side and they were enjoying simple things together. He felt the urge to kiss her and kept asking himself a thousand times when would be there right time to do so. Marie was telling him a story about his family, but he was paying no attention whatsoever, as his mind was trying to work out the best strategy to kiss her.

By the time they finished eating their cake, he put his arm around her and after a few minutes of simply staring at the water in the canal, he finally kissed her. It was a sweet kiss. She responded with another passionate kiss. They remained silent for a while as they both knew this hadn't been just another kiss.

For Andrés, this walk along Little Venice would definitely become an unforgettable moment of his life. Was it here that Andrés de la Vega got to know what love was all about?

On his way back home he asked himself the following question: "Am I in love?" He wasn't able to know the answer to this, as he had never loved any woman in his life before. Throughout his 28 years of life the only love he knew was that of his grandmother. He had never experienced what it was to love someone else. He was confused, but at the same time, he was feeling extremely happy. He just couldn't understand why he was feeling this way.

CHAPTER VI

The walk in Little Venice was followed by a series of dates in fancy restaurants —places Andrés would choose— and also to simpler yet interesting restaurants —which Marie would pick. They loved going to the Barbican Centre on Sunday afternoons and enjoy the London Symphony Orchestra concerts. Andrés enjoyed classical music without any logical reason. He simply felt peace when listening to it. But Marie had lived her childhood with Bach, Tchaikovsky, Mozart, Rachmaninov and many other composers playing at her living room.

She appreciated classical music because she had studied the lives and the legacy of the greatest musicians and so she understood the complexities and the creativeness that these geniuses had gone through in their lives. She was aware of the effort and discipline that each musician in the orchestra had to have in order to play an instrument. And she would definitely appreciate a conductor who knew how to take the best out of each musician and orchestrate a beautiful musical expression.

Andrés was also amazed when seeing how Marie lived a performance by the orchestra. Each composition was lived through her body and soul vividly. She felt each note and each emotion in every melody the musicians played. One time, she got so emotional when the violin concerto in D minor by Bach was played, that she even shed a tear. Andrés was able to now see that this girl was getting him to know and to feel things he had never imagined.

As time passed by, Andrés turned to be a detail oriented boyfriend. At the beginning of the relationship he thought that giving expensive and luxurious presents would show her his feelings. "Which girl wouldn't love to be gifted a Tiffany's necklace from her boyfriend? All of them", he thought. However, Marie was not that kind of girl. She didn't think it was necessary to get material things in order to prove ones love. During one of his business trips to New York, he got her a very expensive necklace. She hesitated a bit but at the end decided to accept it.

Marie really took Andrés by surprise when she told him she wasn't a girl who was interested in money, jewels or anything ostentatious. He got a bit upset to hear this, as he had conceived the idea that by getting her something expensive would be enough to show her how he felt for her. He couldn't get on his mind how a girl could get a bit uncomfortable when receiving an expensive gift. However, little by little he started to realise that this girl wasn't the typical kind of woman he was used to meet.

Without even noticing it, Andrés started to drop his guard. His eccentricities, his ego, and even his addiction for work, all started to diminish without him being aware of it. His daily routine even took a turn and this was reflected at work. He got to a point where his rigid dressing regime of wearing black suits, white shirt and black tie, was left a side for a while. There were days in which he would simply not use a tie, something he had never done before. During the weekends he stopped driving his Aston Martin and started using the tube and the bus, because that's how Marie liked to travel around London. He even started to get a bit late to work and to cut his 10K run each morning so that he could stay in bed with Marie whenever they slept together. Up to this point they were simply sleeping together as they hadn't made love yet.

Andrés wasn't aware of all these changes —even if he had always been a very methodical and conscious person— but he was simply doing what he felt was right. He was being driven by an irrational and unexplainable feeling of love. He wasn't restricting or limiting these feelings he felt towards Marie. Even though they had slept together, Andrés was a bit surprised that after three months of dating, she hadn't showed him her desire to make love with him. And he couldn't care less. He was happy with the simple fact he got to spend time with her.

He was in love with the woman she was and enjoyed every single second he got to share with her. He fell in love with her generosity, innocence, beauty and intellect. He had fallen in love with a woman who accepted and loved him just the way he was. He wasn't sure how this had happened, but he stopped trying to understand the reasons, the logic, the motives, the rationale behind it, and for the first time in his life he decided to flow with what he was feeling. There were times when he was aware he was acting differently, but he wouldn't break his head as he was used to do before meeting Marie.

The love story continued. On a summer Sunday afternoon —the first summer Andrés got to spend with someone in this city known for the rainy and grey days— they decided to celebrate their fifth month together. This was something Andrés had always considered to be utterly corny, but in this opportunity he didn't care. Marie invited him over to her flat which was situated close to Angel station. Andrés got there close to seven in the afternoon. The sun was about to come down and the sky was painted with orange clouds on a navy blue background.

Marie lived in the lower part of a Victorian house which the landlord had converted to an individual flat. This flat had something unusual for any typical London home: it had a very nice and cute garden in the back. Once Andrés entered the main door, she asked him to close his eyes and to stay like that until she said otherwise. He did nothing but to follow her orders. Marie grabbed his hand and led him all the way to the door which took them straight to the garden. When they got there, Marie asked him to open his eyes. What his eyes got to admire in that moment was something he had never seen before. Not even in a Hollywood film. He was surprised by the reflection of about 500 candles she strategically placed all over the little garden.

Marie opened the glass door, and Andrés started hearing Norah Jones playing in the back. He was astonished by all of this. He couldn't believe she had done something like that for him. The man he was before meeting Marie —his fake confidence, his selfishness and his uncontrollable ambition— started to be threatened by the love he was feeling for this beautiful, sweet and amazing Norwegian girl.

The evening was complemented with glasses of red wine, a homemade lasagne and laughter. Love was definitely in the air. Once the main course was finished, Marie brought Andrés' favourite dessert — *crème brulée*. As soon as she put the plate on the table, Andrés stood up and asked her to dance with him. The last time he had danced was when he was 12 years old. The day his grandmother passed away.

Andrés wrapped his arms around her as strong as he could. He got his mouth close to her ears and in a sweet voice he whispered:

—Marie, I want to thank you for all that you've done tonight. I don't know why you did it, but... —Andrés just stopped talking.

Marie moved away from him as she got a bit nervous when he paused. She looked directly to his eyes and said:

—Andrés, everything I've done tonight is because you became someone important in my life, but if you're afraid of anything, let me know now before it is too late.

He put his finger on her lips and giving her a tender look — something abnormal in him —he replied:

—Marie, please, don't say anything else. I don't know how to say this but... —he hesitated once more, but then he recovered his courage and in a shaky voice he said—: Marie, I love you!

Marie was staring at him, and after hearing these words she smiled and said:

—Andrés, I have also got to that point. I love you too.

Andrés didn't wait for a single second to pass by, and he gave her the sweetest kiss he had ever given. Both were living the emotions teenagers experience when they kiss for the first time.

That summer night, Andrés lost his virginity. Yes, he did. He could have had sex with a prostitute in Amsterdam many years ago, and he also had many one night stands with many strangers, but he had never made love to a woman. He had only experienced empty sex. That night, he actually took the time to kiss each part of Marie's body. He kissed her neck and caressed her stomach, her legs and her breasts. He had no urgency to penetrate her. His only wish was for this passion and desire to make love to her to extend for hours.

Marie started to get aroused as she felt Andrés' lips kissing her whole body. The moment they both had been waiting for had finally arrived. It was during this romantic Sunday evening that Andrés made love to Marie. Nothing of what he had lived with as many as 20 women before her, could be compared to that moment. For Andrés it was normal that once he had finished, he would dress up, go to the bathroom, take a shower and would fall asleep. This time it was all different. He laid in bed naked next to her. He rubbed his hands over her back, her legs, her hips. He wasn't thinking about anything else. His mind was completely blank. The only thing he was focusing was on his hands which were caressing the beautiful body of the woman he loved.

Yes, he had made love to the woman he loved, and this love was reciprocated. That night they slept accompanied by the music of Ella Fitzgerald. Before they fell asleep, Andrés kissed her very tenderly and whispered in her ear: "Today you have shown me that love actually exists. I love you, Marie".

The next morning, Andrés came to the office dressed in khaki trousers and a blue shirt. Before that day he had experimented with wearing different shirt colours, but he had never wore a different colour of trousers. Once he got to the reception, he said "good morning, fellows" to all of his colleagues. Each and every one of the people who were there in that moment, and who had known him for about six years, were astonished at what just had happened. He had never treated them as equals, so for them to hear him say "fellows" was something out of this world.

That day, coincidence or not, Tom —the colleague he threatened of firing when he was celebrating his first child being born— had to get approval for his family holidays. Tom walked into Andrés' office and shaking due to the nerves he was feeling, came in and asked him:

—Hi, Andrés… ehmmmm… I would like to ask you for a favour —once he heard these last words, Andrés turned himself away from the computer to face Tom and asked him to sit down.

—What can I do for you, Tom? —Tom was lost. He even thought: "Who is this guy who actually acts like a human being? What did he do with the real Andrés?"

Tom continued:

—Andrés… next week I was planning to go on holidays with my family and I just wanted to get your approval. However, if you tell me that there's work to do, then…

Andrés interrupted him and asked Tom to hand him the sheet of paper he had to sign, and said:

—Hey, Tom, go and enjoy your time with the family. By the way, how is the little one doing?

Tom wasn't able to respond to that. He was at a loss for words. He remained silent for about five seconds. He didn't know what the hell was going on. "Is this the person who once threatened to fire me because I was celebrating I was going to be a father?" he thought. After reflecting on this, he got back to reality and feeling a bit lost he replied:

—He is doing well, Andrés. He is getting to that point in which we're almost able to sleep again every night —. They both smiled.

Tom left Andrés' office with the feeling he had talked to some other person who wasn't exactly Andrés. He told all of his colleagues what had happened and no one believed him, until he showed them the signed document approving his holidays. He feared Andrés was not going to approve them.

This renewed Andrés de la Vega was in love and he showed it with a relaxed attitude towards life. Something he had never experienced before. However, a few days after that unforgettable night at Marie's place, news arrived that Richard Stephens was going to open an office in New York City, and wanted him to be head of the firm in the Big Apple. His dream —before meeting Marie—was to live in New York and conquer the city as he strongly believed what Frank Sinatra's song said about this city: *"if you can make it here, you can make it anywhere"*.

This opportunity could not have come at a worse moment. It got to Andrés' life right when he was starting to enjoy being with a woman he loved, and who loved him, and that was something which was more valuable than what New York and all the money in the world could offer. Richard Stephens gave him no option. It wasn't an offer. It was an order. He had two weeks to sort all of his things and move on to conquer New York City.

CHAPTER VII

It was ten o'clock in the morning when Richard entered Andrés' office. Three minutes later he was walking out from it. He thought he had delivered the best news he could to Andrés, without knowing he had actually turned his life around in a matter of minutes. Three minutes had been enough to turn Andrés back into the man he had always been. Three minutes were needed for Andrés to forget the five months he had spent with Marie. In only three minutes his life had given a 180 degrees turn. The peace and happiness he was feeling started to vanish little by little.

From the moment Richard left his office, Andrés wasn't able to think of anything else but on Marie's naked body lying next to him. He couldn't believe what was going on. He couldn't figure out why he wasn't jumping up and down after his boss had told him that his dream of living in New York City had come true. He was feeling miserable and restless and he just couldn't understand why. "Why now?" He thought. For a split of a second he thought of asking Marie to move with him, to leave everything behind them and have a fresh start. They could just move together and he would do all he could to make her happy.

But his sudden emotion didn't go beyond that. Five months had not been enough to remove the coldness, selfishness and loneliness off Andrés. He had to deceive himself by thinking that those five months had been a beautiful dream and nothing more than that. He wanted to convince himself that his true happiness was waiting for him in New York, the place where he was going to be able to continue building his career and where he would be able to generate even more wealth. From one moment to another, Andrés wanted to throw away all of what Marie represented in his life.

While he was reflecting on this, he started convincing himself that there was no way he could give up his successful life for someone he didn't know that well. Even though he knew he was lying to himself, he polluted his mind with excuses and simply wanted to persuade himself that he had to keep on pursuing his dreams of grandeur. This was the strategy he decided to use in order to mitigate the pain he was feeling and the unhappiness he knew he was going to have to face once he decided to lose the only woman who had taught him to love. He was aware he wasn't being honest with himself, but he knew that if he wanted to continue having things going his way, he had to make choices.

Still lost in his self-deceiving thoughts, he got a text message on his mobile. It was Marie. The text read:

"I just wanted to let you know that I love you and that you have made me feel like no one else has. XXX".

Andrés smiled when reading the text, but without giving it too much thought, he decided to delete it. He decided to avoid any thought relating to Marie, to the last few days and to the five months he had spent with her.

His focus switched to thinking about New York. This was his motivation to force himself to continue striving for a life he knew — deep inside of him— was not going to fulfil him. However, his ambition for more money and power couldn't be switched off so easily. But, was there a limit into how much more he wanted? Was New York the place in which he would actually be happy and fulfil his life after having experienced a true and pure love with Marie? Could making lots of money be compared to sharing a walk in a park or a beautiful sunset with the woman he loved?

Andrés was not planning to sacrifice his ambition —even if he had more than he really needed— for the love of a woman. He didn't have enough courage to accept that the real reason behind his pride and selfishness was his fear of being hurt by the person he loved the most. And that was why no one or nothing could change his mind about starting a new life in New York. Andrés didn't know that the greatest risk there is in life, is to not take any risk at all.

He was not capable of replying to her text message and even less to call her. For four days, Andrés was untraceable and Marie —who was not a naive woman— started to doubt whether she had fallen in love with the wrong person. During those four days of absence, Marie recalled each moment they had spent together —since the day they met in the restaurant— to try to understand Andrés' sudden behaviour. She remembered the first date they had in Mayfair. She also recalled that Sunday morning in the Flower Market in which he had got her a sunflower and the moment they held hands. The very romantic walk in Little Venice also came to her mind. The first time they kissed. She wanted to bring back every memory of that Sunday in which they had made love for the first time.

She wanted to see their story from all angles, as the good lawyer she was. She analysed each thing she had said. She also feared that by saying "I love you" too fast she had scared him off, but he had it said to her in the first place! Even if she tried to think about it for hours and hours, she couldn't understand what was happening with him.

She was clear of one thing though, the Andrés she had met would not simply fade away from the surface of the planet after having lived intense and passionate moments like the ones they had shared in the last few months. She got to the point where she believed the only explanation for his behaviour was that he was a pig who was only interested in having sex with her and now that he had, he would just disappear. There was no other rational explanation to put in plain words what was going on.

On the fifth day of silence, Marie just couldn't cope with his cowardly attitude and decided to call him so that she could confront him. She tried three times but she was directed to his voicemail. She wanted to wait for a few hours until she could get hold of him.

Andrés was well aware Marie was calling him, but every time he saw her name he would press the "end" button straightaway. A few hours later, he got the fourth call. He wasn't used to having more than two missed calls from her, so he decided that this time he had to pick it up. After more than half a minute of superficial chatting, he said:

—Marie, I'm busy at the moment —he remained silent for a bit and continued —. We need to talk. Can you meet me for a coffee after work?

Marie could easily perceive the coldness in his words, but even if she was hurt and was not going to let any man treat her like that, she just couldn't leave aside her feelings for him, and in a saddened voice she asked:

—Andrés, are you OK? I have missed you these days.

Without any type of hesitation and very bluntly he replied:

—I'm doing well. I'll see you at seven —and he hung up.

During the twenty minutes' walk from his office to the cafe they usually met at —close to the Tower of London— he didn't pay any attention to the beautiful sunset which was covering the sky. He didn't notice the yachts sailing in the Thames. His mind was too busy trying to fool himself and trying to remove all of the amazing and intense moments he had shared with Marie.

"Five months of me acting like a stupid teenager cannot change my plans. I must go on with my life and live it as it pleases me". He repeated these words over and over. Deep inside, Andrés knew that the state of happiness he had achieved by spending time with Marie —every second of each day they spent together— was not something which could be bought with all the money in the world. He refused to accept that life had actually granted him with the opportunity to live and experience the most beautiful thing that a human being could ever feel: unconditional and selfless love. He needed to believe Marie was just another person in his life and that she wasn't "good enough" to get between him and his dreams. However, Andrés didn't even know what his "dreams" were apart from making lots of money.

They got to the cafe at the same time, but Andrés was so out of himself, that he didn't notice they were both about to push the door at the same time. Their hands touched slightly, but Andrés instantly took his hands away from hers, as if he was disgusted by it. This was the moment when Marie understood —without having to exchange words— that this relationship and the love he had felt for her had vanished.

The conversation didn't last more than ten minutes. It took him five minutes to order his traditional cafe latte with skimmed milk, while Marie simply waited in the most hidden table she could find so that he couldn't see how devastated she was. Marie was sitting down playing with her mobile and kept telling herself that she needed to reflect self-confidence and that she didn't have to show how hurt she was. However, her saddened eyes betrayed her. Once he got close to the table where she was sitting, Andrés fixed his look in Marie's eyes for about ten seconds, but he was incapable of staring at these sad green eyes any longer. He felt guilty. "Why am I feeling guilty?" he asked himself.

Andrés started the conversation by saying: "Marie, I asked you to meet up with me because…" She interrupted him and said:

—Andrés, I don't quite understand why you are acting this way after all we've lived through.

Andrés tried to stop her, but she continued saying:

—You don't need to explain anything to me as your attitude speaks for itself. It is obvious that you are not happy with me and that I'm not good enough for you.

In that moment, he forgot all the lies he had told himself before seeing her, and simply wanted to ask her to stop talking and kiss her.

—I wish you all the best and believe me when I say that I will never forget how happy you have made me.

She grabbed her purse, stood up from the chair and started running outside of the cafe drying some tears which were rolling down her face.

Andrés was static, speechless and puzzled. He didn't want to understand what had happened. He knew he had made a big mistake, but he wouldn't give in. He wanted to forget about Marie and simply focus on the new chapter of life which was waiting for him in New York.

That night when he got to his flat, he opened up a bottle of whiskey and played Frank Sinatra on his speakers. He was now determined to forget everything about Marie and all that she represented in his life. He would simply archive it all in the memory trunk and that was it.

He told himself it was going to be easier to live by himself, doing what he really wanted to do, whenever he wanted to and with no need to give explanations to anyone. He thought he didn't want to live a life attached to a girl. He just wanted to be himself and adjusting to someone else wouldn't let him be free. However, even if he wanted to ignore it, his heart was broken and sad. But this cold and selfish man had spent so much time under the mask of an emotionless human being that he preferred to ignore the pain he was suffering.

That night he closed Marie's chapter and carried on living a life of unhappiness, loneliness and misery that he was used to before having experienced a glance of true love.

CHAPTER VIII

The next morning, Andrés got back to being the same guy he had been before. He started to live by his strict routine once again. He went for a run to the park —even though he felt a bit hung over from the night before— and wore a black suit, white shirt and black tie all over again. His face showed uneasiness and unhappiness, but moreover, it showed emptiness. He wasn't conscious of how dreadful he looked as there were more important things to think about. Marie had become a simple memory, or at least that's what he wanted to believe. He only had a few days to organise his things before moving to New York and that was the only thing he wanted to think about.

A couple of days after his relationship with Marie had come to an end, he decided to take a day off to sort everything out. He wanted to distract his mind from thinking about her. He had to speak with the moving company and he also had to seek for a way to sale his Aston Martin and his flat in Richmond. Even though he had spent a relative short time with Marie, all of his life in London —including his flat and his car— evolved around her. This was due to the reason that in ten years he had lived in this city, he never enjoyed it until Marie appeared in the picture. And even if she had showed him what true happiness felt like, he still wanted to get rid of her. His pain and sorrow made him take decisions contrary to what his heart was truly asking for. Andrés wanted to show himself —and Marie if at all possible— that she had never meant anything to him. However, he wasn't aware that by denying his feelings, as painful as it could be to actually face them, he was harming himself even more.

On his day off he decided to run a bit more than his usual 10K. Unable to face the sorrow over losing Marie, he wanted to run some extra kilometres so that he could feel physically tired. In this way he could blame the physical effort for the actual heartache he was feeling.

He got back to his flat with pain all over his body, in his knees, legs, back and even in his arms. The strongest pain though, was in his heart. He decided to take a long hot water shower. He never did this. That day he decided to spend about twenty minutes under the shower and felt how each part of his body hurt with each drop of water. His knees resented the pain of holding the whole weight of his body with the slightest movement he made. And it hurt. He couldn't even lift his arms to wash his hair. So much pain was making him feel useless and miserable. Losing control over himself, he shouted so loud in an attempt to let out all of the pain he was feeling. His shout was so loud though, that he got worried the neighbours could call the police if they had heard him. It wasn't the pain of his aching body which made him feel so frustrated, it was the pain of his broken heart which made him feel like rubbish. He couldn't come to terms as to why he felt so devastated.

He finally came out of the shower and saw himself naked in a mirror. For a moment he faced his own reflection. He was such a narcissist who loved to look at himself in the mirror, but this time he didn't have the courage to do it. He didn't want to see his own reflection. He even felt disgusted at himself.

But he needed to be strong and decided to see straight into the man who appeared in the mirror. His body was the same, but his heart wasn't. He looked straight to his eyes and he couldn't face his own look for more than a second. Even if it was hard for him to accept it, he wasn't the same person. He had experienced what many people —even older people — don't get to experience throughout their lifetime: to genuinely love and be loved. The love he experienced hadn't been possessive, jealous, envious or manipulative. On the contrary, it had been true love, full of respect and admiration. However, Andrés' selfishness, ambition and coldness were stronger than the language of his heart.

While looking at himself reflected in the mirror, he realised he didn't have enough courage to face his own eyes. So he decided to start looking at other parts of his body. He started noticing that there were many imperfections which he had never paid attention to. He realised his feet weren't the most perfect ones. His legs were skinny. He really wasn't the perfect man he wanted to believe he was.

He continued observing his body from head to toes. When passing his eyes through his penis and testicles he noticed that there was something which was more than a simple imperfection. He spotted something that wasn't supposed to be there. But it was. He freaked out. He had both of his hands close to this area, and so he started to open and close his left hand very slowly until he reached his left testicle. It was a slow movement. A movement driven by fear. A movement that someone makes when he knows it won't be good news. When he finally touched it, he felt a rounded lump, which was almost half the size of his left testicle. It felt as if he had three testicles. Fear took over each particle of Andrés' body.

In that specific moment, Marie, his Aston Martin, his bank account, his luxurious flat in Richmond and the grandeur life waiting for him in the Big Apple turned all into a less relevant priority for him. He was static with his eyes and mouth completely open in awe and with his fingers exploring the lump he had found under his left testicle. Touching it hurt him.

Touching his testicle, he recalled feeling a sharp pain on the left side of the abdomen for the last few days which he simply didn't give any importance to. His mind was suddenly polluted with thousands of thoughts, but he got stuck with one: "What the hell could this lump be? Cancer?" He decided to get dressed, grabbed the keys to his car and drove directly to the doctor's clinic.

On his way to the clinic —which was located near Westminster— Andrés started to feel pain in his testicle and his abdomen. It was as if his mind —which was now conscious of the existence of this lump— had given his body and mind permission to feel pain and fear. He was distressed by thoughts which could only increase the fear he was experiencing. A disease. A surgery. Death? Even though this intruder had been in Andrés' body for a while —now that he was conscious about it— allowed his mind to threaten his false confidence.

Once he got to doctor Lovestone's clinic —which was a private practice— there were two other patients before him. He was the third person in line and he had to wait. He hated waiting. He didn't want to think what it was to go to a public hospital in London with all the "trashy people" —as he referred to the people who didn't have the financial position he did— and have to be surrounded by them. This was the second time Andrés had to visit a doctor since he had lived in London. His first visit happened because he wanted to get a flu shot as there were many people in the office getting sick, and being an extreme workaholic, he wouldn't allow a stupid sickness to get on his way to making money. "Time is money" was one of his defining mottos.

Back on this second visit, he just couldn't stop imagining the worse scenarios which could unfold. From one second to the other, all of his plans and his own life were being threatened. During this forty five minutes wait at the doctor's clinic, he didn't grab his BlackBerry. Not even for one second. He was just glazing through some magazines in an attempt for time to fly by. All of the sudden the receptionist said in a very strong British accent: "Andrés de la Vega". Andrés stood up from the chair he was sitting in, and as he started walking, he knew he was about to confront a situation he never imagined he would have to face.

The doctor, an older man in his early 60s, had a thick grey coloured moustache, wore reading glasses, had an olive green beret and was dressed with a red shirt and mustard coloured trousers. Andrés' first impression was that this so called doctor didn't reflect professionalism and this made him distrust him. Doctor Harry Lovestone started asking questions to Andrés so that he could complete the patient's profile as this was the first time he was visiting him. Andrés was losing his patience with so many questions and he was not responding in a very polite manner. He only wanted to hear the doctor say that everything was going to be OK and that he could simply forget the whole matter and continue living his life as he had always done. After five minutes of constant questioning, the doctor finally said:

—Well, Andrés, what brings you here?

Andrés, who was quite annoyed by now, shouted:

—God damn it! You finally want to know what the hell I'm doing here.

Doctor Harry noticed Andrés' tension and tried to calm him down and in a very paternal voice he said:

—Andrés, please, tell me, what can I do for you?

Andrés finally let his guard down and with a very nervous voice he replied:

—Doctor, I have a lump in my left testicle and I don't know what it is.

Doctor Lovestone asked him to walk towards the stretcher which was located just a few steps from his desk, and asked him to remove his trousers and underwear. Andrés felt extremely uncomfortable with this. "Oh shit, now I have to show my parts to an old man who claims to be a doctor but who actually looks like a clown", he thought to himself. When Andrés had completely uncovered his parts, the doctor put on some plastic gloves and started to feel both of his testicles and abdomen. He asked Andrés if he felt pain, and he nodded.

The doctor removed his plastic gloves, threw them into the bin, and asked Andrés to pull up his trousers and to wait for him at his desk. Andrés waited for a couple of minutes, until doctor Lovestone walked back to his wooden carved desk.

—Andrés, for how long have you had this swelling in your testicle?

—I just noticed it this morning —replied nervously.

—And what about the abdominal pain?

—I've felt it for a few weeks, but I just didn't care. My job is more important than anything.

Doctor Lovestone removed his glasses, he looked straight at Andrés' eyes, and as a teacher who is about to reprehend his student, he said:

—There is nothing, and I can reassure you with all the years I have lived, that there is nothing more important than your well-being. Both physical and that of your soul.

When Andrés heard the word "soul", Marie's image automatically hit him; but he didn't give it too much importance as he had to focus on what the doctor was saying.

—All right, doctor, whatever you say —. He paused and continued —What do you think is happening to me?

Doctor Lovestone grabbed a sheet of paper and told Andrés that before making any diagnostic, he had to get an ultrasound done and also some blood tests. This could not be performed at his clinic, so he had to arrange for an appointment in a laboratory. They would get the results in about a week, the doctor said. Andrés was growing with anxiety and fear with each word the doctor said. He was evading the one question he feared the most, but suddenly he found the courage and asked if there was a possibility for this to be cancer. The doctor replied:

—In this present time, everything is possible, and that is why you must get that ultrasound and the blood tests done, so we can have a definite answer.

Andrés thought to himself: "One fucking week? I have paid 350 quid for this clown to tell me that I have to get an ultrasound and blood tests done so that I can have an answer in one week?"

Andrés took the laboratory order from the doctor's hand, stood up from the chair, threw the money to pay for the appointment to the receptionist and ran away like a grumpy little kid.

He drove back to his flat filled with fear. New York was no longer his priority. His only priority was to know what has happening with his body. He wanted to call Marie to tell her what was going on, but his pride didn't let him. While he was driving home, he was able to contemplate the beauty of the sky and his eyes wanted to show a sign of weakness, but this emotionless human being was not going to allow himself to drop a single tear. He told himself he was not a weak man and that everything would be back to normality soon. Or at least that's what he wanted to believe.

That night Andrés wasn't able to sleep at all. He couldn't keep his eyes closed and for many hours he kept turning his restless body from one side of the bed to the other. There was a time in which he needed to head to the toilet, but he would have to face the lump in his testicle and that freaked him out. So he decided to stay in bed. About four in the morning, he managed to shut his eyes and was able to sleep due to the mental tiredness he was feeling.

Two hours later, Andrés woke up feeling frightened. He had seen his grandmother in a dream! In his dream, he went back to be a 10 year old little boy who was playing at his grandma's garden mowing the lawn as he used to do during his school holidays. His grandmother appeared with a glass filled with lemonade and as she was approaching him, she handed the glass to him, and in a very sweet voice she whispered in his ear: "My dear Andrés, I am here with you".

That was the moment he woke up feeling restless and could not hold the tears falling down his cheeks. He had not shed a single tear since the day she passed away. That had been 17 years ago. He was now crying because he was afraid. He feared the worse. To think that he could be suffering from cancer gave him the chills. At this time of his life, there was now something out of his control which was threatening to derail him from the path he had planned for his life.

Andrés thought of his family. He wished he had them close to him, even if it was for just one second. He recalled how his grandmother would always make him feel protected. In this moment, a simple hug would do. But he was alone, completely and utterly alone. He fixed his eyes to the white painted ceiling of his room. This moment made him realise how lonely he was.

Lost in his thoughts, a sudden idea struck him: what if he made a short trip to Guatemala to be closer to the memory of his grandmother or to his family, whom he had abandoned for such a long time?

It was in that moment of impulse and vulnerability, that he decided he would have the ultrasound and the blood tests done that morning, and after that he would take the first flight from Heathrow to Guatemala, the country he had decided to forget about. He would spend five days in Guatemala City; he would then head back to London to receive the results from the doctor and to finally know what was going on with his body.

Was the memory of his grandmother what drove him to take this irrational decision? Did Andrés wish to feel closer to the memory of the woman who had loved him and taught him so much about life? The vulnerability that he was experiencing compelled him to be impulsive and he didn't want to understand the logic or motives behind this decision. Life in those moments could take a direction he never expected, and so he flowed with whatever he was feeling. Something inside of him pushed him to do so.

At 6:10am, Andrés wrote an email to Richard saying the following:

"Before moving to New York, I have decided to take some days off to visit my family in Guatemala. I will be in New York in two weeks' time. I hope you don't mind".

Richard received the email and was quite surprised by it. Andrés had never talked about his family during their seven year professional relationship, but he thought it was a good idea for him to see them after such a long time. He replied:

"Sure thing, kid. I look forward to seeing you in New York in two weeks so that you can keep on making me a richer millionaire".

CHAPTER IX

As soon as he received Richard's reply that morning, Andrés took a shower, packed his clothes in a small travelling suitcase and went to his favourite French café to get a ham and cheese croissant and a café latte with skimmed milk. As he was leaving the small shop in Richmond, he was able to see the people who were passing by his side. He never had time to look at other people, but today he was making an exception and decided to sit down in a bench in the middle of a small park.

He observed a young mother walking hand by hand with her little daughter. He also noticed that there was an old man sitting in another bench reading a newspaper and drinking a cup of coffee. While observing these people, Andrés thought to himself: "Everyone seems to be happy. Am I the only person in this world who might be suffering from a terminal disease? Why is this happening to me? What have I done to deserve this?"

What he didn't know was that the old man, sitting in the bench close to him was feeling like the loneliest human being in the world after having lost the love of his life: his wife, whom he had been married to for 40 years and who passed away five years ago after suffering a stroke. The mother who was walking with her little one also was also an unhappy person. Even though she lived a comfortable life, she knew her husband cheated on her with his secretary. Why did Andrés have to believe that everything had to evolve around him? Why was he being selfish, even in this moment? Why couldn't see that he wasn't the only one who suffered?

He decided to take the train to the laboratory as he would then head straight to the airport. During his walk to the station he took a longer path and walked along the banks of the Thames. Before reaching the river, he walked through another small park which local residents used to play cricket on Sundays. He was eager to observe the water, the ducks which were swimming in this part of the river, the trees which decorated the river bank and the little boats which were sailing from all directions. He wanted to feel the wind stroking his face. Every ray of sun which hit him in the face made him want to live even more. Andrés had finally come to face his greatest fear: he was afraid of dying.

He knew that life as he knew it would change after that very morning. He wanted to record that moment in his mind forever. He wanted to remember the walk by the Thames, the old man reading his newspaper, the mother laughing with her daughter and the ducks swimming in the river. He was afraid. He thought of Marie once again. The memory of the first time they had made love invaded his mind. He wanted to believe that all of what he was living was just a dream, that Marie was still part of his life and that the possibility of having cancer was just a nightmare. However, this was not his reality.

He finally made it to the train station and boarded the first train he could to central London. As he got to the laboratory, he was asked to remove his trousers and underwear once again. This time the spectator was an Indian male nurse, who didn't inspire much trust either. The nurse poured some gel in a small device and began to roll it onto Andrés' testicles. Andrés could see a screen that was in front which showed all of what was going on in his testicles, but he couldn't understand what he was supposed to be looking at. The uncertainty of not knowing what has happening increased his nerves.

—Hey, what is this screen showing? Tell me now! —he rudely shouted to the nurse.

The Indian man, with a very strong and difficult accent, answered that he was unable to provide any type of diagnostic as he was simply a nurse. He told Andrés the doctor was the only person certified to provide him with a definite answer once he had seen the ultrasound himself. Andrés rolled his eyes and thought: "Is it possible for someone to tell me what the hell is going on in this place?"

Not having any type of answer, diagnostic, comment or a tiny observation made Andrés lose patience and was convinced he was actually suffering from a terminal disease. He thought that if nothing abnormal was happening to him, either doctor Lovestone or this Indian nurse —whom Andrés didn't understand a word of what he said— would have told him that everything was OK from the first place. But this hadn't been the case up to now.

A man who had always been extremely self-confident, who always seemed to have everything under control, who gave the impression that he knew everything at all times and who permanently looked down on people, was now showing his genitals to a complete stranger wearing only a hospital robe. The newly defined dynamic which included getting naked and having to let a stranger touch his genitals made him feel utterly humiliated.

After having the ultrasound done, he moved to another room in which a female nurse pinched him with a needle and took some blood from his right arm. This test was required in order to determine if any cancer cells had spread to other parts of his body.

Once this test was over, the nurse asked him to lie down for a moment in the stretcher as he was looking quite pale. Andrés, who was dizzy and tired, was desperate to believe now more than ever —that all of this was not real. He wanted to run away from everything.

While he was resting on the stretcher of that clinic, Andrés could not still believe what he was going through. Not even all the money in the world could take him away from what he was living. In those moments, he only wished he had his grandma or Marie close to him. But he had no one. He wanted to cry, but he just didn't allow himself to do it. He couldn't show others that someone like him could be scared. He had learnt it in his professional career; he could never show any signs of weaknesses to anyone and this principle was also applied to his personal life.

The Indian nurse approached the stretcher where Andrés was laying down. He saw fear in his eyes. He saw anxiety. But he didn't see any sign of humbleness in his eyes.

—Mr. de la Vega, we have everything necessary for the doctor to review the tests. You will have your results within a week.

Andrés remained silent. The nurse continued saying:

—For the time being, try to rest a little bit but don't refrain from your daily activities as the mind can play lots of damaging tricks if we're not active.

After hearing these words, he got dressed again. As he left the laboratory, he ordered a cab and headed straight to Heathrow Airport.

It was about 3pm when he got to the airport. He walked straight to the British Airways counter and asked for a first class ticket to Guatemala City. Andrés didn't remember there were no direct flights from London to Guatemala. The only way to fly there was to take a connection flight through New York City, wait for three hours at the airport and then fly to Guatemala. The next available flight was booked already for first class passengers, but there were still a few economic seats.

Andrés was not going to be able to fly first class, something inconceivable to him. Ever since he started working at Richard's firm, he could not come to terms with the idea of flying economic. He showed the customer assistant at British Airways his frequent flyer VIP card, but as much as she wanted to help, all the seats were already booked. The girl tried to calm him down by saying that there were first class seats for whenever he wished to return.

As it was typical of him, Andrés rolled his eyes as wanting to call her a "useless person" and then purchased whatever seat they had available. He complained about the customer service and cursed at everyone at the counter. Making others feel like shit was a way for him to let go off his own feelings, his frustration, his fear, his sadness. The girl at the counter printed the boarding passes and gave it to him as fast as she could. She had gotten extremely nervous.

And this was how Andrés went back to travelling economic class once again. He was going be a regular traveller with no luxury, as he had been before becoming the successful man he thought he was. As he was moving away from the counter, he thought to himself: "Even if I wanted, things could not get any worse at this point".

CHAPTER X

Once Andrés boarded the plane, he saw people who looked like him and who were sitting in first class. They were all dressed sharply, just like him, and had their laptops open and a glass of champagne courtesy of the house on their tray tables. As he walked, he thought to himself: "What are the chances to run into someone I know in this flight? None". To run into a client or a colleague who was on that flight would be embarrassing for him as he'd have to explain why he was travelling economic.

As he was passing the last seat in the first class section, he heard a woman calling his name:

—Andrés de la Vega, is that you?

He couldn't believe it. There was actually someone who knew him in that plane. This was the last thing he wanted in that moment, and there it was: a woman in that plane knew him. He turned around hoping that this person was someone unimportant. His eyes met with Mia, the girl from New York whom he had almost lost his virginity with, a few years back. Andrés, without knowing how to react, simply replied:

—Yes —he paused and taking a long breath, he continued —Yes, it is me.

At the time they had met in New York, Mia was a law student at university; and was now working as a consultant for the American Government on global warming issues. She had to travel quite often around the world to participate in conferences and meet with leaders from other countries. She said:

—Ever since that night in New York I didn't hear back from you. I thought I would never see you again.

Andrés didn't know what to say as he was speechless. The only thing he could think of was to find his seat and forget about what was happening. Even though Mia didn't know him at all, she noticed he looked quite concerned.

—Andrés, are you OK? You look a little pale.

He wanted to put an end to this accidental conversation for the stupid shame this woman brought to his memory and which for a second time   —coincidence or not— found him feeling vulnerable and humiliated.

—Yes… Mia, right? —he asked.

With this answer he wanted to show her that she was a ghost from the past by pretending not to remember her so well. However, he definitely knew the name of the woman who —according to him— had humiliated him a few years back.

—I am fine. Hope you have a safe trip —he said and continued towards the economy section.

Mia raised her hand in an attempt to say good bye, but he had already disappeared. Andrés continued walking with his head down as he was embarrassed for travelling in economy class. He felt as if people were judging him for travelling there, as if they knew him! He got to his designated seat, which was located in the last row next to the toilettes.

His seat was the one between the window and the aisle. On the window side, he had an American man who was two meters tall and weighed nearly 250 pounds. In the aisle seat, there was an English girl who had a lot of make up on, wore a leopard print mini dress, had high heels on and smelled like cheap perfume. Andrés couldn't believe he was going to spend seven hours on board this plane next to these two characters. When he sat down, he thought of going back and keep on talking with Mia as he wanted to take his mind of all that he was experiencing, but his pride didn't let him. He decided to stay in his seat for the whole flight. All he wanted to do by this time was to fall asleep and to forget all that was happening in his life. Even if it was just for a few minutes.

The guy sitting next to Andrés noticed that his flight partner was feeling tired and decided to start a casual conversation to make him feel at ease.

—Hello! My name is Bud. You look too elegant to be travelling with us in economy class —he said joking.

That was a good observation indeed, Andrés thought. He couldn't stop dressing with elegance, as he felt this was his personal trademark. And even if that comment came from a nobody —as he considered Bud to be— his ego appreciated the comment. He was pleased to know that people around him could perceive he was not in the place someone like him deserves.

—This summer's weather has been really good here in London, don't you think? —Bud said.

Andrés thought to himself: "This can't be happening. Here's another idiot who can only talk about the London weather". He ignored what Bud had just said, turned his iPod on and fixed his eyes on this tall American guy, trying to tell him: "Please, fuck off. The last thing I want to do right now is to talk to you".

Bud was just trying to be friendly with the guy sitting next to him as they were going to share the next seven hours of their lives. But he got the message and understood that Andrés was a person of very few friends, so he decided to continue with his own routine. Andrés asked for a glass of whiskey on the rocks. He was not used to drinking as much as he had those last few days, but he needed it. He wanted to relax, given that the idea of sharing a long haul flight next to an obese man and a girl who looked like a whore —and who both snored and dribbled while sleeping— would definitely not help him calm down.

The aircraft finally took off. The returning to Guatemala adventure, after so many years, had already begun. Precisely when the plane took off from the Heathrow runway, he realised what he was doing. When the flight captain turned off the seat belt light, Andrés recognised he was actually flying to Guatemala and he hesitated. What was he doing on board a plane flying to the country which he had always wished to forget? His grandmother was dead. What the hell was he doing trying to cling to a simple memory for his own sake? Was he really flying all the way just to visit her grandma's graveyard? If he could have made the airplane return in that specific second, he would have done it immediately. But he obviously couldn't. He weighted the idea of getting to New York, spend a couple of days in the city and then head back to London as soon as he could to see his doctor.

Thousands of thoughts invaded Andrés' mind and made him doubt. He couldn't see clearly why he had taken that stupid decision of going back to Guatemala. He wanted to fall asleep, but he simply couldn't. He checked his emails on his BlackBerry over and over again. He attempted to read financial magazines and newspapers he had bought in Heathrow, but nothing interested him. He kept on putting and taking off his earphones in order to watch a move or listen to some music, but nothing could really grab his attention.

Even if he tried to keep himself distracted, he couldn't. The only thing he could think of was the many stupid and illogical reasons why he was on board that flight. He was so scared to face his fears. He was scared to talk to himself. He was afraid of accepting the situation he was living in that very moment. First, he had lost the woman who selflessly taught him the true meaning of love, of giving without expecting anything in return, of freedom. He had lost it all because of his fucking greed. He let go a woman who loved him for who he was. He lost her because he had preferred to make more money instead of building a life with her. Not just that. Now he was facing his own mortality. What he had never imagined, or even considered, was now a real possibility in his life. Could he have cancer? Andrés didn't want to think about Marie or this disease, but he was trapped in these thoughts.

Very harmful thoughts haunted Andrés during the long hours spent on that flight. Whenever he recalled the moments he shared with Marie, his heart would race faster. Then the word "cancer" would attack him and he surrendered easily to fear. What frightened him the most was the uncertainty of not knowing what was going on with his life. Not having control over the situation really bothered him. He thought that if there was a God, he would not let this happen to him.

It was a common practice during his business trips to see Andrés working on his laptop for the whole duration of the flight. He was always thinking about numbers, the next strategy to use, the next company to purchase, the profits that he would generate and how he would spend his bonus money. But today, everything was different. He not only felt humiliated for having to travel with trashy people —as he labelled them—, but moreover, he was becoming increasingly anxious as he was starting to understand that whatever was about to unfold in his life was out of his control.

At this point, his strategic mind changed its direction of thought. That afternoon, inside this plane surrounded by white clouds in the sky, and sitting next to two people he got to hate in such a short time, his strategy now turned into thinking: "what will I do if I have cancer?" Now his mathematic mind revolved around: "how long will I be able to live if this has already spread in my body?" His purchase thoughts now became focused on: "which doctors will be able to cure me?" And finally, on his bonus, he now wondered: "who will be next to me through this?"

The seconds and minutes aboard this plane felt as if there were eternal. With each second he felt even lonelier and more scared. Andrés was used to planning long term goals, but now that long term period seemed uncertain.

CHAPTER XI

During the seven hour long flight to New York, Andrés had not been able to read a single page of any of the magazines he bought, nor listen to a complete song on his iPod. He tried desperately to avoid any thought relating to his situation, but his mind didn't let him and that's why this flight turned into a real torment. He wanted to escape from his own thoughts, but his mind imprisoned him with tragic scenarios and with fear throughout the whole journey.

The plane finally approached New York City's John F. Kennedy airport. Bud, his companion who remained silent for the whole duration of the flight, tried to make a last attempt to start another conversation with Andrés and asked him about his purpose of travelling to New York. As expected, this was another failed attempt. The girl sitting next to him had not troubled Andrés during the course of the flight. However, her smell —that of a cheap whore— disgusted him and he found a way to let her know just that.

When the girl woke up as the plane was about to land, Andrés stared at her and with an ironic tone, he said:

—I hope for the sake of humanity, that one of your purchases while staying here in New York includes an original perfume.

She tried to ignore the comment, but still feeling offended by it, she said bluntly:

—And I really hope that someone who looks as important as you do, can buy a bit of respect towards others —Andrés turned his face, but she continued —, oh no, I forgot, you can't buy that, you arrogant prick.

After twenty long minutes waiting for all the passengers to get off the aircraft, Andrés was able to escape. He promised himself that he would never, ever, fly in economy class once again.

He was hoping not to run into Mia on his way out, as he wasn't in the mood to chat with anyone, and even less with her. Once he made it to the gate, he saw her kneeling down trying to get some papers from her luggage. As she wasn't facing his way, he sped up his pace, but she did manage to see him walking by. She shouted:

—*Bon voyage*, my friend, I hope you feel better.

Andrés decided to ignore her and simply walked away.

His next adventure was to queue in order to get through US Customs. This was another situation he really hated. He couldn't understand why there wasn't a queue for business people or for people who travelled first class. He detested having to wait in line and mingle with all kinds of people around him. On this occasion, there was a man from the Dominican Republic queuing up before him. He was tall, with dark skin, well built, white hair, and was wearing shorts and a red flowery shirt. He looked in his mid-50s and seemed very excited, something he couldn't hide.

When Andrés joined the queue, this man turned towards him and with a very strong Dominican accent from Santo Domingo, he said:

—Excuse me; do you know how long are we supposed to wait here?

Andrés didn't feel like chatting to anyone, and so he ignored him. But the man asked once again:

—Hey, excuse me; do you know if this will take very long? —he said this with his eyes wide open with excitement and with a huge grin on his face —I'm asking because my son is waiting for me outside. I haven't seen him for 15 years now, and I will get to see my newly born granddaughter.

For a second, Andrés wished he had someone waiting for him too. He wanted to think his grandmother or Marie were going to be waiting for him at the airport, that he was going to be able to hug them and that he was going to feel protected and safe with them. But this was definitely not going to be possible. There was no one waiting for him anywhere. When he realised how lonely his life was, he felt an enormous feeling of emptiness filling his heart. Knowing he was not going to be able to ignore this guy in front of him forever, he replied keeping his eyes fixed on the ground:

—Taking into account the number of people queuing, I guess it won't take more than 20 minutes —said Andrés with a sad voice.

His sight was still fixed on the floor as he said these words. He was feeling empty and worthless.

This Dominican man was part of the third generation of fishermen on the island. He lived in a small house which he had built himself by the seashore. He went fishing everyday by dawn and his wife was responsible to sell the fish he got in the local market. He had five sons and three of them had migrated to the US. Fifteen years had gone by without being able to see them, but he and his wife were extremely proud of their achievements ever since they left home. Perhaps, for someone like Andrés it was easier to judge them and even label them as underachievers, given that they had lived their lives as "simple" mechanics. However, this Dominican man, felt proud of them because they were living a simple and honest life, without many material possessions but with a lot of love. Moreover they were setting an example to their children of hard work and dignity. The happiness that this man was experiencing after having landed in the US didn't require any words to describe it. He was anxious to see his sons and his newly born granddaughter. This feeling was heavier than the sadness and pain he could have felt after having lived apart from them for so many years.

On the other side, there was Andrés. A young, successful and rich man with a secured future. But there was something missing nonetheless. There were no real expectations or dreams which could make him live a life with a purpose. He had no commitments in life. He was living his day to day to get richer only. To see this humble and simple old fisherman with such an excitement made him feel even emptier. Even if he had a family, he had chosen to walk away from them.

The fisherman was called through the immigration booth, and he went on without any problem. Andrés did too. Andrés knew he would never run into this man ever again, and for a brief moment he felt joy for him. He recalled his grandma telling him when he was a little boy that "we are all energy, Andrés. Whenever you're truly happy, this happiness irradiates to everyone around you. Similarly, whenever you feel sad, you will make others around you feel sad as well". Although Andrés was a very logical and intellectual human being, he knew that her grandmother —with all the eccentricities of her heart— was right. Even if he was feeling empty and trapped by fear, this fisherman's happiness had filled him with a surprising hope.

This brief moment of reflection —which was not very common for Andrés— was followed by a walk towards the gate in which he would board the plane to his final destination: Guatemala. As he was approaching the gate, he started noticing the different type of people that he was running into as he was getting closer and closer to the gate. The last time he had been "close" to his country, was the day he left home ten years ago, so he had forgotten what it was to fly from the US to Guatemala. It was usual for him to spend time at the VIP rooms during his business travels while waiting for the plane to depart. However, this time it was not going to be possible. He was so tired, that even finding the VIP room was too much of an effort for him. So he decided to stay in the gate for over three hours with all the "other people" as he considered them.

He realised that over three quarters of the passengers were men who had migrated illegally to the US, and were now going back after many years of absence —some for the first time ever since they left home— to visit their families. The majority of the men sitting there were wearing jeans, cowboy boots and belts, colourful long sleeve shirts and cowboy hats.

Andrés noticed a group of four men sitting together waiting to board the plane. Instead of taking a carry-on bag, they were bringing stereo systems, TVs and video game consoles packed in big boxes. He heard one of them speaking Guatemalan slang and saying in Spanish: "Oh man, my kid is going to be so happy with these gifts. I can't wait to see his face".

He also observed some other people, who looked a bit more like him: executives and wealthy Guatemalans who had been on holidays or shopping in New York and were now heading back home. They were dressed in a similar style to him. Men were wearing elegant suits and others had designer polo shirts and jeans. Women were styled just like any European or American fashion model. They were all playing around with their "smart phones" and iPads just like in any other developed city Andrés had travelled to.

Even if Andrés didn't feel Guatemalan anymore, due to all the time he had been away, he found it amusing to see how the people he related to, were obviously uncomfortable with sharing this space with the more simple and humble group. From this scene, he was able to realise that within the same country, the type of people, the social classes and the realities, were polarised. He had always heard European people who had visited Guatemala saying that the country was simply beautiful but that the social differences were extremely obvious. It was right at that moment, in one of the gates at JFK, that Andrés was able to see this reality with his own eyes after more than ten years of exile. He could see now this sad reality through the eyes of a foreigner too.

Listening to the very unique Guatemalan slang, he was able to transport himself to his childhood for a few seconds. Overhearing some Guatemalan words reconfirmed him that he was about to go back to his past. He started to feel frightened about it too. His mind started to play tricks again as if wishing to make him go into a deeper state of fear. What was he going to do there exactly? He would get to his grandma's grave, and then, what? Would he see a doctor there as well? What if he was diagnosed with cancer? Would he be treated in London or in Guatemala? How long would he need to stay there for? What if his family didn't wish to see him after all that time? What if he lost his job in New York?

Before reaching this point in his life, fear wasn't something that would get in Andrés' way. This was something he rarely felt. He was a self-confident man who was used to achieve each goal he set for himself. However, now it all was different. Everything was out of his control. Now more than ever, each second that ticked the clock started to feel as an enormous weight he was just unable to carry for long. He was scared. He wished for a second to have Marie close. A simple kiss and a hug would do. But she wasn't there.

After having spent the three hours waiting in the gate, Andrés heard the announcement on the speakers asking passengers going to Guatemala to start boarding the plane. Twelve hours had passed since Andrés had the ultrasound and the blood tests done, and so he was relieved to hear that he was to begin the last trace of his journey. This calmed him a bit. Andrés was so exhausted and overwhelmed by the whole situation that he didn't even check whether there were any first class seats available. What could be worse than sitting next to an obese American guy and a cheap looking girl through a complete transatlantic flight? He thought that there could be nothing worse than that. But he was wrong.

This time he didn't have to sit next to the toilets. He sat in the window seat with the view to the wing and the turbine of the aircraft. Once he sat down, he started to get anxious to see who was going to be his flight partner for the following five hours. The stewardess were about to "cross check" the plane, when all of a sudden he heard a baby who was wrapped around her mother, crying as if there was no tomorrow. The mother of the baby was literally running into the airplane as she was about to miss it. Mixing Spanish with English she shouted: "Ay please, don't leave without me". Andrés was aware luck hadn't been on his side so far that day, so he immediately knew who was going to be sitting next to him. And his guess was correct!

The young mother seemed like she was in her early thirties. She had dark skin, curly hair up to her neck; she was chubby and was wearing very tight white jeans and a white blouse with a neckline which exposed her breasts and belly. She was in high heels, also white, and wore many cheap looking "golden" necklaces and bracelets. Her baby girl was about five months old and would not stop crying. She was carrying a bigger than accepted carry-on bag in one hand, and her baby on the other arm. After finally making it to her seat, she saw Andrés and in Spanish she asked:

—Excuse me; can you please carry my daughter for a sec while I place my bag?

Andrés didn't react to this question. His English influence was too much. After ten years of living abroad, he had lost the dimension of how open Latinos are. In England, it was very unlikely that a person would ask a stranger to carry her baby. Not even for a second. Andrés wasn't sure how he was supposed to act. He was so influenced by the European mentality, that he was afraid that people would confuse him with a paedophile if he actually carried the baby for a brief moment. He was so tired that carrying a crying baby was the last thing he wanted to deal with. However, she insisted and asked him once again:

—Please, do you speak Spanish? —she implored.

Andrés was still not reacting. The young mother, noticing she had to speed up the process of placing her bag as she was being asked to take her seat, just handed the baby to Andrés. He was surprised by the whole thing that he grabbed the baby as if the little creature was a supermarket bag. The girl wasn't being able to place the bag on the compartment as it was just too big and heavy. She kept pushing it over and over again, but it wouldn't fit in. After a couple of minutes of failed attempts, and of noticing Andrés disgust in his face for carrying her baby, the stewardess approached them. She asked the girl to please give her the bag as they were going to have to check it in because it was impossible to fit it there. This wasn't said in a very polite manner though. Finally, the girl sat down, took her baby from Andrés' arms and in limited English she simply said:

—Thank you for holding my baby.

Andrés had never held a baby with his hands before. He had always been scared of their fragility. To him, becoming a parent in the short, medium and long term was simply out of the picture. He believed babies were an unnecessary expenditure which required too much effort. If he wanted to continue living up to his plans, being committed to a woman and having kids were activities which were definitely missing on his list of priorities.

The little baby girl didn't stop crying throughout the first half of the flight until her mother started to breastfeed her. Andrés couldn't believe what his eyes were seeing. Seeing this woman's breasts out and about made him feel so uncomfortable he started to sweat. How could this woman be breastfeeding her baby in front of him? How could she be showing her breasts to all the passengers? How could this lady feed her daughter like this?

Little did Andrés know that this woman came from an indigenous village in the *Verapaces* —northeast Guatemala—, a very humble place in which people firmly believed in the power of natural breastfeeding. To indigenous people, it was extremely important for mothers to breastfeed their children because this created a bond between the mother and the baby. In Andrés' mind, all XXI century mothers had to feed their children with baby bottles, so that they didn't have to put other people around them in uncomfortable situations as the one he was experiencing in that very moment. How mistaken and isolated was Andrés from the reality of the world!

His selfishness had led him to become self-centred and always expected other people to do what made him happy. According to Andrés, everyone was supposed to live up to his standards. His egocentric mind-set trapped and isolated him inside a bubble. Inside this bubble he couldn't care less about the other seven billion inhabitants of this planet.

Andrés wasn't aware of other realities which were stratospherically different to his, especially of those people from his own country. The girl sitting next to him, for example, had migrated to the US as a *mojada* —or illegal immigrant— when she was just 12 years old. This was the first time in 20 years she was going to be able to visit her family back home. Something she had dreamed for a long time. She only hoped that her family would recognise her after all those years. Even if these two characters had lived abroad for quite some time, their realities were completely different from each other.

The girl, on one side, had always worked as a cleaner. Her circle of friends had always been other illegal immigrants. Her day to day, ever since the first moment she set foot in the US, became a survival routine so that immigration wouldn't deport her back to Guatemala, where she had no opportunity to access a dignified life. Her mission in life was to work as hard as she could, so that she could send her monthly 100 dollars to her family back home which helped them eat. Before leaving to the US, she had always heard from other people around her, that she could opt for a better life in that country, the so called "American Dream". However, her daily struggle made her realise in a short time that things weren't as the Hollywood movies portrayed it. Dreaming of the day she was going to be able to reunite with her loved ones became her strength and hope to wake up each and every morning. And that day finally arrived.

On the other side of the spectrum, there was Andrés, a young man who fled his country to study in a respected university in England. He was someone who had achieved a very highly regarded and enviable professional position in a relative short time thanks to his hard work. The people he networked with were either from his same university or from other well-known universities from around the world. Andrés was used to travelling around the globe on business trips and staying at the best hotels in town. Andrés didn't go to England because he had to work to feed his family back home or because he had no opportunities to access a decent life, as was the case of the girl sitting next to him. He left because his materialistic ambition made him.

In that same flight, two individuals were returning home after many years of absence. One brought with him material wealth, a university diploma, a respected professional position, an enviable bank account; but he was also bringing with him a possible terminal disease and a lonely heart. The girl next to him was coming back with three thousand dollars she had been able to save over the years, a daughter wrapped in her arms and the hope to see and feel part again of her family which helped her to get through all the hard work, sadness and humiliations.

By the time the baby girl fell asleep, Andrés almost automatically fell asleep as well. It had been almost thirty hours since he took the decision to make that trip, and so he was able to sleep for a while due to all the physical and emotional exhaustion he was feeling. After a couple of hours of sleep, he woke up as he heard the voice of a stewardess announcing that they had landed to their destination. "Welcome to Guatemala City", she said in a very broken Spanish. When he heard these words, he knew that there was no way out from it. He was now in the place he always wanted to forget about. "What the hell am I doing here?" he asked himself one more time.

CHAPTER XII

It was shortly before midnight when he reached his final destination: the Aurora airport in Guatemala City. As he was getting closer to the exit doors, he noticed that for every person arriving, there was a group of about 15 people —the majority were men and women from very humble villages— who had gathered to greet their loved ones at the airport. They came from villages far away from the city, but they did not want to lose a second to be next to the people they missed the most. Some of them hadn't seen each other for decades even.

Andrés saw an old lady in a striking purple *guipil* —the Guatemalan indigenous traditional costume women wear— who, upon seeing her son, started crying of excitement. She ran as fast as her legs allowed her until they met and embraced in what seemed like an eternal hug. Andrés overheard the lady who whispered in her son's ears: "I was afraid that after 20 years I was not going to be able to recognise you, but you're still very handsome, my son".

Even if it was hard for him to accept it, he would have loved to be part of the Guatemalan "folklore" in that very moment. For a second, he wished for his family to be there to embrace him as well. But they weren't there. They didn't even know he had decided to visit Guatemala, so how could they be there for him?

Andrés decided to walk away from the arrivals area and started looking for a cab. He walked by these waves of people who were waiting for their relatives and friends. This young man, who had been born in the same country as most of them, now looked and walked like an English aristocrat. He really stood out from the people there, not only because of his fashionable sense of dressing but because of his despicable attitude.

As he was walking by, he thought to himself: "this doesn't even look like an airport but more like a bus terminal". He stood up in front of a sign which read "Taxis" and taking a deep breath he asked himself: "what do I do now?"

The original plan he had outlined included a visit to the village where his grandma was buried, he would meet up with his family —if there was time— and after five days in Guatemala he would fly back to London. He took his BlackBerry out of his pocket and noticed that it had signal from a local company which allowed him to make calls but not to browse the Internet. He was not going to be able to order a taxi online, but he'd have to trust a local cab driver to take him to the nearest hotel. He also realised that he didn't have too much charge left on it, but he decided to charge his mobile once he got to the hotel. He felt as if being naked when his mobile wasn't working.

For a moment he considered calling his parents, but he didn't have their number saved on his phone. Nor did he have the number of any relative or friend who could get his parents' phone number for him. And even if he did, calling anyone in the middle of the night after so many years of absence would just worry them. Or so he thought.

He approached a cab which was parked close to where he was standing, and he spoke his first words in Spanish after many years of not speaking it —only when it had been really necessary when doing business —, and asked the cab driver with a very exhausted tone of voice:

—Can you take me to the nearest hotel?

The cab driver realised that this guy wasn't the typical Guatemalan man and knew he couldn't drive him to a cheap hotel.

—There are many fancy hotels around here. I'm guessing you're looking for one like that, right?

At this point, Andrés was too tired to think, but knowing he hadn't booked any hotel, he remained as alert as he could.

—Yes, take me to the closest one possible, please —he answered.

He opened the door of the cab and got in immediately with the carry-on bag he had brought with him all the way from London. Andrés couldn't believe he was actually back in Guatemala. The cab left the airport zone and reached the city within a few minutes. Andrés' eyes got lost at the sight of the lights posts in the streets, the cars which were driving pass them and at the buildings which decorated this metropolis —some he still recognised and many others he didn't. There was a flashback to his childhood and the memory of his grandma hit him harder than ever before.

Perhaps the biggest fear for him to go back to Guatemala after all those years was because he preferred to ignore and stay away from the pain and sorrow that the loss of his grandmother represented in his life.

However, in that very moment, he needed to be close to her, even if his logical and rational mind could not understand why.

They finally made it to the hotel which was located in the city centre. He requested a room for the three following nights and asked to receive a morning call by 7am. He also asked for information about car rental, as he was going to drive to a nearby town the next morning.

As the receptionist was entering his personal details in the computer, she asked:

—Excuse me, sir; I need to make a copy of your passport. Are you Guatemalan?

Andrés felt offended by this question, and without saying a word, he simply threw his British passport —which he had recently gotten— in the counter as wanting to show that he did not belong there anymore. How could she think that he was like all these ordinary people? He thought. No. He was a British citizen and didn't belong to that world of savages, as he had previously referred to them.

Andrés signed all the required paperwork and went straight to his room. Once he got there, the remaining energy he had was used to brush his teeth and to put on his silk pyjamas —which he had bought in Edinburgh a few years back. Andrés got into bed and by the time his head touched the pillow he felt into a very deep sleep. For the first time in many years, he was able to sleep like this. The physical tiredness, but overall, the mental and emotional roller coaster he had been through in the last 30 hours had worn him out completely.

The following morning, the phone at Andrés' room rang at exactly seven o'clock. When he heard the first ring, he tapped the phone with his left hand in an attempt to snooze what he thought was his alarm clock. But the phone kept ringing and realised he wasn't going to get an extra five minutes of sleep. Still asleep he picked up the phone and just heard a voice which said:

—Good morning, sir, this is your morning call.

Upon hearing these words, Andrés immediately opened his eyes and fixed them to the white ceiling of the hotel room. Everything in his mind was just like that ceiling he was staring at. Five minutes passed until he realised once again where he was. He opened and closed his eyes, swallowed saliva over and over again and his right hand kept scratching his head non-stop. He wanted to believe this was all a dream, that he was waking up at his Richmond flat and that he was late to take the train and head down to the City of London for work. He wanted to cling to the idea that he was going to be able to live his daily routine as always.

When he realised that he was 5,500 miles away from his flat in London and that he was actually in the country he had left ten years ago, he jumped from the bed as a kid waking up from a terrible nightmare. It took him about ten seconds to become conscious of his reality. He became aware that he was in Guatemala, that there was a lump in his testicle, that he had let go a woman he really loved and that he had no one who was waiting for him anywhere in the world.

He decided to take a shower, and after that he dressed like an aristocrat who is about to spend his summer holidays in Ibiza. He chose to wear blue cotton trousers, a white long sleeve shirt, a brown sweater wrapped around his neck and brown chamois leather loafer shoes with no socks. As he was getting dressed, he realised he had forgotten to charge the battery of his mobile as he simply surrendered to bed. But he didn't give it too much importance as he was going to drive down to the village where his grandmother was buried —*Los Manantiales*— and he would get back that same day. After that short trip he would decide if he was going to visit his family or not.

He wanted to tick off the list the visit to *Los Manantiales* and get over the main reason of his stupid decision to travel all the way to Guatemala. After that, he was going to be able to continue with his life as usual. Or at least that's what he was trying to believe.

Once he finished grooming himself, he walked down to the hotel reception. He saw that there were many guests who had a similar appearance to his. There were many American businessmen who were wearing suits, ties and most of them were carrying their leather laptop bags with them, a sign that they were executives, just like Andrés was. Having all these people around him made him feel like home, even if it was for a brief moment of the day.

He walked towards the reception, where there was a girl named María, and he said:

—Last night I requested information for renting a car. Did you find something?

The girl thought to herself: "first of all, good morning, you spoilt brat", but with a fake smile she replied:

—Yes, sir. Can you please tell me your name?

As arrogant as he could only be, he replied:

—De la Vega, Andrés.

She turned her eyes back to the computer and realised that no one had requested any information under that name. She then looked back to Andrés and said:

—Of course, Mr. De la Vega. You can go ahead and eat breakfast and I shall bring you all the information you requested to your table.

María pretended to be looking for information on the computer —even if the screen was blank— as she didn't want to deal with an angry Andrés.

—Just one more question before you go, sir. What kind of car do you have in mind?

Andrés who was already making his way to the restaurant, turned around, and feeling like the almighty he responded:

—I'm sure that it is very difficult to get a Range Rover in this country, am I right?

What María didn't know was that this conceited man had never ever driven a Range Rover, nor a four by four vehicle. What she was conscious about though, was that she was dealing with an arrogant imbecile. She tried to be polite and patient —given that this was part of the job— and calmly said:

—It is possible, sir. But sadly, given the violent situation the country is going through at the moment, we wouldn't advise you to take such a car and expose yourself unnecessarily.

Andrés thought: "Violence? What is she talking about?" But he didn't want to dig deeper as that would only show he wasn't aware of the situation and he hated to be taken as an ignorant person. Somehow confused and nervous, he replied:

—OK… just get me any four by four vehicle you can find, as soon as possible.

María agreed with another fake smile and told him she would have all the information required by the time he was done with his breakfast. As he walked away, she started making calls to car rental companies and managed to reserve a 2007 Hyundai Santa Fe. It was a four by four car, just like he had requested.

Ten minutes after their first encounter, María walked towards the table where Andrés was sitting in, and noticed he was reading the New York Times very anxiously. She thought to herself: "Why is he reading the news from another country and not the ones of the place he is at?" But she didn't say a thing and just handed him a paper with the car rental confirmation which he had to sign and said:

—Your car will be here in half an hour, sir. Do you need anything else?

Andrés thought of asking for a mobile charger, but he considered that he still had a couple of hours left of battery which would be enough to go and come back from his short trip. He still had his eyes on the newspaper and without making any visual contact with her, he said:

—No, thanks. That's all.

He finished his breakfast. He had ordered a continental breakfast and a cup of tea, just to show that he wasn't a local guest. For a second he thought of ordering the typical Guatemalan dish, but he didn't want people around him to confuse him with a local. Half an hour later he heard his name being called from the reception as his car was waiting for him outside.

Andrés stood up from the table and headed towards the hotel lobby. The guy from the agency who had brought the car to the hotel handed him the keys. Andrés freaked out and pushed this kid against the car and desperately asked:

—Do you know how to get to *Los Manantiales*?

The kid got scared at Andrés' attitude and fearing his reaction replied:

—Eh… no, sir… I have no clue of where this place is.

Andrés —who was letting his nerves take over his actions— put his hands on the boy's shoulders and said:

—I need to get to *Los Manantiales*, and I have no fucking clue how to get there, do you understand?

The kid, who must have been about 19 years old, recalled that this village was close to a somehow bigger town called *La Mina* which was located north of Guatemala City. However, he was so nervous at Andrés' way of acting that he had a mental block.

Once this kid reacted to what was going on, he aggressively removed Andrés' hands from his body and still a little scared he told him:

—I know that there is a town close by called *La Mina*, but I don't know how to get there. All I know is that you have to take the *Atlántico* road and there you will have to follow the signs to *La Mina*. Whenever you get there, you will have to ask someone for directions to *Los Manantiales*.

Andrés took his hands off the kid and felt embarrassed for what he had done, but he was so nervous, exhausted and lost that he wasn't being able to control his impulses. He walked away from the boy, and like a child who knows he has misbehaved, he said:

—I'm sorry; I didn't mean to hurt you. The *Atlántico* road is the one which takes you to Izabal, right?

Andrés didn't know how he had been able to remember that, but it seemed like he was right. The boy replied:

—Yes, precisely that one.

Andrés took the car keys, turned on the engine and the GPS in his mobile. However, he wasn't aware that in a country like Guatemala —and especially in a little village like *Los Manantiales*— the GPS systems were useless.

The new adventure was about to begin now. He was heading to a place which he never ever imagined he would have to go to: the little village of *Los Manantiales*. Something as irrational as needing to be close to the memory of his grandmother had driven him to break all sorts of attitudes and structures he had built for so many years. Because of fear, of having to face his mortality and the need to feel part of something, took him all the way to this situation.

CHAPTER XIII

August in Guatemala is still considered to be part of the rainy season. In the mornings people can still appreciate the sun and light summery warmth. It is during the afternoons, around 3pm, that it is usual to see rain making its magical appearance. It is as if God has automatised the hours for sunshine and rain, because only a few days a year did this synchronisation fail.

This morning was not the exception. When Andrés got into the car, it was about 8:03am and the temperature was 25 degrees Celsius. Like a genuine Brit —which he was trying to imitate as much as he could— he felt happiness to see and feel the sun during this time of the year as in London, autumn had started earlier than expected.

Andrés had no idea as to which direction to take in the road. He tried to use —once again— the GPS in his mobile, but he realised that when he typed "*Los Manantiales*" the application didn't recognise it. He tried with "*La Mina*", which was the town the boy of the car rental had suggested as a first stop, but this place wasn't recognised either. Andrés had to trust his instincts and out loud he said: "Grandma, I have come all the way here for you, please take me to where you are". He felt silly to hear his own voice pleading to a dead person, but very deep inside, he felt a rare state of peace.

As Andrés was driving, he was being guided by a combination of instincts and memories from his childhood. He made it to the very open and wide *Reforma* Avenue and remembered when his father used to take him and his sister to the Independence Day and Christmas parades which took place in this long and famous avenue of Guatemala City. An image of his dad carrying him on his back when he was just a little boy so that he could enjoy the whole show hit his mind.

At this time it was rush hour in the city and cars were moving slowly. While he was stuck in the traffic jam, Andrés was able to appreciate and observe how the city had grown in the ten years he had been away. There were also many places —buildings, restaurants and shops— which remained as if time had never passed by them.

All of this made him feel like a kid once again, and without expecting it, a short lasting smile was drawn on his face. He thought about his parents, his sister. He wanted to call them in that very moment, but he had forgotten to check his email and search for a telephone number which would probably be in one of the thousands of emails he had saved in his inbox.

Once he was able to get to the end of the *Reforma* Avenue, he had to drive through the Historical Centre of the city in order to find the *Atlántico* road. After so many years abroad, he wasn't aware that the Historical Centre was considered —by many Guatemalans his age— to be a danger zone due to the high levels of poverty and criminality. Andrés wasn't conscious about this, not only because of having lived so many years away from home, but moreover, because his father's office was located in the heart of the Historical Centre, and for Andrés this area reminded him of a relatively peaceful childhood. This was an area he and his sister knew like the palm of their hands and therefore it was a zone in which they felt comfortable and at ease.

It had been relatively recent that the new "centre" of the city had "moved" to the area in which Andrés was staying at. There was also poverty in that area, but there were more modern buildings, huge American look-alike shopping centres, first class restaurants and luxurious homes which made the new "centre" be more cosmopolitan, and allowed for poverty to be hidden and to be less obvious to locals and foreigners alike.

In contrast, the authentic Historical Centre was decorated with old colonial houses, old buildings and with more simple people. To many Guatemalans, this was a "danger zone" area but to Andrés —even after all those years in exile— it felt like home.

As he toured along the avenue which crossed the whole Historical Centre, he was able to observe the Post Office building, the Main Square, the Cathedral and the monumental National Palace. This was more like the "European" classical area of the city, whereas the new "centre" had turned into a mini American city which was built to please the needs of a tiny portion of the Guatemalan society, a society in which classism and racism continued to be the bread and butter of its inhabitants.

Andrés continued his journey through the Historical Centre of the city, and stopping at a red light, he looked up towards the *Cerro del*

Carmen —a small hill which for a long time was considered to be one of the landmarks of the city. This hill reminded him of his cousins who lived close by. They had never seen each other again after their grandma's death, because of the inheritance problems between his father and uncle. Andrés remembered the close relationship he and his cousins had during their childhood. What could have happened to them? Would they still be living in Guatemala? His father's office was located close to the *Cerro del Carmen* too.

The frivolous and selfish Andrés seemed to have disappeared during the forty five minutes' drive through the city. The memories of his family hit him. He felt a very deep state of peace which was not normal in him. He felt like he belonged somewhere. "Can these memories make me feel real joy?" he asked. "No, there was nothing special about them", he automatically responded to himself. Those memories from a very distant childhood didn't belong to him anymore. He didn't want to spend too much time thinking about these silly memories and focused back on continuing with his journey once again.

A few minutes later, he finally made it to the *Martí* Street which would take him all the way to the *Atlántico* road. As he was driving this long street, he started to notice the other reality of the city. In this side of town, there was poverty in every direction he would look at. He saw how overcrowded all public transport buses were. These buses —or *camionetas*— must have had capacity for eighty people, Andrés thought, but he observed how there were more than one hundred people squashed with each other like sardines. He noticed that no one was making use of bus stops. The bus driver would stop wherever he felt like it. He was able to see all the contamination that cars, *camionetas* and any other vehicle were creating in the streets. Each time he stopped at a traffic light, he would see little kids begging for money or doing their best to juggle things in the air in order to get some money. In about an hour, Andrés had been able to discover the two completely opposite realities of Guatemala City.

Before this trip to his hometown, Andrés had travelled on business trips to many of the so called "developing" countries such as Malaysia, Thailand, Mexico and even Nigeria. However, as his purpose was for business only, he had only experienced the luxurious side of these cities. He always stayed at the most expensive hotels and ate at the highly acclaimed restaurants as recommended by high-elite critics. Whenever he travelled, he never felt the need to see beyond the financial centres, and he was definitely never interested in seeing the poorer side of any city.

Andrés was a stranger to poverty in the world. The only way he ever got close to it, was through newspaper articles or by watching the news. As he was driving, he recalled a documentary he watched a few years back about malnutrition in the African Horn. This documentary shocked him, but decided to turn the TV off when they showed a severely malnourished one year old toddler. He felt disgusted by the image and decided this situation had nothing to do with him. Today, many years later, he was observing glances of poverty with his own eyes. He was impacted by this, and also feared for his life a little bit. He even thought of simply going back to the hotel, but if there was a strong characteristic of this young man was his perseverance. He was determined to visit his grandma's graveyard and he was going to do it no matter what.

He kept on driving and finally made it to a long bridge —at the end of the *Martí* Street— which would connect him to the Atlántico road. As he was crossing the bridge, he noticed a sign which read "*La Mina* - 18 Kms". He was glad that he was on the right path and even thought he would get there before he had expected. He tried luck with the GPS on his mobile once again, but this time his mobile didn't even turn on. Andrés felt unprotected without his mobile. This meant being disconnected from the world! He blamed himself for not having charged the phone the night before. He got so scared he even considered the possibility of putting an end to this trip. It was the first time in his life in which he acknowledged how attached he was to this gadget. In a single second, a mobile phone without battery had taken away the peace he was starting to feel.

Andrés was blank. He was in a real state of shock, as when someone tells a kid that Santa Claus is not real. "How is it possible that I can get so worried over a stupid phone?" he asked himself. Maybe he knew the answer to this question but he was not willing to acknowledge it. "All human beings must feel the same", he told himself in an attempt to justify his fear. He had read many articles and books which stated that it was normal for human beings to be addicted to the Internet, their mobile phones and social networks. Given this, he thought he was just being "normal" himself.

He also recalled a few articles which talked about the modern human being and its addiction to be constantly "connected with the world". These articles stated that people with this "social disease" were simply trying to find ways to call attention, to fill in the emptiness they felt and moreover, to evade themselves. As he read many pieces of information on this subject, Andrés always tried to convince himself that he was none of the above. He wanted to believe that he used technology for the practical purposes which made his life easier. Just for that. Making life easier meant resolving all his mundane needs with a "click": grocery shopping, checking the weather forecast, purchasing plane tickets, reading newspapers, checking his work and personal email, etc. His whole world revolved around this device. He had become attached to it, even if he didn't want to fully accept it.

It was very difficult for Andrés to acknowledge his weaknesses. "If I had any weaknesses I wouldn't be where I am", he repeated regularly so that he could feel better with himself. However, this silly experience of having no mobile and being disconnected, made him acknowledge that he was dependent on this device. But, why was this?

He kept on driving, but he was now feeling insecure and nervous at all the things that could happen if his plan didn't unfold as he was expecting. What would have happened if he hadn't realised his phone was dead? As he continued driving through the Historical Centre he was actually living the present moment, his "here and now", and he was feeling at ease with himself. Now that he was aware of this "disconnection" with the world, he lost his serenity and was worrying about what could happen.

He doubted if he was going to be able to make it to the final destination and got distressed while his mind was bombarding him with negative outcomes. After twenty minutes driving, he finally reached a sign which read "Exit to *La Mina* - 1 Km". He pushed the lever down to turn the right blinker of the car, although he noticed that nobody else was using blinkers when changing lanes. However, as he was pretending to be a British citizen, he kept on doing it thinking that this was the "proper" way of driving. When finally entering the road which would take him to *La Mina*, he had no idea what the days ahead were about to unfold.

CHAPTER XIV

The distance to get to *La Mina* from this new road —which was actually paved— was about 10 kilometres. The scenery was beautiful. There were mountains which looked as if they had been painted with different shades of green. The road went up and down between slopes. The sky was clear, the wind was smooth and the sun was shining beautifully. The weather and the landscape felt perfect. It was quarter past nine in the morning when he reached this part of the road. He assumed that *Los Manantiales* —where his grandma was buried— was about fifteen kilometres from where he was, which would allow him to get back to the city by midday.

In less than fifteen minutes, he was entering the little town of *La Mina*. He was certain he had reached this little town as he drove through a very long single-lane street which could only fit one car or bus. Even if it was a one lane street, Guatemalans —being as cheeky as they were— could make cars and buses drive in both directions.

On one side of this narrow street, he observed local indigenous women selling fruits, vegetables and grains which were being kept in large baskets. Although Andrés was driving with the car windows shut, he was still able to hear the horns of all vehicles driving from one side to another and the yelling of bus drivers who attempted to "organise" the traffic jam.

Andrés couldn't believe that there was no authority organising traffic in this place. He couldn't come to terms to understand why a wider road hadn't been built yet and why local authorities hadn't moved those ladies somewhere more hygienic for them to sell their agricultural products. He also noticed that the overcrowding buses phenomenon was the same —if not worse— as what he had seen in the city. This narrow street was a complete chaos, but somehow, it all flowed!

After a few minutes stuck in traffic, he finally made it to the other end of the street, which took him straight to the *Plaza Central* —or Main Square— of the town. This was the typical Guatemalan built square which included a small cathedral and a tiny market. He thought this would be the best place to ask for directions to *Los Manantiales* as he had not seen any signs providing indications on how to get to there.

Andrés parked his four by four vehicle close to the *Plaza Central*. Before leaving the car, he tried to turn his mobile on once again, but he simply confirmed his phone was dead. He got off the car and walked towards a bench which was nearby. In this little town, there were no more people who looked like him, he observed.

La Mina's population was mostly of Mayan origin. However, not everyone in this town —especially men— wore their typical costumes. From his spot on the bench, Andrés noticed a group of men talking to each other, close to where he was. They were wearing jeans, t-shirts and some of them were sporting football shirts from international teams like Barcelona and Real Madrid. "How can people in this remote place know who Messi and Ronaldo are?" he wondered.

He saw another group of women who were all wearing their traditional *guipiles*. A few of these women were breastfeeding their babies very close to where he was sitting. He recalled the scene in the plane which made him feel so uncomfortable, and wondered once again, why would mothers still do this in public? He just couldn't understand it.

A five year old boy with snot all over his face approached him. His t-shirt and trousers had so many little holes in them, his shoes had no soles and he was carrying a small wooden box. When the boy got close to Andrés he asked him: "shoe shine?" This kid, at five years of age, was already working as a shoe shiner in the *Plaza Central* of *La Mina*.

Andrés set his eyes on this kid, who seemed to have his mind somewhere else. Seeing this little boy dressed in rags and having to work being so young shining shoes of strangers, touched him in the deepest of his heart. After a few seconds of staring at the kid he started a conversation with the little one.

—And why aren't you at school? —Andrés asked a bit annoyed.

The little boy simply stared back at him, smiled and replied:

—Because my parents don't let me. I have to work so we can all eat —and he continued offering his services —. Can I shine your shoes? It is only three *quetzales*.

Andrés made his currency conversions and came to the conclusion this kid was charging 20 pence or 0.20 of a pound for shining shoes. Andrés' indifference and greed were paralysed for a few moments as he stared at this young shoe shiner in this little square in *La Mina*.

He took his wallet out and discovered he only had one hundred *quetzales*. He wanted to give this boy all of his money, but he was afraid there were not going to be many cash machines around there, so he took a twenty *quetzales* note —about 1.30 pounds— and in a broken voice he said:

—I don't need you to shine my shoes, but here you go, here are twenty *quetzales* because I really liked you.

The little boy saw the note and was so astonished and excited that he couldn't help opening his eyes and mouth as if he was about to receive the greatest gift of his life. Andrés wasn't sure if the money was going to be spent by this boy or his parents, but to see this kid's bright eyes, was priceless. Andrés reflected on this boy's situation and he was certain that his birthdays and Christmases were not filled with video games, computers or toys all children dream of. He felt great sorrow.

The little one, whipping off the dry snot from his face, took the note and said:

—Thank you, young man! My grandma told me that I was going to receive a gift from an angel on my birthday.

Andrés was destroyed by this comment. He felt so sad for this little boy. And how could he think that he was an angel? What could he actually buy with twenty *quetzales* which could make him so happy? Andrés stared at him a bit longer and in a friendly tone he said:

—No, I'm not an angel —he smiled and continued —: What will you buy with this money on your birthday?

The kid put his little hand on his mouth, he set his eyes on the sky, and just like a little Socrates who is wondering about the meaning of life, he replied:

—Well, I'm definitely going to buy some *tortillas*, *chicharrones* and... —he paused for a moment and suddenly he shouted —: a Coca-Cola! Today everyone at my house will be able to eat enough food.

Andrés wasn't able to hold it any longer. He looked down to the floor and his eyes filled with tears, but he didn't shed a single one. He touched his eyes with his right hand just to make sure he hadn't dropped a tear. In that moment, he got up from the bench and said good bye to the kid. As he started walking, he heard the little one running towards his mother who was nearby: "Grandma was right! Look what I got", he said while showing her the twenty *quetzales* note. Andrés turned his head and saw the little boy hugging his mother with a huge smile on his face.

As he was walking towards the middle of the square, Andrés started to question himself. What would have happened if he hadn't met the kid in that specific moment? If the kid hadn't received a gift from anyone, would he have come to the conclusion that his grandma was a liar and that there were no angels? Why did this kid approach him? And above all, he just could not fully understand, how this little boy, with his dirty little face and dressed in rags had made him feel so damn vulnerable.

Andrés was used to deal with the toughest and ruthless businessmen in the world, from New York to Hong Kong; and none of them had ever made him feel as vulnerable as this little boy had done in a town located in the middle of nowhere.

He then decided to keep on walking and headed towards a group of youngsters, who were hanging out in the middle of the square. Andrés asked them for directions to *Los Manantiales*. At the beginning, they were very surprised to see someone dressed as fancy as Andrés was, in a town like *La Mina*. At first sight, they even confused him with a drug dealer. They were not used to seeing people like Andrés in town. Any "stranger" was automatically associated with a drug dealer and that scared the locals. The four teenagers he was chatting with, simply responded that they didn't know where *La Mina* was and they walked away. Andrés didn't quite understand their behaviour but continued walking around the square hoping to meet someone who could help him.

Andrés hated asking for directions. He kept thinking that this situation which made him interact with all these people wouldn't be happening if his mobile had been working properly. However, he wasn't being conscious that not having his mobile would have meant losing direct contact with people from that little town. He continued walking and saw a green fluorescent painted office which had the word "Town Hall" written on it.

He walked towards this public office and saw that there was no one inside. The wind breezed through this small office and Andrés saw how some papers flew away from a tiny desk located next to where he was standing. Nobody was there to pick them up. For a minute he examined and analysed each and every metre of this reduced space. Seeing there was actually no one, he decided to pick up the documents and put them back into the desk. In that moment, he heard someone coming in through another door. It was a chubby woman, with purple tainted hair and long pink painted nails who was wearing a flowery long dress and was eating a piece of bread with black beans in one of her hands. When she saw Andrés putting the papers back, she shouted:

—Thank you so much for this! You're so handsome —and she winked at him.

Andrés felt embarrassed at this and blushed. He couldn't understand all the sensations that this little town was causing him.

—What can I do for you, gorgeous? —she asked.

Andrés, who was a bit intimidated and nervous, replied:

—Hmmm… I just wanted to know how to get to *Los Manantiales* — he made a pause —and hoped that you could help me.

This chubby and funny looking woman, who had a piece of bread in her mouth —but couldn't care less—, continued talking while eating at the same time:

—OK, and what is it that you want to do there? Looking like this —referring to his aristocrat look— you will not get there alive —and she busted into laughter.

He was not used to give explanations to anyone, and even less, to a stranger. But he realised if he didn't talk he wouldn't get any directions to the village, and he just wanted to leave that place as soon as possible. "In England, no one would ever ask me why I want to do something. I ask and people respond. They don't need to know why I do certain things", he thought to himself. However, he was aware that he wasn't in England —not even close— and so he had no choice.

—I want to go to the cemetery there and see the place where my grandmother is buried —and he lowered his head down.

As he finished uttering the last word, she received a phone call and picked it up. As the seconds started passing, Andrés noticed she was not going to hang up and help him. Once again, he got back to observing each and every single angle of that office, as he was getting very uncomfortable with the whole situation. Andrés started to lose his patience as he was able to hear the whole conversation which wasn't even work related. At all!

—Yes, darling. You should definitely leave that son of a bitch and find another man —she said as she took another bite of bread with beans that she was still eating.

The conversation kept on going for another three minutes, until Andrés couldn't take it anymore. He couldn't understand how someone who was supposed to be a public servant was wasting her time talking stupid and irrelevant things with a friend, instead of working. He was very annoyed, and told himself: "If this is the type of people who is supposed to look for the well-being of this town, then they are really screwed up".

He was leaving the so called Town Hall when he saw an older man with grey hair —maybe in his early sixties— who was resting next to the door. He seemed tired. This man was just getting to *La Mina* after having walked four kilometres in two hours under the intense morning sunshine. He carried with him a sack of corn tied up to his head and back with some ropes.

This old man could have easily reach *La Mina* by bus, but that meant an expense of about five *quetzales*, which he preferred to save so that he could purchase more food for his family. And this was the reason why he walked all the way to this town instead of using the public buses. He walked that same route once a week so that he could sell his product in the market. If he was lucky, he would get thirty *quetzales* for the sack, which would allow him to buy beans to feed his family for an entire week.

He was sweating heavily and was drying his face with a handkerchief when Andrés ran into him outside the small office. Andrés wasn't planning to talk to him, but this old man had overheard the conversation with the lady from the Town Hall, and so he said:

—Excuse me, young man, *Los Manantiales* is about eight kilometres from here.

Andrés hadn't paid attention to him, but once he heard his voice he turned around and saw how tired he looked. Andrés said:

—Thank you, sir. But how can I get there?

This old man stared at him and said in a funny voice:

—I hope you have a big car, because otherwise you won't make it there, my friend.

Andrés told him that that wouldn't be a problem. The old man continued:

—You have to turn to the right once you get to the cathedral which is there —and pointed towards the little church —and then you have to keep on heading north. Keep going straight that entire road until you reach the end of it. Once you get there, you will see the beginning of a dirt road. Be very careful with the *camionetas* coming from the opposite direction, as the drivers can be quite daredevils.

Andrés felt relieved after being able to talk to someone willing to help him. No matter how sweaty this stranger was, Andrés extended his hand and said:

—My name is Andrés. Very nice to meet you, sir.

—Andrés, you never know what life has planned for us. My name is Federico but you can call me Fede. I'm from a little community called *El Diamante* which is about four kilometres from the place in which your grandmother is buried —he paused and felt ashamed for what he had just said —. Sorry. I overheard your conversation and that's why I know you're going there to visit your grandma.

They shook hands and Andrés felt honesty and sincerity coming from this stranger. He was used to deal and negotiate with people who only wanted to take advantage of him. This made him develop and live his life within a polite but hypocritical environment. He was used to live in a Machiavellian world in which the most important thing was to screw others where only the strongest character was able to win. However, this old man, a complete stranger to Andrés, in less than five minutes had reflected purity which turned into genuine trust.

There was something that still wasn't clear to Andrés. *Don* Fede had said "community" and not village or town. "Didn't he live in a town like *La Mina*?" he wondered.

—Thank you, sir! My town is a bit further away from here —and smiled —. See you later —said Andrés in a friendly manner.

He thought of offering him a ride to his town, but he couldn't waste any more time. He was very anxious now and so he got into the car and took a deep breath.

By the time Andrés got back to his "comfort zone" —which was the car— he started feeling pain in his testicle and abdomen, something which hadn't happened through the whole morning. He couldn't understand how this had happened, and he tried to ignore the pain, but this was impossible to do. He turned on the car engine and continued with his journey. He drove towards the cathedral and headed north until he got to the dirt road which would take him to *Los Manantiales* as *don* Fede had described.

CHAPTER XV

Don Fede told Andrés that *Los Manantiales* was about eight kilometres from *La Mina*, so even if the whole journey there was going to require driving through a dirt road, the trip shouldn't take that long. At least that's what Andrés thought. This road connected several communities which were all divided by mountains. There were flat parts along the road but there were also other sections of the road which had steep slopes heading up and down skirting the mountains. Andrés had never seen and even worse, he had never driven, on a road as challenging as this one.

At the very beginning of the dirt road, he noticed a few vehicles driving through, but there weren't too many though. Most of the vehicles were old and rusty pick-up trucks and lorries which were transporting animals, sacks of fruits, vegetables and grains which were grown in the nearby communities. He also saw one or two chicken buses —or *camionetas*—, but not too many either.

As he started venturing more into the road, he suddenly stopped seeing other cars driving around him. He felt as if he was driving through a desert, as the only visible thing to Andrés was all the dust rising as from the dirt road. Within ten minutes, he hadn't been able to advance a single kilometre because of the bad state of the road. Occasionally, he ran into a chicken bus here and there, and *don* Fede was right, those guys drove like maniacs!

Andrés couldn't understand how could they drive so crazily and irresponsible at a speed of 80 kilometres per hour through extremely steep slopes and risking the lives of all passengers. He realised people around those communities had no other option but to take these chicken buses to move from one place to another, as owning a car was simply an impossible luxury in this remote part of the world.

As he reflected upon this reality, Andrés concluded that *lassaiz faire* and the capitalist concept of market competitiveness wasn't an option here. Instead, people lived within a "take it or leave it" dynamic. Andrés also became aware of all the effort and chaos *don* Fede had to go through every week as he walked to *La Mina* carrying the sack of corn with this back and head in order to be able to feed his family.

During this journey he also noted the little houses —or better put, huts— which were built along the dirt road. He observed bamboo sticks being used as walls and different sized tin sheets which were used as roofs. Kids were running and playing around their huts. There were also men, wearing hats to cover from the sun, who were cutting the grass and bushes with their machetes. Once in a while he saw a few *tiendas* —or little shops— selling sodas, some seasonal fruits, snacks and few basic hygiene products such as soaps and shampoos. These tiny shops were built just like the huts he had seen throughout his driving experience. This very unequal and imperfect construction was supposed to cover people from the cold and warm weather. He wondered what would happen to them when it rained.

After thirty minutes venturing through the mountains and passing by a few communities, the road started to get narrower. Andrés had to slow down a bit as he needed to be more careful in case another vehicle and, even more so, if one of those chicken buses came from the opposite direction.

Only one vehicle —coming from either direction— was able to go through this stretch of the road, and therefore the law of the strongest one applied here as well. Each driver here was at the mercy of the other drivers. There was no law and order in this part of town. This resembled the Wild Wild West.

At one point, Andrés was about five metres from crashing into a chicken bus, whose driver didn't seem like he was attempting to stop and give him way. By instinct, he turned the wheel in a quick movement, and managed to escape a severe accident.

He wasn't used to being in a place in which there was no law to protect him. He was sweating like crazy and cursed the bus driver: "I hope you die, you careless son of a bitch", he said. Having no mobile and fearing the worse might happen as he drove through the "jungle of savages" he got frightened and wondered if he should continue driving. Each second he was living inside that car was a new experience for him on so many levels. He wondered a thousand and one times why he broke the methodical routine of living his life. If he had stayed in London, this would have never happened to him.

As he was coming to the end of this stretch of the road, he noticed that there was a wooden made bridge he had to cross in order to get to the other side where *El Diamante* community was located. This bridge was about forty metres long and about five metres wide. After *El Diamante*, there were about three or four more kilometres until he could reach *Los Manantiales* —according to what *don* Fede had indicated him in *La Mina*. Andrés was becoming increasingly anxious, as he ignored where he was at that point or where he was supposed to get to.

When he was faced with this bridge, he saw on the other end, an old and wrecked pick-up truck carrying more people than it was capable of which was heading his way. Andrés reversed his car so that the other driver had enough space to pass by when he got to his end. As the pick-up truck was crossing the bridge, the wooden boards started to tremble. The boards were swinging from one side to the other flirting with the air. Andrés realised that those supports holding the wooden boards could collapse in any second.

It was hard for him to understand why people from these communities risked their lives like that. What would happen if those supports simply broke when he was crossing the bridge? He imaged the headline on the morning newspaper: "A suicidal crazy man has killed himself in the middle of nowhere". Andrés had never faced death in so many different ways, as he had done those last couple of days.

The pick-up truck which was carrying about fifteen women and little kids, who were all squeezed in the rear part of the truck, finally crossed the bridge. The driver honked his horn as thanking Andrés for his patience. Andrés was so nervous that he didn't know if he had to honk his horn back in order to thank him back for this gesture. At the end he didn't. He just wanted to get over and done with this situation.

It was now his turn to cross the bridge. He always considered people with phobias —like fear of heights or darkness— to be weak people. According to him, he didn't suffer any type of phobia. Of course, he wasn't aware of any, because he had created a lifestyle which never allowed him to leave his comfort zone. He had never been a person willing to take risks as he wanted to prevent situations like the one he was experiencing at the time! He was well aware of his strengths, and found a way to live a life around these, without considering or taking into account his weaknesses. His life had become a rigid routine from the moment he opened his eyes in the morning until he went to bed at night. He had never been willing to put himself in a position which could threaten the way he lived his own life.

However, at this very moment, when facing forty metres of unsteadiness and the possibility of a free fall, panic took over him. Even though he had the air conditioning on, he was sweating as if he had been walking many kilometres in the desert. He was breathing heavily and felt his heart racing. He told himself that if he had made it all the way to that place, there was no way he could simply go back. He encouraged himself by thinking that once he crossed that bridge, he would be a step closer to the memory of his grandmother. Courageously, Andrés started screaming like a mad man, pushed the petrol acceleration pedal, and ventured into the bridge at a speed of ten kilometres per hour! It took him about one minute to cross the bridge, but he was so afraid that it felt like hours to him.

When he reached the other side of the bridge, Andrés was now screaming —not of fear— but as someone who has won his first gold Olympic medal. He started hitting the wheel drive with excitement and raising his arms to the sky as if he had achieved something that no other human being had achieved before. Some kids who were passing by saw him celebrating and approached him. Andrés realised how childish his attitude was, but... he didn't care! He lowered the car window and started giving "high fives" to these kids, who were as excited as he was. He faced his fear and by overcoming it, he felt satisfied with himself.

He decided to continue with his journey. After almost an hour of driving through dust, steep slopes, moving bridges and crazy chicken bus drivers, he believed he was getting closer and closer to *Los Manantiales*.

Once he crossed the bridge he saw a sign which read *"El Diamante"*. There were only a few houses alongside the dirt road, but didn't pass through a school, a church, a cathedral, a shop or a main square. He started to wonder where all the people lived in this part of the world.

When he was about to leave *El Diamante*, he realised he had to drive through a very upward steep path covered with a thick layer of mud to get to the next community. This was steeper than any other part of the road he had driven through that morning.

Halfway this narrow stretch of the road, Andrés had to turn the wheel drive very slowly so that he could border the mountain and continue his way to the top. Due to the rain from the previous day, there was dry mud on the road which now felt like quicksand because of the morning sun effect. This made it very difficult to manoeuvre the car. However, Andrés thought if chicken buses and old rusty pick-up trucks could drive through it, he was not going to have any problem with the more modern car he was driving.

He hesitated for a couple of minutes but once he recalled what it felt to cross the moving bridge, he felt confident he was going to make it through again. He started playing with the four wheel drive functionality of the car. He had no clue as to what he was trying to do, but as he started driving up the narrow slope, he decided to shift gears crazily, from third to first, from first to second, from second to third. He then turned on the four wheel drive button. There was a red light turning in the main car board. He didn't pay attention to it. He kept pressing the petrol acceleration pedal as hard as he could and kept shifting gears. He wasn't moving as fast as he wanted. The moment to slightly turn the steering wheel had come. As he was turning it, the car suddenly stopped. He thought that pressing the clutch, the accelerator and the brake all at the same time had choked the car. He removed the key, took a deep breath and put it back in.

"Come on, you son of a bitch, work!", he kept screaming out loud as he was putting the key back in and pressing the accelerator and the clutch pedals at the same time. "Come on, you can't do this to me!" he kept repeating over and over again. But the engine wasn't starting. The lights, the radio and the board were all turned on, but not the engine. Andrés tried one time after another. He was screaming, swearing, sweating. As he was swearing he started moving ferociously inside the car. He wasn't being conscious he was in such a steep path at the moment, that the strong movements he was making slid the car backwards because of the mud on the road. When he became aware of what was going on, he looked through the rear view mirror and realised the car was sliding back and that it was getting closer to the edge of the road where there was a deep and wide crack.

Andrés simply shut his eyes, and waiting for the worse thing to happen, pulled the break handle with all the remaining strength he had as a last attempt to save himself. The car was half a metre away from completely falling into the huge crack, when it suddenly stopped. The break handle had nothing to do with this. The weight of the car was being held by a stone which was stuck on the rear left tire.

Andrés felt the car was static. He opened his eyes in a slow movement, and trying as hard as he could to remain steady, he was set his eyes on the co-pilot rear view mirror. He saw the fragile position the stone was stuck under the tire. Maintaining the balance of the car was the most important thing in that moment. A slight movement could be fatal. Keeping the position of his body was important so that the stone could still hold the weight of the car and prevent it from falling. In one sudden movement, he pulled his body forward —still in a sitting position— having the steering wheel against his chest. Andrés felt the stone moving a few centimetres after this. He was frightened. In that moment, each centimetre was vital for his survival. He thought the best way to get out was to open the door on his side slowly, but then he realised that this would put too much pressure on the left side which was supporting the weight of the car. He then decided to lay his body horizontally, with his head on the passenger seat and his feet next to the steering wheel. He was sweating like never before in his life and his heart was beating rapidly. He lay down for a few seconds, but felt the car kept on sliding. "How long would that stone be able hold the weight of the car?" he thought desperately.

Very slowly, he started pulling his legs towards his chest to end up in a foetal position. He unlocked the door with his right hand. In one single and rapid movement —using the very little strength he still had—, Andrés jumped out of the car into the air and fell into the muddy surface. As he hit the ground, he hurt his right leg and shoulder with a few tiny stones. He also scraped his hands, knees and face. Once lying down in the ground in agony, he witnessed how this grey machine with black windows was falling abruptly into the crack on the edge of this dangerous road covered with hundreds of stones and mud.

Andrés felt like crying because of all the rage and pain he was feeling against life in that moment. But tears simply wouldn't drop. Not even then. Lying on the ground, he was only able to move his left hand. He fisted his hand and started hitting the ground over and over again, in an attempt to let out his frustration, regardless of the pain he was feeling.

In that moment, his mind went blank. There wasn't an external world anymore. Only his body, his soul, the mud and the stones around him were present. He didn't think of Marie, his grandmother, London, New York or cancer. He wasn't thinking at all. He simply noticed how his eyes started to fill with tears. He raised his head as much as he could towards the sky, and being unable to move his body, he implored: "God, what do you want from me?" As he finished saying these words, his head bounced back and hit the ground. He was not able to move again and fainted.

Andrés's body remained motionless for a few minutes, until a stranger —*don* Rómulo— who was driving his red old pick-up truck from the opposite direction, realised the dramatic scene and started running towards the body lying on the ground. Initially, *don* Rómulo thought that this had been a murder. As he was getting closer and closer to the body, he noticed that this young man was still breathing. He then rapidly grabbed Andrés' body with his arms and found that this young man was not conscious.

CHAPTER XVI

Andrés remained unconscious after fainting as he fell to the ground. He hadn't suffered any brain damage directly, but the accumulation of so many emotions which were so unfamiliar to him —especially those experienced that morning— had lowered his blood pressure causing his collapse.

A couple of minutes after *don* Rómulo found Andrés' body lying on the ground, a lorry showed up. This lorry was heading to a close by community to deliver vegetables from *La Mina* when he ran into *don* Romulo's screams calling for help. The driver came down from the truck and told *don* Rómulo to take Andrés to *El Diamante* as fast as he could. In the meantime, he was going to stay in that spot looking after the crashed car. *Don* Rómulo carried Andrés' body —still unconscious— to his pick-up truck and drove as fast as he could to the house of *El Diamante's* community leader —*don* Constantino. Upon his arrival to *don* Constantino's home, all of the kids who were playing outside ran towards *don* Romulo's pick-up truck filled with excitement as they saw him carrying the body of a complete stranger out of his vehicle. This created exhilaration in this tiny community.

Don Constantino heard all the noise that was generated outside his house —which was located on top of a small hill— and walked down to see what was going on. He walked towards *don* Rómulo with calm and sobriety, regardless of the excitement and agitation in the environment.

—Rómulo, who is this man and what is going here? —he asked vehemently.

—I don't know, *don* Constantino —replied *don* Rómulo, who was feeling startled by all of what had unfolded in the last few minutes.

Not knowing where to begin to tell the story of how he ran into Andrés' body, he took a deep breath and said:

—I was driving back to *El Diamante*, when I saw a car crashed into the crack which edges the road, and then I noticed a body lying on the ground —he paused to take another breath and continued —: when I got next to him, I realised he was still breathing and I was told to take him here.

Don Constantino took a close look at this stranger; he put his hand below Andrés' neck to check if he was still alive and when noticing he was having fast pulsations, he said:

—Please take him up to my house, and tell my wife to give him a glass of water with sugar and ask her to put Aloe Vera on his wounds.

Don Rómulo grabbed Andrés' heavy body and started carrying him up the hill to *don* Constantino's house. Once he reached it, *don* Constantino's wife —*doña* Rosa— came out and *don* Rómulo gave her the instructions *don* Constantino ordered. She took Andrés by his arms, and laid him on a small mattress which was on the floor. She boiled some Aloe Vera and then applied it to his wounds so that he could heal. He was still unconscious. *Doña* Rosa then lifted Andrés' head with so much care —as if he was one of her own kids— and gave him sips of water with sugar so that he could react.

In the meantime, *don* Constantino asked *don* Rómulo and other men who had gathered around his house, to make the best effort to take this stranger's car out of where it had fallen and to bring it back to *El Diamante*. The men were a bit reluctant to follow *don* Constantino's orders as they all considered that if Andrés was somehow related to the *narcos* around there, they could easily get in trouble.

Don Constantino —as tempered as he was— asked them to do as he said. All the people from the community learnt about the situation which was taking place in *don* Constantino's house and the kids, who were all very excited about what was going on, started jumping into the truck that was being deployed to take out Andrés' car from the crack it had fallen into.

The leader of this community walked back to his house and asked his wife about the sudden visitor. *Doña* Rosa knew very well her husband was a wise man, but she shared the same fear the people in the community had towards this stranger. If this man was a drug trafficker, then they would be in trouble.

—Constantino, who is he? —she asked her husband as she cleaned the face of this man who had unexpectedly arrived to her house.

—Rosa, I have no idea, but whoever he is, he is still alive and needs our help.

Doña Rosa who was staring at Andrés asked her husband:

—But, what if he is a…?

Don Constantino interrupted her and said:

—Well, if he is what you are all afraid he may be, then let God judge him, but not us. God doesn't discriminate who we need to help.

Doña Rosa knew his husband was right and nodded. In that moment, they noticed Andrés was attempting to open his eyes, but he wasn't able to open them completely. He tried to say a few words, but he could only mumble.

With that maternal love only women can show, *doña* Rosa caressed Andrés' hair and face and whispered:

—Everything is going to be all right, young man. We're here with you.

All of the sudden they heard someone rushing inside their house. It was *don* Fede —the older man who met Andrés earlier that morning in the Town Hall— who was on his way back from *La Mina*. As he was passing by *El Diamante*, he heard what had happened and decided to give a hand as he recognised the crashed car and knew who the driver was. *Don* Fede was agitated after running so fast up the hill to get to *don* Constantino's house, but when he saw Andrés being held by *doña* Rosa, he said:

—*Don* Constantino —he said while taking a deep breath —I met this young man, Andrés —he breathed again —today in *La Mina*. He was heading to *Los Manantiales* —he paused for a second and continued —as he wanted to visit his grandmother's graveyard.

Don Constantino and *doña* Rosa stared at each other wondering what someone like Andrés was doing in such a remote place where no one — not even the mayor of *La Mina*— would visit. These communities were so far away from everything that it felt as if they were lost in time.

El Diamante, just like *Los Manantiales* and other neighbouring communities were completely isolated from any technological and even social progress. About two hundred families lived in each community. About sixty percent of the population were children and teenagers between the ages of 0 to 17, and the rest were adults and elders. In terms of gender, around sixty percent were male and forty percent female.

Each community had a leader who was responsible to look after the safety of the population, and of keeping order in case of any conflicts amongst its inhabitants. The leaders were usually land owners who employed people from their own communities to work with them. In this way they generated jobs and also goods which were then traded with other communities. Leaders were also responsible to liaise with the Town Hall at *La Mina*. Sadly for the population of these communities, the bureaucrats from *La Mina* didn't quite care about the conditions these small communities lived in. The leader position was appointed by an Elderly Council. This council was formed by a group of elders who were still considered to be the wisest people and who had the capacity to elect the best fitted person to lead their community. In this remote place, as in many rural areas in Guatemala, the presence of the state government was inexistent and so they depended on these leaders to give some sense of direction and order to the people.

Within these communities, the objective wasn't to grow in abundance or to improve their economic indicators. No. Their only aim was to be able to survive day in and day out. People lived in very precarious conditions. For example, electricity was considered a luxury and only five percent of the families had access to it. The majority of the families had to survive with candles they bought on a weekly basis so that they could have some light —even if it was only for a few hours— each night. To own a TV was more than a luxury in these places. The few who owned a TV was because they had received it from a family member who had migrated to the United States in search of the "American Dream". Owning a computer was impossible to think of, and the Internet was a concept which was too progressive to be understood by people in these areas. However, mobile phones were easier to spot. Each family owned at least one.

People with more resources to survive —*Don* Constantino's family for instance— planted and harvested their own pieces of land and sold as much as they could in *La Mina* market every week in order to get some money. This exchange in the markets gave them the opportunity to access other products like beans, chicken and other vegetables and fruits which they didn't harvest themselves.

The most common product grown in *El Diamante* was corn. The majority of its population survived working for the people who owned the land. Each worker earned about forty *quetzales* —approximately five dollars— each week. This was only possible though if they were lucky enough to be employed by land owners, and provided the weather was favourable for harvesting. Other men in the community —the minority — worked as truck drivers delivering goods to and from *La Mina*.

In this community, people got married very early in their lives. The most common age for couples to get married was between 17 and 18 years old. The women, once married, turned into housewives who were in charge of looking after their simple home, their kids and husband. The progressive concept of gender equality didn't exist here because there were no other job opportunities apart from working in the corn fields. Moreover, because of their idiosyncrasy, people in these communities still portrayed women as the protector of the house and the men as the one responsible to provide all the material needs to their family.

The use of contraceptive methods was inconceivable; not only because of a religious restriction but because people felt like it wasn't the natural thing to do. Taking birth control pills or the use of condoms weren't even an option to improve family planning which would in turn help these communities improve their quality of life. Therefore, this was one of the reasons why people here had numerous children, even if they were aware it was almost impossible to provide a decent life to the little ones.

There was a primary school but the majority of parents preferred to see their kids working in the fields, as this represented an extra income for the household. They weren't interested in their children's education and their long term development and search for opportunities. For an outsider this could seem like bad parenting. However, as people were merely living to survive it was hard for them to conceive the idea of a "long term" future.

Here, life was lived with a short term mentality: to survive day after day. Their daily goal was to be able to feed themselves and to protect their families from sudden changes in the weather. Being able to provide food to was the sole dream of each member of this community. To think about education, a university degree, a professional job, art, culture or sports was something which didn't really fit the mind-set of these people.

Their houses —or huts— were simple and fragile. Parents and children had no option but to share the same roof as there were no walls allowing for any sort of privacy. The outside walls were commonly made of bamboo sticks or pine tree wood boards. The roofs were tin sheets — for the lucky ones who were able to afford it— or pieces of plastic or nylon. For those unlucky ones who could only afford to have pieces of plastic or nylon as their roofs, the rainy season turned into a complete agony. The surface of all these huts —regardless of the type of roof they had— was simply the earth and mud in which they were built.

Inside the hut, the four walls created a multifunctional space which was used as a bedroom, living room and even kitchen. The average size of these houses was about nine metres square. This reduced space witnessed the lives of all families day by day, year after year, without any privacy whatsoever. It was normal for everyone in the family to share the same mattress until kids reached their adolescence so that they could maximise space.

Women cooked in *comales* —a Mayan built type of flat pan— and also used huge pots which were heated with wood collected by children in the fields and in the mountains. It was common to see mothers cooking with the assistance of their daughters. Their daily meals consisted of black beans and corn tortillas. For special occasions, such as birthdays, Christmas or local festivities, they would kill chickens and pigs and make a banquet within their limited possibilities.

The huts didn't have a bathroom built inside. In these communities, people were used to dig "black holes" close to their homes in order to do their necessities. Each family was supposed to dig a hole in the ground of a specific depth once in a while. This was used as a pot which was then filled with excrement from each member of the family. Once the hole was completely filled, they covered it and dug somewhere else. It was common to see flies hovering around these places which emanated disgusting smells.

Access to public health was almost impossible to think of. There were some people who were able to pay for the bus ride to *La Mina* and to pay for a visit to the doctor —sometimes a decent one but most of the times a useless one. For the majority of the population, on the other hand, it was very difficult to afford the bus ride and moreover, to pay to see a doctor and the medicines which were then prescribed. In this community, people were used to natural medicines instead, which were made of herbs, plants and other natural sources to cure their diseases. However, their most frequently used "medicine" was God. To these people, faith was part of their daily lives. Moved by their blind faith, some were able to heal and others died in peace with the hope of a better life in heaven.

Life expectancy in this community was about 50 years for men and 52 for women. Taking into consideration that these people were exposed to many germs and infections due to their poor hygienic and sanitary practices, this was considered to be a high mean for a rural population in Guatemala. And it was considered to be a higher mean for women especially, given that by cooking inside the huts, they got used to breathing contaminated smoke on a regular basis.

Although, the conditions in *El Diamante* were precarious, *don* Constantino —and his father— had strived to improve the quality of life of people in their community. They had created many job opportunities so that men from the community could access a source of work to be able to provide to their families. They also employed children and teenagers who wished to work —but who were also committed to their education. *Don* Constantino created a fund which was financed by the profits generated from the sale of goods sold in *La Mina's* market. The money from this fund was used to support those families suffering critical health issues, and it also contributed to maintain the little church and to support the local children's football team.

Doña Rosa, *don* Constantino and *don* Fede were all very surprised by the reason which moved Andrés to drive all the way to that remote place. They were waiting for him to react so that they could help him get back to wherever he was coming from.

Andrés finally opened his round eyes. Once he became conscious again, he felt a strange smell close to him. It was the Aloe Vera plant *doña* Rosa had rubbed on his face and other parts of his body in order to heal the wounds from the accident. He started to move his eyes from one side to the other in an attempt to understand what had happened and why he was there. He tried to stand up, but the pain in his legs, arms, chest and face was too strong. Suddenly he realised there were three people standing in front of him. He automatically recognised *don* Fede. Without saying a single word, he raised his left arm and pointing to *don* Fede, Andrés smiled.

Doña Rosa felt moved to see Andrés like this and said:

—Sleep, son, we will be here with you.

Andrés had never met this lady before, but he felt protected with her —as he did with his grandmother. *Doña* Rosa caressed his hair like a mother would do to her child, and he fell asleep once again.

CHAPTER XVII

Three hours had passed from the moment Andrés was taken to *don* Constantino's house until he finally became fully conscious. He had fallen asleep on a small mattress which *doña* Rosa had put on the ground for him. He was once again rolling his eyes from one side to the other in order to get familiar with the place he was at.

He tried to regain his mobility by opening and closing his hands over and over again. He was observing this simple movement with astonishment. His hands then moved towards the pockets of his trousers. He felt his wallet. He was missing his mobile but he assumed it was inside the car. However, that was now completely unimportant to him. He was eager to know what had actually happened all that time. The last thing he remembered was jumping off the car and hitting the ground. He also recalled a vivid dream he had in which his grandmother was caressing him tenderly. This hadn't been a dream though. Andrés confused the hand striking his hair as part of a dream, but it had actually been *doña* Rosa looking after him.

He was now realising that all of the surroundings were completely new to him. He observed the walls made of wood. He also touched the surface which was made of stone blocks and the roof which was made up of different sized tin sheets. He noticed the entrance to the room he was lying in had a red cloth which played the function of a door. It was very warm inside. Next to the mattress where he had been lying all that time, there was a small wooden table covered by a flowery plastic-made cloth. There were five chairs, all very old and rusty.

He wasn't able to spot a couch in this reduced space. However, he saw a few images hanging on the walls, including that of the Sacred

Heart of Jesus and another of the *Virgen Morena de Montserrat*. He also saw a calendar and a Rosary which were hanging from the same nail on the wall. These were all the "decorations" this simple house had.

The walls, which were made of pine wood boards —not all cut in homogenous size— allowed for people to see through the gaps of the boards. Even though it was warm outside, he was able to see that clouds were starting to turn a bit grey. He also realised he was on top of a hill. In that moment he wondered whether he had been kidnapped. "What happened after the accident?" he asked himself nervously. He was trying really hard to remember what had happened, but nothing came to his memory.

All of the sudden, he noticed someone moving the red cloth in front of him, and saw *doña* Rosa coming in with a glass full of water. Andrés got scared, as he had never seen this woman before.

—Have I been kidnapped? —he asked startled.

Doña Rosa smiled. She walked towards him and knelt next to the mattress. With one hand she was holding Andrés' head and with the other, she was holding the glass of water so that he could drink it. With a tender voice she said:

—No, son. You have not been kidnapped. You had an accident and that's why you were brought here.

Andrés felt relieved after hearing he hadn't been kidnapped. "That would have been just what I was missing", he told himself in silence. However, he was still feeling anxious to understand what had happened. *Doña* Rosa noticed his anxiety and said:

—Don't worry, son. You will get better soon and you will be able to go back home as if nothing had happened —she smiled —. My daughter is on her way with the mobile phone so you can get in touch with your family, because I can't imagine what I would be feeling if one of my kids went through something like this and I wasn't informed about it.

"Get in touch with my family? What does she mean?" he asked himself. Andrés didn't even have a phone number to call. He had no one to get in touch with. No one!

As Andrés wasn't saying anything back, she continued with the monologue she had started:

—My name is Rosa and my husband's name is Constantino. We have three kids: Juan, who is 16 years old, Marina who is 12 and Pedrito, who is six —she remained silent for a second and then proceeded —: are you married?

Doña Rosa noticed Andrés staring aimlessly. "Maybe he hasn't fully recovered yet", she thought to herself. At that moment, Andrés tried to sit on top of the mattress with all the remaining strength he had left and he made it. He drank a bit more of water and with his look fixed to the image of the *Moreneta de Monsterrat*, he finally spoke and said:

—My name is Andrés de la Vega —and he extended his hand to the lady, as he used to greet his work colleagues —. And if you ask me right now, why am I here, I wouldn't be able to respond to that as I don't live here in Guatemala. I live in England.

—She was not an intellectual woman, but she knew England was a faraway country in Europe. Therefore, *doña* Rosa was intrigued by the background of this stranger. Andrés continued:

—I arrived to Guatemala last night, and the only thing I wanted to do was to get to *Los Manantiales* to see my grandmother's graveyard and head back home.

Andrés couldn't believe he was giving explanations to a stranger, but even if he was sitting in an old mattress in a house completely foreign to him, he felt secure with *doña* Rosa. He trusted her. This was something similar to what he experienced with *don* Fede that morning in *La Mina*.

—She died many years ago but... —his voice broke for a moment and as he regained his strength he continued and said —I felt a need to be close to her.

His eyes started to fill with tears. This emotionless, cold, vain and superficial human being was now showing the sadness, loneliness and emptiness of his soul. Seeing this young man devastated awoke the maternal instinct in *doña* Rosa. She hugged him as strong as she could.

This scene didn't last for long as *don* Constantino and his three kids entered the small room where Andrés was being looked after by *doña* Rosa. *Don* Constantino was coming back from helping all the other men who were attempting to take Andrés' car out of the crash scene. After a few hours of work, and with the effort of many people, they had been able to take the car out from the crack it had fallen into.

The car made it all the way to *El Diamante* pulled by a truck. All of the rear part of the car had been damaged, and the left side windows were all broken into pieces. *Don* Constantino asked his men to place the car in the community's warehouse. This was used to storage all the corn sacks which were then transported to *La Mina*. The car would stay there until Andrés decided what to do next.

Don Constantino walked towards the young man, and extended his hand as Andrés dried the tears off his face.

—Nice to meet you, young man. My name is Constantino and I'm very happy to see you're feeling better —he paused and then continued —. It looks like your car won't be able to work today, but the people from the community managed to get it out from the rift. The engine doesn't seem to work, but we brought it all the way here, so that you can tell us how we can help you to get back home.

Andrés wasn't sure what to do or say to thank them for their help. Somehow humble and at ease, he looked straight at *don* Constantino and said:

—My name is Andrés and I want to thank you, *don* Constantino, for... —he froze for a second.

Andrés wasn't used to express his feeling and emotions as these had been ignored for quite a few years now. It was difficult for him to express gratitude and saying "thank you" required a lot of effort from him. Prior to this moment in his life, his day to day evolved exclusively around him: his decisions, his pleasures, his plans. Nonetheless, he couldn't ignore what these strangers had done for him.

He was feeling a bit silly to hear himself say these words out loud, but he continued:

—I'm really thankful with you and your family for all that you've done for me on this disgraceful day.

Don Constantino interrupted Andrés when he said these last words. In a calm temper and in a somehow intellectual tone, he said:

—No day is disgraceful, Andrés. If God is giving us the opportunity to open our eyes in the morning, whether it is cold or warm outside, each day is both a gift and a blessing.

Andrés listened to him, but didn't give too much importance to what he had said. Whenever Andrés heard the word "God", regardless of the place, language or country, he always felt uncomfortable with it. However, he recalled that a few hours earlier, before passing out at the crash scene, he had asked God, in despair, what He wanted from him.

It was about three in the afternoon when everyone at *don* Constantino's house heard the sound of a lightning. Andrés got scared by it and the children laughed at him. For them, hearing the roaring sound of a lightning during the rainy season was normal, and to see an adult getting scared like a little boy was amusing.

The three kids were feeling a bit shy with the presence of Andrés in their house. They had never seen anyone dressed like him before. Even if his clothes were dirty and ripped from the accident, they could notice he came from a different place. They felt intimidated. When they entered into the room with their father, the little one —Pedrito— hid behind *don* Constantino's legs so Andrés couldn't see him. The girl —Marina— was holding a mobile phone with her. Whenever Andrés crossed a look with her, she turned her head somewhere else. However, she never lost the opportunity to have a quick glance at him whenever he was looking elsewhere. The eldest —Juan—, was a teenager who looked at Andrés with admiration as if this newcomer was the hero of a Hollywood film.

Doña Rosa who was sitting beside Andrés asked Marina to hand her the mobile phone. The girl gave it to her, and she then passed it on to Andrés. He took it in his hand and noticed this was the simplest form of a mobile phone he could think of. This phone could only make and receive calls and send text messages. It had been a long time since he saw a phone like that one.

All of the family members were eager to know who he would call, what he was going to say and do. He continued to look at the mobile screen trying to think which number to dial. He thought he would call the car rental agency, but the phone number was inside the car — hopefully— and he didn't want to bother anyone no more.

He also considered checking his email to search for a phone number. However, once he realised the conditions these people lived in, he felt stupid asking for Internet connection. Something inside of him —a feeling or an emotion which he couldn't rationally explain— wanted him to remain in that very same place.

Andrés continued to flirt with the phone in his hand as he was feeling hesitant and doubtful. The sky turned greyer and greyer as the seconds passed by, until another lighting strike was followed by some light rain. Listening to the never ending sound of "tac tac tac" from the rain dropping on the roof, he convinced himself it wouldn't be safe to head back home that afternoon as he didn't want to experience any more adrenaline driven adventures.

As the rain started falling down, the three kids and *doña* Rosa ran outside. They picked up the clothes which were drying under the sun, covered the accessories *doña* Rosa used for cooking and they also covered the big holes in the walls with pieces of nylon so that water wouldn't get in. Andrés stayed alone with *don* Constantino. This wise man perceived the hesitation in Andrés, and said:

—If you want to, you can stay with us tonight. This rain will make it very hard for your family to come and pick you up. Tomorrow morning we can talk with *don* Fede's cousin who is a mechanic and we can call a crane in *La Mina* to pick you up —he paused for a second and he concluded saying —: Only if that's what you want of course.

Andrés felt a huge relief to hear those words. His body was full of pain and he just wanted to rest peacefully, and somehow magically, that little house and that humble family were providing him with it. He decided this was the best decision he could take. He'd stay one night with them, he would rest and the following morning he would call the car rental agency and everything would be back to normality.

CHAPTER XVIII

It was about seven o'clock in the evening when the rain stopped. The sky was getting darker and Andrés was sitting alone in the tiny room he had been resting the whole afternoon. As the rain ceased, he noticed how some water had filtered inside the walls and roof of that simple house.

He removed the Aloe Vera *doña* Rosa had placed on his wounds and made an effort to get up from the mattress. In an attempt to roll himself closer to the edge of the mattress, he heard a cracking noise coming from his back. He bit his lips and closed his eyes so that he wouldn't scream in pain.

Andrés gathered as much strength as he could in that moment and tried to stand up by using his arms to support himself. His first attempt failed. His weak arms couldn't hold him for too long and he fell down again onto the mattress. He tried once again and this time his shaky arms managed to hold him for a few seconds. With his right foot he pulled a chair which was a few steps from where he was. He used this tiny chair to support his arms and finally managed to stand up. He started taking small steps, and even if the pain was very strong, he was happy to see he was able to walk again.

He walked towards the red cloth they used as a door, and as he started to remove it, he was able to appreciate something he had ignored for a long time: a majestic dark sky with millions of white dots. From this mountain the stars seemed to be so close to him that he even felt he could grab them. He noticed only a few lights were turned on from the homes around the mountain. Andrés recalled what Marie had told him one night when they were together: "Here in London you can't appreciate so many stars by night because of the thousand lights there are in the streets". Now he was going to be able to tell her —if they ever met again— that she was right: stars can only be fully appreciated in a place in which they are allowed to be seen!

Ever since the rain had stopped falling, he smelt food, but didn't know where this was coming from. While he was admiring the beautiful stars he started playing with the different constellations formed in the sky. As he was playing to be an astronomer outside the room, he realised *doña* Rosa and Marina were preparing dinner. They were making some *tortillas* in the *comal* and they were cooking black beans in an enormous pot, scrambled eggs in a small cooking pan and were heating coffee in an old and rusty percolator. The *comal* was outside of the house, next to the room in which he was staying, and was only covered by a piece of nylon. Next to the *comal*, there were many lit small candles as electricity during the rainy season wasn't too reliable.

When *doña* Rosa saw Andrés finally coming out of the room, she said out loud:

—Andrés, we're about to have supper. I told Constantino we needed to prepare the best meal we could for our foreign guest of honour —and she smiled —. We're only waiting for Juan and Constantino to come back with a delicious cheese my sister-in-law makes herself.

Andrés couldn't believe what he had just heard. To them, he was a guest of honour when he was actually feeling like an intruder. He wanted to be polite and replied:

—It smells delicious, *doña* Rosa —and smiled back.

These words of appreciation had never come out of his mouth, and he was aware of it. He knew he was going to have to eat whatever he was given, but he was afraid to feel disgusted by the food *doña* Rosa and Marina were preparing. Within his delicate taste, black beans were definitely not an option. He had grown accustomed to eating fine Italian and Spanish dishes every day, and to drink his café latte from the French boutique coffee shop in Richmond. The only way for Andrés to eat eggs, was *a la benedict*, and not scrambled as *doña* Rosa was cooking them.

Even if he was a cold and selfish man, he couldn't ignore *doña* Rosa and Marina's enthusiasm and affection while cooking for him, for the "guest of honour". He was having an internal dilemma as he was fully aware he wasn't going to be able to reject the food they were preparing, but he was also aware of his "fine" taste and how he responded to food prepared like this.

As he was walking towards *doña* Rosa and Marina, he noticed that there was another room next door about the same size as the one he was staying at. There was a little head popping in and out of the door whenever Andrés looked that way. It was Pedrito, who was intimidated by this stranger. Andrés kept on playing the hiding game and he noticed that every time the little boy hid behind the door, he would naively giggle inside the room. They played like this for a few minutes, until Pedrito finally came out of the room, and without saying a word, he lift his right hand and asked him to get closer to him putting one of his fingers up to his lips in an attempt to let Andrés know that this would be a private and secret encounter.

Andrés wasn't used to interact with kids, as he always thought they had never smart to say; but he was willing to give this little boy a chance as it would be rude not to please the youngest of the family. Andrés was walking slowly and painfully, but he managed to get to Pedrito. The little boy, without saying a word and only by moving his hand up in the air, invited the guest to come inside the room. Andrés accepted the invitation and walked in. As he was walking inside he noticed there was a small table with one candle on top which lightened a couple of notebooks and a pencil.

Pedrito, still in silence, asked him —with another hand gesture— to come closer to him as he wanted to tell Andrés a secret. Andrés, who was in a lot of pain, made a great effort not to let the kid down; and trying not to show the pain he was feeling, he finally knelt and managed to get his ear close to the little boy's mouth. Pedrito put both of his tiny hands around his mouth as wanting to protect his words. He whispered into Andrés' ear:

—Are you from another planet?

—Andrés wanted to burst into laughter after hearing this question, and when he was about to respond to that, he noticed that one of the notebooks the boy had on top of the table had the drawing of a huge brown circle and it had "Jupiter" written on it. Andrés decided to keep on playing the game. He whispered back into Pedrito's ear:

—Promise to keep a secret? —Andrés asked.

Pedrito nodded with his head.

Andrés continued to tell his story:

—Yes, I am from Jupiter and I am here because my spaceship crashed.

The child was so astonished to hear this that he covered his mouth with both of his hands. He couldn't believe he had met someone who was from "another planet".

—And why are you here all by yourself? Is your family back in Jupiter? And is your wife from Jupiter too? —asked Pedrito filled with excitement.

Andrés couldn't help reflecting on this and repeated in his mind the same questions Pedrito asked: "Why am I here all by myself?" He realised he was the only one to blame for having walked away from his family. Even though they tried many times to get in touch with him, he always found the perfect excuse not to talk to them and for them to know nothing about his life. He never visited them and never gave them the opportunity to come to London and stay with him for a while. He thought about Marie. Not only had he ran away from his family, but he had also left the only woman who had loved him for who he really was. And he did this because of a stupid job!

Friends? Andrés didn't really have any friends around him. Most — if not all— of his colleagues despised him. Richard Stephens —his boss — was perhaps the closest there was to a friend, but they didn't share anything else besides work. Suddenly, Andrés realised something he had tried to ignore for a long time: he was all alone in life.

While he was experiencing this sad revelation, *don* Constantino and Juan got back to their house with a black plastic bag. This bag contained the delicious cheese they had picked up from *don* Constantino's sister house.

Andrés knew Pedrito was still waiting for an answer and without thinking twice, he whispered:

—I am alone because I have to learn and experience how you humans live.

Pedrito's eyes opened widely out of excitement and he said:

—I will help you —and winked his eye to Andrés.

Doña Rosa shouted from the kitchen:

—Pedrito, Andrés… dinner is ready!

Pedrito grabbed Andrés' hand and guided him to the *pila* —a wash basin— where *doña* Rosa washed all of their clothes on one side and the dishes on the other. Pedrito was taking his role as a teacher very seriously so he decided to take Andrés to the *pila* as he wanted to teach him how humans must wash their hands before they eat a meal. Andrés smiled and they both washed their hands together. Then they walked towards the dining table which was located in the room he had rested the whole afternoon.

The table was small, but they managed to accommodate six plates, six cups and six spoons. The room was lit by a candle *doña* Rosa put in the middle so that they could all see each other's' faces while eating. There were only five chairs, but Juan had brought a plastic box from his aunt's house which was used to carry soft drinks to make up for the missing chair. Andrés didn't know where to sit, but he considered he would have to sit on the plastic box, given that he was the outsider.

Although Andrés had become a capricious and often rude man, his parents had impressed upon him the values of respect and prudence. Given the type of job he did and the people he surrounded himself with, these values were pushed to the background. However, with this people, the respectful and affectionate Andrés from his childhood was coming out again from wherever it had been hidden all those years and which was close to getting rotten.

He was about to sit down on the plastic box when *doña* Rosa firmly told him to sit down at the head of the small table. Andrés glazed at *don* Constantino as wanting to confirm his wife's strong position. *Don* Constantino nodded with his head and with a smile on his face. Everyone sat at the table and *doña* Rosa started serving equal portions of black beans, scrambled eggs and a cup of coffee too each member of her family including Andrés. Without requesting permission, *doña* Rosa grabbed some of the cheese with her fingers and sprinkled it on top of Andrés' plate. She told him the black beans with cheese were simply delicious.

Andrés really hated it when people touched his food with their hands. On many occasions, when he noticed a waiter or anyone else in a restaurant touching his food, he would immediately request a new dish and would make a big fuss over the situation. This time around he had to set aside his spoilt brat attitude and eat whatever was being offered to him. In this place, unlike all other places Andrés had travelled to, eating was not a routine. In *El Diamante*, eating was considered to be a luxury.

Andrés was about to grab a bite, when *don* Constantino asked Pedrito to give grace for the food. All of the family members closed their eyes, lowered their heads and grabbed each other's hands.

This scene moved Andrés wholeheartedly. He realised how the years had gone by without being able to enjoy a simple meal in the company of other people. It had been a long time since he felt part of a family. In his daily life, he shared each meal with his only companions which included his laptop, BlackBerry, newspaper and the iPod, whenever he was in the mood to listen to some music.

Andrés was a person who had the capacity to pay for a fancier and more elaborate dinner, unlike these simple scrambled eggs, black beans with cheese and *tortillas*, but even all the money in the world was not able to pay for the love and affection with which *doña* Rosa and Marina had prepared this food to please him, to please a complete stranger. That family didn't know who Andrés was. They didn't know how wealthy he was. They did it simply because they were honoured to have him in their home.

Ironically, this was a normal moment for *don* Constantino family's daily routine. However, for Andrés —a rich man who had more money than this family could even conceive— this simple moment was lived with happiness and joy.

Andrés also closed his eyes, lowered his head and grabbed Pedrito's hands on his left, and *doña* Rosa's hands on his right. Pedrito made the sign of the cross and said:

—Dear God, we thank you for our daily bread, because we have a roof to cover from the rain and for our health. Bless this food we are about to eat and thank you for letting —he meant to say the *Jupiterian* but he didn't want to break his promise to Andrés, and continued— this friend into our home.

When the little one finished saying grace, Pedrito tightened Andrés' hand as wanting to show what a good accomplice he had been by not sharing his secret. Andrés smiled.

Eating dinner with this family was filled with lots of laughter and funny stories, mostly told by Pedrito who had an immeasurable imagination, while *Don* Constantino also shared with Andrés stories about *El Diamante*. He talked about the lifestyle of most families living there, and about the difficulty of selling their products in *La Mina* because the household demand had diminished for their more rustic and organic products due to the rapid expansion of chain supermarkets in the more rural areas.

Doña Rosa told Andrés that her three children attended school and that Juan also worked part time. Marina helped her with different chores at home and Pedrito only studied and had fun playing around. They told him that it was very sad to see so many kids not attending school because their parents didn't allow them to go as they preferred their children to work and generate some income than receiving education. But *don* Constantino and *doña* Rosa were well aware of the importance of education in their children's lives and that was why the supported them with this.

Something that impressed Andrés from this people was the capacity they had to never complain about the conditions they lived in. They knew life in this community was tough and things were getting even more complicated as time passed by, but even then they didn't complain or said anything negative about their lives.

Doña Rosa grew fond of Andrés in a very short time —maybe because she saw loneliness reflected in his eyes just like a mother does— and treating him as if he was one more of his children, she continued with the conversation.

—My boy, it's true that things are difficult around here and even if we don't eat big banquets, there hasn't been a day we missed a meal. Even if it rains on us, we still have this simple roof, which is not perfect but still protects us. And we also have clothes to protect ourselves from the cold.

Andrés could not believe what he was hearing. According to his western standards, this people lived in the worse conditions possible. He couldn't see how this was a decent lifestyle for anyone. He couldn't come to terms as to how this people in the XXI century could live under these circumstances. But to them, this survival and simplistic lifestyle gave them enough peace to face each day as it came. Maybe they hadn't experienced another reality to compare both worlds and have enough information or tools to confirm that they were completely happy with what they had —or didn't have—, but was this necessary?

Andrés thought about his own so called problems. He didn't have to work in order to feed himself or others. Food for him was something he took for granted. He even recalled many times when he didn't finish a whole meal because he didn't enjoy it or because he felt disgusted by it, and simply threw it away. He didn't live in a house filled with holes which allowed for the water to get inside whenever it rained. In his little bubble, his current dilemma was whether to build a bigger attic in his house so that he could have a bigger 3D TV. These were two different worlds, two opposite realities, in which neither *don* Constantino's family nor Andrés could compare with each other. However, what surprised Andrés the most was the easiness and genuine peace that this people lived in regardless of all the difficult external circumstances which surrounded them.

Andrés was a very intelligent man but he had stopped being honest with himself for such a long time. That was why he was afraid to acknowledge he was an unhappy person regardless of all the material things he had accumulated throughout his life. It was during this meal, next to these five simple —yet authentic human beings— when he realised the real reason that had separated him from achieving a genuine inner peace. He concluded that this lack of peace was due to the constant and never ending need to accumulate material wealth and for it to never be enough which in turn had also isolated him from the people who loved him the most.

This man had achieved what the Western society expects from us at a quite relatively young age. And he had even exceeded it. He had everything a person could dream of having. However, he had attained all of this material wealth sacrificing the most important thing in a person's life: his true essence as a human being. He had become a person who lived to work. He felt useless if he wasn't sitting at his office, if he wasn't making money. He was a man with no interest in life apart from his work, and if someone came between his plans or his professional success, he always figured out a way to get rid of that person. This had happened with his colleagues and with Marie.

He had accumulated more than he could have ever imagined when he took that plane to London ten years ago but his greed had no limits. He asked himself: "Why do I always want more? What is my limit? How much more do I still need to sacrifice?"

At one point, Pedrito interrupted his mother who was talking and said:

—Mom, do you think Andrés can stay with us for a bit longer? I promised him that I'd show him some things that I'm being taught in school —he was referring to their secret with Andrés about "getting to know how to live like a human".

Doña Rosa looked at Andrés who was all blushed, and then returned her face towards Pedrito:

—We have no problem with him staying as long as he wants, Pedrito.

Pedrito turned his head to Andrés and winked at him. Andrés blushed from head to toe. Marina, who hadn't shared a word with Andrés because of her shyness, said smiling:

—I really hope you can stay longer. That way mom can feed us more food than normal, just like tonight!

Everyone around the table laughed at this.

Andrés didn't know that due to his presence in their home, *doña* Rosa had cooked food which they would have eaten in two days if he hadn't been around. They were so excited to have him over that they didn't mind sharing the little they had.

As they finished eating their meal, *don* Constantino invited Andrés for a short walk around *El Diamante*. If he was to leave the next day, he had to see a bit of the mountain they lived in, their little piece of heaven as they liked calling it. Andrés finished drinking his cup of coffee; he thanked *doña* Rosa and Marina for a delicious dinner, and stood up from the table. Walking a bit clumsy still due to the pain he felt, Andrés followed *don* Constantino towards an encounter with a beautiful dark and starry night.

CHAPTER XIX

Pedrito asked his mother if he could join his father and Andrés, and she agreed. He ran out of the door as fast as he could and held on to Andrés' hand. The little one had grown fond of his *Jupiterian* friend in a very short time and Andrés —even though he found it hard to show his feelings—, also felt connected to the kid.

As they were leaving his house, *don* Constantino told Andrés that they would walk just a little bit towards the top of the mountain so that it wasn't too painful for him. The only lights in *El Diamante* at that point at night were coming from burning candles —which were slowly coming to an end—, the millions stars decorating the dark and immense sky and the bright half-moon.

Andrés was amazed by the beautiful spectacle they had in front of them, and *don* Constantino was well aware of this. Andrés had never been to a place in which the light shining from the stars and the moon were enough to guide them through the night. He felt it was possible to touch the moon and the stars with his own hand. He felt close to the sky. *Don* Constantino, who was also appreciating the *Tres Marías* constellation, said:

—This is why I call this place my little piece of heaven —and smiled.

Don Constantino, whose eyes were also lost in the starry sky, continued walking and without losing sight of the beautiful stars, asked Andrés:

—Tell me, young man, what is someone who has travelled all the way from England looking for in a place like *Los Manantiales*?

Pedrito once again winked at him. His father didn't know Andrés came from Jupiter —as he had been told— and felt privileged to be the only one to know his secret. Andrés winked back at the little boy.

As he was trying to come up with the best answer, he asked *don* Constantino if they could sit down for a bit as his body started aching once again. Both of them headed towards a long tree trunk which people in the community used as a bench. The view before them was mesmerising. They sat in a flat piece of land with no trees which could get in their way. Andrés felt as if he was in the balcony of a medieval castle.

He was able to observe three other mountains in front of them, with only a few houses still lighted by the burning candles. However, what impressed him the most of this place was the monastic silence surrounding them. The only thing he could hear was the silence of the night and the wind freshening his face. Nothing else. "How can something so simple give me peace?" he wondered.

He got back to the conversation with *don* Constantino. Andrés who was now looking more relaxed and at ease compared to the previous days, replied:

—You will think I'm crazy when I tell you the reason why am I here, because I can't fully explain it to myself either.

Don Constantino smiled and replied:

—Andrés, even if you don't quite understand what you are doing here, let me tell you that there is a reason why God brought you all the way to this remote place. Even if you find it hard to believe, His plans are simply perfect.

Andrés wasn't able to fully understand these words. He hadn't heard the word "God" so many times in such a short period as when he was a student at a catholic school. Andrés continued:

—A few weeks back, I started to feel some pain in my abdomen, but I really didn't pay attention to it. However, a couple of days ago, I noticed that I had a lump in my left testicle.

Don Constantino wasn't looking at the stars anymore. All his focus was on Andrés.

It was almost impossible for Andrés to express his internal feelings and emotions, but *don* Constantino's paternal and caring eyes —just like *doña* Rosa's— allowed him to speak up.

—I saw a doctor a few days ago and he asked me to do some tests in order to know whether it is a cancer or not, and most importantly for us to know which are the next steps to take.

Don Constantino was still a bit lost, as he was trying to understand what a trip to *Los Manantiales* had to do with all of this; but he kept on paying attention to what he was saying:

—*Don* Constantino, this is the first time in my life in which I don't have things under control. Things right now aren't going my way —he paused to take a deep breath and continued —, and I'm very scared of what can happen to me.

As he said this to *don* Constantino, Andrés' voice broke a bit and he lowered his head. Suddenly he felt *don* Constantino's arm around his back wrapping him in a hug. Andrés burst into tears with his head lying against this humble man's chest.

—Let it out, boy. Cry as much as you need to, and let your soul free itself from all fear and sorrow.

Andrés who had his eyes shut, could only think of Marie and about his family. The feeling of emptiness hit him hard in that moment. Regardless of all the money and power he had, he was all alone. He felt frightened about the possibility of having cancer. Each thought and each image which came to his mind made him cry more and more. As his need to cry increased, he felt *don* Constantino holding him even tighter. Pedrito, who was playing a few steps from where these two men were sitting, noticed what was going on and approached them.

Andrés was sobbing, and with his face covered with tears and his mouth drivelling like a little boy, he said:

—I don't want to die, *don* Constantino! Why is this happening to me? Why is God punishing me? —and in a whisper he said —, I am so scared, and I have no one to lean on.

Don Constantino was holding him even tighter now. In the arms of this man —a simple farmer with a noble heart— Andrés felt loved and appreciated. Realising the power of the words he had pronounced out loud, the ability to fight God and feeling protected in the arms of a man who understood him, made him feel as if he had broken a lock within his heart.

In that moment, he recalled the day his grandmother died. While she lived —*doña* Anita told Andrés and his father— that whenever she died, they had to unlock an old trunk she kept in one of the rooms at her house. When this sad day arrived, Andrés and his father went to her house after the funeral ended. They didn't speak a word on their way to *doña* Anita's house, but both of them knew what they were supposed to do when they got there.

Once inside the house, they walked straight into the studio. They found the trunk which was medium sized and occupied half of the small room it had been kept at. Both of them felt the excitement of being treasure hunters. Even though they were sad about their loss, they were both also very intrigued by what they were about to find in that old rusty trunk. They imagined that once they opened it, they'd find jewels, real estate titles or perhaps a good amount of money. Andrés' father broke the lock with a lot of effort. The moment of truth had finally arrived. Andrés, who was 12 years old at that time, decided to open the trunk in one sudden movement.

The dust which came out of the trunk resembled a sand storm as they weren't able to see anything in this studio. They ran outside as fast as they could so that the air could get clearer once again. Andrés and his father waited for a few seconds before they went back as they were intrigued and overly excited. To their surprise, they didn't find any jewels, money or real estate titles. There was only an empty trunk with a couple of pictures and a handwritten letter by *doña* Anita, which read:

"Guatemala, 23 November 1981

To Rafael and my newly born grandson who will be named Andrés:
I am guessing you were expecting to find immeasurable wealth in the form of jewels, money and other material things in this trunk, right? I'm sorry for letting you down, but the few possessions that I'm leaving behind will be found in my will.

I could have filled this empty space with many material things but the only legacy that I want to leave you can't be measured or touched. What I want to leave you is a simple message for you to live a fulfilled life. Never stop loving and being loved. Never let your hearts become like this old trunk which has been locked for so many years. Don't let your hearts get rusty because you aren't making use of them. Even if you believe there are many risks in loving, you will find that it isn't true, because someone who loves selflessly cannot expect anything in return. And if I don't expect anything back, what can I lose?

I leave you with two photographs: 1) Rafael, this picture was taken the day you were born and the moment in which all the family welcomed you to our lives. Never forget how much we loved you. 2) My little grandson, this picture was taken yesterday, the day your family was welcoming you. Never forget how much your parents love you and will always love you.

Love and family are the most precious legacy I can leave behind, and I hope you can make the best of it and that you both can share it with others throughout your life.

with love, Grandma"

Being such a young kid when he read this letter, Andrés didn't quite understand the value of the message left by his grandmother. He even felt disappointed because inside this trunk there wasn't anything he could touch which could make him happy.

Sixteen years later, in the middle of a starry night, sitting in a majestic view point in *El Diamante* and wrapped around the arms of a farmer, Andrés finally understood the value of the letter which was kept somewhere in his London flat. At that moment, he realised his heart had actually become like this trunk: it had been locked for many years, it was empty from any feelings and emotions and it was dusty as it hadn't been allowed to feel.

His grandma had tricked him once again and had brought him all the way to this remote place, where he was now able to recognise how empty he was feeling. It was in this place, where Andrés recognised that there was no love in his life. However, coming to terms with this reality —as tough as it was— allowed him to free himself.

Feeling liberated from these locks and ghosts which imprisoned him for so many years, allowed Andrés to feel human again. *Don* Constantino took his arms away from him after seeing he had recovered his normal self. Andrés was drying the tears in his eyes when he said:

—Forgive me, *don* Constantino, as I'm not a man used to crying and to share my feelings, and even less with someone who doesn't know me.

As Andrés finished saying these words, Pedrito decided to approach him and hugged him. Andrés felt so much tenderness with that little creature around his arms. He realised this was someone who didn't know him at all but who was showing him love and care as if they had known each other for years.

Don Constantino told Andrés his wife had shared with him the fact that he wanted to go to *Los Manantiales* to visit his grandmother's graveyard. He offered him to take Andrés there, if he was willing to stay one more day with them, so that he could actually do what he intended to do in the first place. If he had got there all the way from England, the least he could do was to spend one more adventurous day and reach his destination. Andrés thanked him for his kindness and agreed to stay one more day.

They got back to the house after spending a few minutes enjoying and appreciating the beautiful spectacle before them. When they got back to the house, Andrés found that the mattress he had slept at the whole afternoon had now some more blankets so he didn't have to suffer from the cold weather at night. Andrés thanked *doña* Rosa for her kindness and a bit worried he asked:

—Where will you sleep, *doña* Rosa?

—We usually sleep here —and pointed her finger to the mattress — but tonight this bed will be used by our guest of honour. We will sleep in the other room with the kids.

Andrés was aware the other room was the same size as this one, or even smaller. How could they all sleep together on the same mattress?, he wondered.

—But, *doña* Rosa…

She interrupted him and said:

—No "buts", you sleep here and if there's anything else you need, let us know, OK?

—Good night, *doña* Rosa —said Andrés.

—Good night, son —replied *doña* Rosa.

Andrés thought: "how can someone who has so little can give everything to a complete stranger?" He remembered the letter from his grandmother: "true love is the one which is given without expecting anything in return". He lay back on the mattress, thought of his grandmother and smiled. This Andrés —who was physically shattered— but who was slowly healing his soul fell into a deep sleep in just a matter of minutes.

CHAPTER XX

While sleeping, Andrés felt a bit of cold, but the blankets *doña* Rosa had left him next to the mattress helped him get through the night. The first thing he heard in the next morning was the "qui quiri qui" sound of a rooster. Behind the red cloth —which they used as a door— he noticed the sun was already shining. He wanted to convince himself that it was going to be a good day. His body wasn't aching as much as the day before, and the testicle and abdominal pain weren't too intense either.

Andrés stood up from the mattress and realised it was eight in the morning. He had slept over ten hours non-stop! This was a sign that regardless of the physical pain he was experiencing, he had found some mental peace which had allowed him to sleep that long.

He left the small room and found *doña* Rosa washing her family's clothes in the wash basin. Her three kids had left to school early in the morning, and *don* Constantino left earlier than usual, as he went to *don* Romulo's house to borrow his pick-up truck, as his was broken.

—Good morning, Andrés! Did you have a good night's sleep?

Even if he had slept on a mattress, and not on a comfortable king size bed as he was used to back home or in the hotels he usually stayed at, he woke up feeling rested.

—Very well, *doña* Rosa! —he shouted —. Those blankets you left me really covered me from the cold.

—Fancy a cup of coffee, son?

—I would love to! —responded Andrés feeling excited.

He also wanted to take a shower very badly, to go to the toilet and to change the dirty clothes he had on, but he remembered he didn't have any other clothes with him. Feeling shy, he asked *doña* Rosa:

—Excuse me, *doña* Rosa, where can I take a shower and…?

She interrupted him and started laughing as she could see that what was about to unfold was something Andrés never imagined even in his wildest dreams. Andrés only smiled as he didn't understand *doña* Rosa's cheeky laughter.

—While I prepare you the coffee, you can take a shower, and I'll give you one of Juan's shirts —she said studying Andrés from head to toe, and continued —: But don't worry, as you can see, we're poor but clean people —and smiled at him.

Doña Rosa asked him to get closer to the *pila* and when he got next to her, she pointed her finger to a tiny hut which was about five metres behind their house. That was the location of their latrine. They didn't use the black holes as most of the families in the community did because they were aware of the hygienic issues caused by these. *Don* Constantino's house latrine consisted of a hole connected to a basic water system which cleansed their necessities.

She gave him a roll of toilet paper —a little rough, he thought— and headed to the tiny hut. In this reduced one meter square space, there was a hole covered by a wood board. The hut's walls were also made of bamboo sticks and covered by tin sheets.

Andrés walked into this latrine and was unsure as to what position to use to sit down. He started putting toilet paper around the hole, but the urine and excrement smell were too strong for him. He decided to take a piss out under a tree and delayed taking a dump until he was able to find a more decent toilet. He didn't tell *doña* Rosa he had preferred to pee under a tree, as she may be offended by it. He wondered how these people could deal with this situation and the horrible smell every day of their lives.

After this experience, he decided it was time to take a shower. *Doña* Rosa told Andrés that people in that community were used to shower with *"guacalazos"*. This meant people would fill a bucket with cold water and they would then use this to wet their head and body as they rinsed it with shampoo and soap.

She gave him a tiny shampoo bag and a small soap shaped as a cricket ball, which was also used to wash clothes. She told him he could use as much water as he needed, but the truth was that they only used half of a bucket each, as it was a very difficult task to fetch water from the foot of the mountain every day.

She handed him a towel and a short squared sleeve shirt from Juan. She told him she was going to clean his room while he took a shower so that he wouldn't feel embarrassed to be naked close to her. Andrés was standing in front of the *pila* with an empty red bucket —of about 20 centimetres tall and 30 centimetres wide— a small shampoo bag and a soap used to wash clothes —and apparently to clean people too. He was too embarrassed to get completely naked, but he was feeling too dirty from the accident the day before that he couldn't care less.

He finally decided it was time to get undressed and halfway he decided to keep his underwear on. He filled the red bucket half way with cold water, and bit by bit he started splashing water on his face, hair, chest and back. The water was freezing, but given that the weather was warm, he didn't complain.

He started rinsing his hair with the shampoo and the rest of his body with the soap. He felt the roughness of the soap. All of the sudden he realised all of his body was covered with white soap, just as if he had been poured with sun protector lotion! There were some kids who were passing by *don* Constantino's house and noticed the awkward moment this stranger was going through. And so they decided to hide behind some bushes and to simply enjoy this funny episode. In the meantime, Andrés started jumping from foot to foot as he didn't want to get dirty from the mud on the ground, but this was an impossible task!

He knew the only way to rinse off the soap and shampoo from his body was to pour all the water from the bucket onto himself. The kids who were hiding couldn't hold their laughter, but Andrés wasn't aware of their presence. He was about to pour the whole bucket of water, when the kids —not being able to keep it together anymore— started laughing so hard that Andrés turned his body in a sudden move to see who was there, and in that short moment he tripped in the mud and fell to the ground. From one second to another, Andrés was on the ground once again. The kids laughed out loud at this and ran away from the crime scene. This time around, Andrés didn't get upset. On the contrary, he started laughing at himself.

Doña Rosa heard some noises and so she ran outside. Seeing Andrés on the ground laughing like a little boy, made her laugh with him. After this, Andrés repeated the "*guacalazo*" ritual once more, making sure that there were no more spies. After succeeding at it he was able to feel fresh again. He had to borrow Juan's underwear as his got dirty with the mud after epically falling to the ground.

He was now wearing Juan's underwear and shirt and his own dirty trousers from the day before. His brown chamois leather loafer shoes were all ripped, but he couldn't care less. The Andrés from two days ago would have felt disgusted by this, and wouldn't have accepted to take a shower with a bucket; but this new Andrés was now feeling free and none of this bothered him at all.

As he was enjoying a cup of coffee and some scrambled eggs *doña* Rosa had prepared for him, he heard *don* Constantino coming back home. It was a fact that this morning's breakfast was nothing compared to his traditional café latte and ham and cheese croissant from his favourite French patisserie he was used to eat every morning. The biggest difference was that this meal had been prepared for him especially. He felt silly thinking this, but thought to himself: "this was prepared with love... and all of it for me!". *Don* Constantino got closer to where Andrés was, and when seeing he was wearing one of his son's shirts, he couldn't help but to laugh at him. He said:

—Now you're actually looking like one of us and not like a *Jupiterian*, as Pedrito says.

On their way to school that morning, Pedrito wasn't able to hold the secret, and had told his father that the guest who was home was coming from Jupiter and that he was going to teach him how to live like humans do. *Don* Constantino found it amusing, but didn't want to ruin his son's excitement so he told him they would help him reach his goal.

Andrés smiled and knew Pedrito had told his father the story from the night before. He realised how pure a child can be.

—I'm glad I now look like one of you —replied Andrés smiling.

—Are you ready to go to *Los Manantiales*, Andrés? —asked *don* Constantino.

—Yes, I am! Let's make it to the place which brought me all the way here.

They walked all the way down the mountain until they found *don* Romulo's pick-up truck on the dirt road. Andrés didn't feel the need to ask about the car. He didn't want anything to spoil the happiness he was experiencing at that moment. He felt proud of himself for being closer to the place where he originally intended to get to, even if there had been many difficulties along the way.

Both of these men hopped into *don* Romulo's pick-up truck, which was an old and rusty Toyota truck which "did the work" as his owner used to say. Once *don* Constantino started the engine, they realised how old this car was as the gearbox was extremely hard to manoeuvre. They could hear some marimba playing in a radio station which didn't have a very clear signal and decided to begin the journey to *Los Manantiales*.

Andrés smiled at this scene and asked himself, "where am I?" This wasn't a complaint now. He was now simply enjoying the moment.

CHAPTER XXI

Don Constantino told Andrés *Los Manantiales* was only four kilometres away. However, due to the rain —as Andrés had experienced the day before— it would take longer as he had to drive more careful because of the road conditions.

As they were driving through the dirt road, they faced some up and downward slopes once again. This time around Andrés was more worried about trying to appreciate the green fields than with the current state of the roads. That day, unlike the previous day, he had no rush or pressure to be anywhere at a set time. There was no timetable today. That was why he decided to enjoy his surroundings.

He noticed men working while kids ran away in the fields. He observed the immense blue sky and allowed the sun shine to penetrate him thoroughly. The freedom he was immersed in allowed him to appreciate the energy arising from nature in those fields, in the sky, and even from the dust in the wind.

Twenty four hours before, this would have all seemed like a curse to him; but now, with a new attitude, Andrés had the capacity to see all of this beauty as a blessing. Once again he started to appreciate the legacy his grandma left him, which up to that day, he had not valued. She used to say that "nature was filled with energy, and that this was the place where we must recharge our batteries".

The drive to *Los Manantiales* was supposed to last thirty minutes. During this time, *don* Constantino shared more stories about *El Diamante* and the struggles of its inhabitants. He told Andrés that as the leader of the community he was very saddened to see the majority of the parents in that area not understanding the value of educating their children.

He told Andrés that his predecessor —who had been his own father — believed education was the only tool there was for the community to progress and develop. That was why *don* Constantino had finished up secondary school in *El Diamante* and then he had studied high school in *La Mina*. Studying in the bigger town of *La Mina* required him to take a bus every day for two years so that he could graduate with a high school diploma.

—I was aware of the economic effort my father was doing to provide me with bus fares, books and my uniform. And that was why I devoted myself to do the best I could —said *don* Constantino —. And that is what I'm trying to replicate with my kids. This is the only legacy that I can leave them so that they can become better human beings and can succeed in life.

Don Constantino kept on sharing his story with Andrés. After high school, he was accepted in the state university in Guatemala City to study a degree in agriculture. This required him to move to the big city into a tiny flat in the city centre which he shared with six other people. Having lived all of his life between *El Diamante* and *La Mina* and then moving to the city was a drastic and shocking change for him.

He told Andrés that the most difficult thing to adjust to was the fact people in the city were perverse and always tried to get a short cut for everything. People didn't care if they stepped over someone else as long as they achieved their goals. However, his biggest difficulty was to live in a grey area filled with buildings, buses, cars and people running from one place to another the whole day every day. He was overwhelmed by all of this.

As Andrés listened to *don* Constantino, he recalled his busy life in London, but he didn't say a word. *Don* Constantino continued telling him that even if it had been a very difficult period of his life, he knew this was the price he had to pay to achieve his objectives. He had a responsibility to make his dreams come true, and even if he had to get through all of this chaos in the city, he had to finish what he had started.

As they were passing through a small town called *El Chijín* , *don* Constantino paused for a second and told Andrés he wanted to show him a very special place for him which was a twenty five minutes' walk from that spot. Andrés was in no rush to get to *Los Manantiales* and told him that he'd be honoured to go with him to such a special place. *Don* Constantino parked the car in an empty piece of land and asked Andrés to follow him.

During their walk, *don* Constantino continued sharing the story of his life. He told him that by the end of the second year of university, he started to feel very ill. He blamed it on the city lifestyle that he was emerged in, but didn't give it too much importance. However, there was a day when he couldn't keep up with the pain any longer. Urinating became painful, and it got worse as he started peeing blood. When this happened he got really scared and went to the public hospital in the city, and the doctor who treated him only said: "I'm sure this is because you have been drinking a lot and that's why you're bleeding. Take more care of yourself, boy", he said.

Don Constantino had never tasted a drop of alcohol in his life, and with this "diagnose" by the so called doctor, he started panicking. The following weekend, he went back to *El Diamante* to visit his family. His parents noticed how sick he looked from the second he got home and asked him to stay with them for some time so that he could heal as soon as possible.

Don Constantino's mother and many other elder ladies from the community started giving him natural and homemade remedies. They would congregate at his house all day long to pray for his recovery. But nothing seemed to work. By that time, there was a Catalan missionary priest called Jordi who was passing by *El Diamante* by pure coincidence. *Don* Constantino's father, who was the leader of the community at that time, would open the doors to his house to every missionary who passed by his land, as he considered it to be a blessing by God. Welcoming father Jordi was not the exception.

When the priest got to *El Diamante*, *don* Constantino's father told him about his son's ill fate. *Don* Constantino had become weaker to the point where he preferred to hold his urine as it was too painful to pee. He was sweating a lot and was looking extremely pale. By this point of suffering, he was looking like a mere ghost. *Don* Constantino was twenty one years old at the time, but his faith was as solid as a ninety year old man. Regardless of his sickness, he was keeping a genuine positive attitude. He smiled and even accepted the possibility that his time to depart this world could soon be approaching. He was feeling happy to be even closer to God if that was his fate.

Father Jordi talked to *don* Constantino, and seeing how irrevocable his faith was and how surrendered he was to God's will, he asked don *Constantino's* father if he could take his son to a "sacred" place he knew. *Don* Constantino wasn't feeling strong enough to do a pilgrimage, but he told his father and father Jordi that if it was God's will that he was going to find enough energy to get through an eight hour journey. *Don* Constantino, his father, father Jordi and a mule crossed a mountain and a couple of rivers until they made it to the most beautiful place he had ever seen. And he healed.

After telling Andrés the end of this story, *don* Constantino stopped in front of a huge bush which covered them both, and looking straight into Andrés' eyes he said:

—Andrés, I have brought you to the most sacred place there is for me. Not even my kids have come here with me.

Andrés felt flattered by this, but also compromised by this kind gesture. *Don* Constantino walked through the tall bushes and got lost inside of them. He shouted and asked Andrés to do the same thing. Andrés, who was a bit scared, kept crashing into the bushes and wasn't able to get through as easy as *don* Constantino had done a few seconds earlier. *Don* Constantino asked Andrés to extend his arm. And so he did. From the other side of the bushes, *don* Constantino pulled Andrés with all his strength. Andrés passed through the bushes and fell down on the other side.

As he stood up from the ground, he was able to admire one of the most beautiful landscapes his eyes had ever appreciated. Before him was a natural pool divided by three majestic waterfalls. The water which filled this natural beauty was almost transparent. From where Andrés was standing, a huge rocky mountain could be appreciated. Between the water and the mountain, there were many tall and bright green trees decorating this beautiful scenery. While Andrés stood silently beside him, *Don* Constantino said:

—As you can see, no human invention has intervened in creating this beautiful place.

Andrés agreed. He only wanted to contemplate what his eyes were observing at that moment.

Andrés was a bit confused as to why *don* Constantino had brought him there after telling him the story of his miraculous healing.

Don Constantino was walking towards the water filled with excitement, and asked Andrés to follow him. Andrés who was astonished by what he was seeing, simply followed the orders of this wise man. *Don* Constantino said:

—This is the place where I came with my father and with father Jordi when I was ill. We were here praying for a long time, Andrés. I felt as if God had asked me to come all the way here, and with a lot of effort we finally made it.

Andrés wasn't paying attention to anything else but to the words *don* Constantino shared with him. Feeling a bit fatigued from the walk, and mostly for the emotions that he was experiencing, *don* Constantino continued saying:

—I surrendered my life to God in this very place, Andrés! I didn't ask him to heal me. I asked him to give me enough strength to face the pain which was killing me and to accept whatever I had to live through.

Andrés was very confused. He couldn't understand how *don* Constantino could surrender his life to God. He couldn't understand why he asked for enough strength to endure the pain and didn't ask God to take the pain away for once and for all.

—When we got back home from this pilgrimage, I started peeing normally again. My faith in God saved me, Andrés.

Andrés was puzzled at these words. Nothing made sense to his rational mind.

—Can't you see it, Andrés? —he asked.

—What is it that I have to see, *don* Constantino? —Andrés asked desperately.

—Last night, up in the mountain, you were complaining for the things that are happening to you —he made a long pause waiting to see any type of reaction in Andrés, but there was none so far —. You are not the only person suffering, son —said *don* Constantino in a softer voice.

Andrés lowered his head, but *don* Constantino kept on talking:

—The memory of your beloved grandmother has brought you all the way here from a country which is thousands of miles away. Do you really think that this desire to visit your grandmother's graveyard was the only reason to be here?

Andrés didn't know what to say. He didn't even know why he had taken the decision to come there in the first place. He wasn't sure why things had unfolded the way they did. And he didn't understand why he had come across these people.

—God is talking to you, Andrés! Whether you believe in Him or not, God is talking directly to you. This illness and the memory of your grandmother have made you come to this place.

—But what does God expect from me? —shouted Andrés.

—I don't know, Andrés. That is something that you and Him will have to figure out.

Don Constantino, who was also very excited for what was going on and for the conversation they were having, asked Andrés to sit on the edge of the water. He asked him to remove his shoes, to fold his trousers up to his knees and to simply feel this delicious water with his bare feet. Andrés obeyed *don* Constantino's orders and felt the warm water touching his feet.

—Now close your eyes and try to focus your mind on feeling the water, listening to the waterfalls and on seeing your heart —said *don* Constantino.

—How can I "see" my heart? —asked Andrés feeling frustrated.

—In the darkness that is created by having your eyes shut, look out for your heart and let it talk to you.

Andrés tried with all his strength to do what *don* Constantino was asking him to feel. It was easy to focus on the water touching his feet and to hear the sound of the waterfalls, but he simply couldn't "see" his heart. He was very nervous because he didn't know how to do this. *Don* Constantino remained silent. Andrés finally started to let go off the pressure he had put on himself. Bit by bit, he was able to fully concentrate on the water wetting his feet and on the sound of the waterfall, and he felt peace.

Don Constantino, who perceived Andrés' calmness, said in a soft voice:

—Andrés, I want you to think about the things or the people who make you really happy in your life. You don't have to say it out loud, just think about it; create an image or focus on a word that defines your happiness.

The first image which emerged in that moment of relaxation was that of Marie. He recalled what this woman had changed in him in such a short period of time. Being around her, he learned how to surrender, and he learned what it felt to be truly loved. He remembered the first kiss in Little Venice and the first time they had made love. He then thought about his childhood, he recalled the many summers he spent with his grandma. The image of his father praying with him before going to bed at night came to his mind as well. He felt his mother's strong arms embracing him every morning before going to school.

He never thought about his job, his flat in Richmond, his Aston Martin, New York, his many trips around the world, his bank account or even his bonuses. After reflecting for a few minutes, *don* Constantino said:

—That is the voice of your heart, Andrés.

Don Constantino then asked Andrés a question he would never forget:

—Now that you have been able to see what makes your heart happy and joyful, do you have it in your life today?

At that moment, Andrés felt as if his whole body had crashed against a thick wall. Andrés knew what the answer to that question was, and ever since he heard the word "cancer", he started realising that no matter how comfortable and secure his life was, he had nothing which would make him feel genuine happiness.

Even if they only knew each other for a few hours, *don* Constantino knew Andrés was not a happy person. "Human beings say it all with the reflection of their eyes", used to say this humble farmer. And Andrés' eyes were lost, alone and empty.

—Andrés, ask God to help you face this illness, and commit yourself to give something in return —said *don* Constantino in an attempt to get to the deepest point of this cold man.

Still with his eyes shut, Andrés finally was able to "see" his heart. He recognised the emptiness inside of him. He knew there was no love in his life. He knew his daily life had no purpose and no commitment. He knew he was living exclusively for him, and no one else but him. He knew he was the only person responsible to push away the people that loved him the most. Andrés started to burst into tears. His heart spoke:

"Here I am, God, talking to you, after such a long time. I know my ambition for material wealth and comfort has turned me into an empty man. However, an illness and the memory of grandma have brought me all the way here. This adventure has made me question the way I live my life and the way I see it. I have experienced how people who don't know me and who are materially poor, have given me everything they have expecting nothing in return. They have comforted me, they have fed me and they have loved me. I have come to understand after so many years that you manifest your beauty and generosity by gifting us with starry nights, with orange sunsets, with a blue sky, with the rain, with the trees, with the fields, with the sea. I can now see that I'm an empty man because I don't have anyone who loves me or who I love. I surrender this life of mine to you, even if it seems that is worth nothing. I want to recover it; I want to give it a purpose and a meaning. In exchange, I will make the greatest effort I can to stop being like my grandma's old trunk. I will ask forgiveness to my family and Marie. I will work very hard against my egocentric way of living. I will help *don* Constantino's family and to *El Diamante* community as much as I can, because I know they have done so much for me. Finally, I please beg you to give me enough strength to face whatever I need to face and that I can heal completely".

Even if this was a short conversation and perhaps a bit dry, it was the first one in many years. Andrés had now spoken to God and to his heart once again. Andrés opened his eyes and saw *don* Constantino who was still sitting next to him praying in silence.

Andrés interrupted his prayer with a hug. He thanked *don* Constantino for taking him to this place where he had finally felt fully liberated. This was the place in which he acknowledged what his heart had to say. This was the place where he had come to accept how empty his life was. He thanked *don* Constantino because for the first time he had surrendered his life and illness to God.

They remained embracing each other in a hug for a while, until *don* Constantino decided it was time to continue their journey to *Los Manantiales*, because otherwise they'd have to wait there for a couple of hours until the afternoon rain passed. Before leaving that magical place, Andrés grabbed a sunflower from the ground and told *don* Constantino that these were his grandmother's favourite flowers and that he would take it with them to her tomb.

CHAPTER XXII

On the way back to the place where *don* Rómulo's pick-up truck was parked, *don* Constantino continued with his story. When *don* Constantino, his father and father Jordi got back from the pilgrimage, he stopped urinating blood. "My faith saved me", he told Andrés. When he was in front of that beautiful natural pool of water, *don* Constantino promised God and himself, that if he was healed, he would go back to *El Diamante* after finishing his university degree and help as many families as he could possibly do, especially those who were having many problems sustaining themselves.

Father Jordi grew fond of *don* Constantino and gifted him an image of the *Virgen Morena de Montserrat* so that he could always remember the experience of faith they lived together. Andrés recalled seeing the image of a Virgin Mary in the room where he had slept the day before and assumed that was her.

A year later, *don* Constantino's mother passed away, and he decided to drop out of university to come back home and support his father and siblings who had lost such a central figure in their lives. Andrés was impressed by *don* Constantino's attitude to make radical decisions thinking of others and not only about himself. "If my mom or dad had died during the time I've lived abroad, would I have had the courage and detachment to leave behind a life full of opportunities for the sake of my family's well-being?" he wondered. He immediately knew the answer was a resounding no. And that was why he admired the courage shown by *don* Constantino.

They finally made it to the car and started the old engine again.

Andrés didn't feel the 25 minutes' walk from that magical place to where the car was parked. Chatting to *don* Constantino was such an enlightening experience which felt timeless. He was learning so much from this man, especially about his humbleness and the simple way of living life. Andrés considered that *don* Constantino and his grandmother would have got along well if they had met. They got back en route to *Los Manantiales* as they continued with their conversation.

—It wasn't an easy thing to decide to come back to *El Diamante* after having lived in the city for a while —said *don* Constantino.

—But, how did you know it was the right thing to do then? Didn't you hesitate to leave a great future ahead of you because of your family? —asked Andrés eager to find out the perfect recipe to take important decisions in life.

—Andrés, what you heard while resting your feet in the water a few minutes ago, that voice which told you what makes you a happy man — he paused briefly to dry the sweat from his forehead —, that is the voice which told me I needed to get back to my family.

Andrés was astonished. He had never taken a decision moved by what his heart asked him; and that was the reason why he felt empty and lonely. *Don* Constantino continued:

—The voice of our hearts is the only one which should guide us in life. It is the one who actually knows what the best decision we need to make is. It knows what is best for us, even if we don't actually agree with it, or better put, if we prefer to ignore it.

—But what happens if whatever my heart is saying is not what I want for myself? —asked Andrés feeling frustrated.

Don Constantino smiled and replied:

—That voice is never wrong, Andrés, because it is the voice of God.

Andrés remained silent and analysed each word *don* Constantino had just said. Andrés was having trouble saying something back which made sense to him. What he had experienced those last few days unfolded the way they did because his heart got tired of being ignored. Facing his mortality, his loneliness, getting to a place in the middle of nowhere and experiencing poverty, were all signs which were needed for him to react and realise life isn't just about accumulating wealth, material assets or titles.

These days had shown Andrés that contrary to what he believed; love actually existed in the XXI century. Each situation he faced ever since he visited the doctor in London up to that road trip on board an old and rusty pick-up truck allowed him to confirm he was part of a plan too. That was the reason why *don* Constantino told him the night before that every event in life happens for a reason —whether we understand it or not— as it is all part of a Perfect Plan.

Don Constantino wanted to dig deeper on this topic and said:

—Personally I think that there are four key elements we must be fully aware in order to live a fulfilled life. First, you have to know and accept yourself. Don't be afraid to recognise your weaknesses and mistakes, as you will only be able to hear the voice of your heart clearly when you accept yourself completely. Second, you must set goals in life which have a purpose, and the outcome of achieving these shouldn't be for your own well-being only. Don't be afraid to think about others. Third, you must master the ability to respond with a positive attitude if God changes your plans along the way. Not everything will unfold as you desire or at the moment you expect. When this happens, don't ask yourself, "why me?", but rather ask Him, "what do you want from me?" And the last, and most important element, is to never stop loving. Love yourself, love your family, love your friends, and love your enemies. This is the most difficult thing to achieve, Andrés, but it is the most important one. You may be able to master the first three, but without this fourth element, everything will be worthless.

Andrés paid attention to *don* Constantino like a pupil does to his master. He wanted each and every word to be engraved in his mind and soul. Andrés realised he was not the same person as the one who boarded the plane from London a few days back. Or better put, he didn't want to be that same person anymore!

The journey continued and the conversation never stopped between these two antagonistic characters. *Don* Constantino told Andrés how a year after being back in El Diamante, he met *doña* Rosa.

—She was so beautiful, Andrés —said *don* Constantino, feeling as in love as if he had just met her —. Her family lived in another community and then they moved to *El Diamante*. From the moment I saw her the first time, I knew she'd be my life partner.

Andrés couldn't help it and laughed at *don* Constantino.

—Life partner? Do you mean your wife? —Andrés asked.

—No, Andrés. You may think living surrounded by poverty automatically makes us ignorant people, but my father taught me that a woman will never be your possession, as many men think. A woman who decides to be with you walking a path together will not be your woman but your life partner.

Andrés felt embarrassed because *don* Constantino was right: his prejudice against people in this community made him label them as ignorant. He knew *don* Constantino was an exception to the rule, but still believed these people could be somehow savages.

—The heart of a woman is deeply hidden within God. Therefore, we must find Him first, just so that we can fully appreciate women — said *don* Constantino.

Andrés thought about Marie and realised how right *don* Constantino was. He had the love of a woman who loved him, but he didn't appreciate it at the time. He wasn't able to appreciate this love because his heart was empty and blindfolded by his selfishness and the fear of getting hurt.

It was passed midday when they both noticed a wooden board which was hung on a little shop with the words *"Los Manantiales"* painted in white. Andrés laughed at himself when he realised how silly he had been by trying to find this remote place using the GPS on his mobile phone.

Don Constantino got off from the pick-up truck and asked a couple of people about the location of the community's cemetery. The owner of the shop told him they would have to walk about ten minutes north of where they were. They were now on the last bit of their adventure. Andrés knew he was not going to find a cemetery like the one in Arlington, Washington D.C. —where JFK was buried— so he was very curious as to see how a cemetery looked like in such a random place on Earth.

They made it to something that looked like a cemetery, but they doubted if this was the actual place. It was a piece of land without any grass of about 30 metres long and 20 metres wide. There were some tombstones with cracks on them. Others had no tombstones, but you could still perceive there was a hole where they had stood for many years.

Andrés hadn't attended his grandma's funeral because he was still very young and his parents decided not to take him all the way there. That's why he had no recollection of the place where his grandmother had been buried. *Don* Constantino asked him for her name.

—*Doña* Ana Marisol Muñiz —said Andrés, feeling proud.

Each one of them walked in a different direction and started reading each tombstone searching for *doña* Anita's. Andrés observed many tombstones during his walk. There was one of a man who had lived forty years only and died in 1910. He was impressed to see kids who died very young. There was a shared tombstone for a couple of little girls —Luisa and Juanita— who had lived just two years, from 1970 to 1972. He realised people in this place lived only a few years because of all the mass murders there were in Mayan communities as a result of the Civil War Guatemala experienced for more than 30 years.

They were both getting to the end of the small cemetery when *don* Constantino suddenly took his hat off and called Andrés. He ran up to where *don* Constantino was standing. Her grandmother's graveyard was there! The tombstone read:

Doña Ana Marisol Muñiz
8 October 1908 - 5 January 1993
Thank you for your example of love and humility. Love, your family.

Andrés recalled the last morning he shared with his grandmother before she passed away. He told *don* Constantino she had been a special lady who shared and irradiated her love every place she went to.

—I don't doubt it, Andrés —said *don* Constantino —. She was and will forever be special. See where she has brought you!

They both smiled. Andrés knelt to clean the tombstone and to place the sunflower he had brought with him —knowing it was her favourite flower. As he was touching the tombstone he felt the wind caressing his face.

He winked at the tombstone and said out loud:

—Thank you, grandma!

Even if Andrés was very sensitive due to all of the emotions he had experienced the last few days, he didn't shed a tear. Not because his heart was cold again, but because he was filled with happiness. He was now aware that from that moment on, everything would depend on him. It was going to be up to him to have the right attitude and enough courage to make the necessary changes in his life which would allow him to live with meaning and purpose.

He acknowledged he had a difficult task before him as he was going to have to break free of the memory of his grandmother. He knew his grandma hadn't left him and would always be there with him, but it was now up to him to start building and living a life by detaching himself from the need to depend on others, in this case his grandmother.

The initial objective of flying to Guatemala —driven by an impulse — to see her grandmother's graveyard was now fulfilled. Andrés imagined this scene as being dramatic, filled with tears, fears and complaints. But it wasn't like this at all. The path which had taken him all the way there —something he had never imagined— was all part of the Perfect Plan God had for him. By experiencing a reality foreign to him he had been able to question his life. He realised that the most important thing was not getting to the end, but enjoying and learning along the way.

God's plan for him didn't include travelling comfortably from London to Guatemala and being driven all the way to *Los Manantiales* and back. Experiencing the true adventure of leaving his comfort zone had created an avenue for him to question his life, his solitude and his egocentric lifestyle. He faced death in many occasions. From the moment he heard the word "cancer" all the way through the car accident. And he was going to have to continue facing it through his illness. He faced once again his country's reality in the New York airport and saw with his own eyes the classism which divides the nation. He experienced first-hand what it was to live in precarious conditions. He experienced what it felt to survive without any type of organisation or government which could help improve people's lives. He experienced a type of spiritual richness —which he had never felt before— by interacting with a poor farmer family. He had recognised the voice of his heart, of God. But most importantly, he had been able to surrender his life and illness!

With this reflection, Andrés appreciated the perfection of God's plan which had been made possible by the help of his angel, of his grandmother. Now it was up to him to have the courage and bravery to trust and follow his heart's voice and let it guide him in making the best decisions for his life.

CHAPTER XXIII

After bidding farewell to his grandmother, Andrés and *don* Constantino walked back to where they had parked the pick-up truck, next to the little shop near the entrance to *Los Manantiales*. It was about three in the afternoon already and the rain was about to make its daily appearance. Once it started raining the journey back to *El Diamante* was going to take longer than usual.

As they both walked by the little shop, one lady who was passing by recognised *don* Constantino and approached him. She seemed nervous and scared and both of them felt the tension.

—You are *don* Constantino, the leader from El Diamante, right? — she asked in a worried tone.

—Yes, ma'am, how can we help you? —said *don* Constantino a little troubled by the look of this woman's face.

—*Don* Constantino, my son who is a bus driver... —the lady seemed stressed and paused repeatedly — has told me that some people from a drug cartel have murdered ten people in the community of *La Guajira*.

La Guajira was about two kilometres away from *Los Manantiales* opposite to *El Diamante*.

—And do people know why this happened? —asked *don* Constantino feeling worried.

—They're saying that these people wanted to kill the community leader because they had some unresolved businesses, but as they couldn't find him, they killed all the men working on his land. That's what my son told me, but as you know, they love making things up and we don't know what to believe in anymore —said the lady moving her head from one side to the other.

—Thank you so much for the warning. We will be very careful on our way back —*don* Constantino said.

Andrés couldn't believe what he had just heard. Just a few kilometres away from where they were, there had been a mass murder. Inside the car, Andrés who was frightened and didn't quite understand what was going on, asked *don* Constantino:

—Should we call the police?

—My dear Andrés that would be the worst thing to do —*don* Constantino replied sadly.

Andrés wasn't able to understand what this meant. "How come calling the police was the worst thing to do after ten people had been murdered?" he wondered.

—So, what can be done? Are we going to allow them to kill more people? —asked feeling irritated by *don* Constantino's passive attitude.

—See, Andrés —said *don* Constantino in a fatherly manner —, this doesn't just happen in small communities, but sadly it is the daily reality of the whole country.

"Every day? How can this happen every single day and no one is able to do anything about it?" he asked himself not necessarily sure if he wanted to know the true answer.

—I'm sure you are not aware of the situation which Guatemala is going through at the moment, but we're living a very tough period due to the violence generated by drug trafficking activity and organised crime.

As he was observing *don* Constantino while he was talking, Andrés recalled a few stories he had read in the BBC about Guatemala, and drug trafficking was a recurrent subject. However, he never imagined the real extent of this problem. *Don* Constantino continued:

—In the newspapers people say there are about 16 daily murders in Guatemala. Drug trafficking affects small communities like ours and also poor neighbourhoods in big cities as they use these places to recruit members. It also affects owners of businesses around the country as they are victims of extortion by organised crimes and gangs. And above all, it affects the whole country because drug cartels have enough power to manipulate the legal system. The death of these ten people, just like other thousands of deaths related to this, I'm sure will never be cleared. Here you will be better off if you pretend to be blinded by it, if you don't say anything against them and if you pray to God not to let you be in the wrong place at the wrong time.

Andrés got scared to hear all of this. How can a fourteen million people country deal with this reality? For a second he was grateful to live in a place in which life was a right and not a luxury.

—Are we going to be OK, *don* Constantino? —asked Andrés afraid of receiving an answer.

—I hope so, Andrés. This happened two kilometres away from here, and we're heading the opposite direction.

Don Constantino noticed Andrés being too tense and thought he was feeling this way because he was a stranger to this reality after so many years living abroad.

—Andrés, we will be fine, don't you worry. God is here with us — he said it with a lot of confidence in his voice.

Andrés tried to calm down and allowed his eyes to get lost by observing the grey and cloudy landscape which was now being accompanied with some rain. After spending several minutes in silence inside the car, Andrés turned his head towards *don* Constantino and said:

—I really admire you, *don* Constantino —said Andrés out of the blue.

The leader of a community of 600 people smiled, but didn't understand what this young man actually meant. His humbleness was such that he didn't think he was someone worth admiring. Andrés continued:

—How can you possibly live this lifestyle each day of your life? — the killings in *La Guajira* had affected his peace and serenity —. And I don't mean to offend you, but you live in a small house filled with little holes which gets wet inside whenever it rains. You can barely provide a good living to your three kids, and on top of that, you have to be responsible for the well-being of a whole community. And on top of that you have to deal with cruel and rough violence each and every day of your life. You are the leader of a community, *don* Constantino! You are supposed to live more comfortably. You don't deserve this.

Don Constantino was focused on the road because driving through the rain could change things in a split of a second. However, he heard all of what Andrés had to say, and with a smile drawn on his face, he replied:

—What would you think if I told you that each morning I walk my kids to school, I thank God for giving me the opportunity to see them grow one more day? That each time I can give work to someone new I feel happy because I know that he will be able to feed his family? That I feel proud with the modest house we have as it was built with the hard work of my wife and I? Even if it has little holes and it isn't close to being a mansion, it was built with love because we wanted to provide a roof for our children. What would you think if I told you that having a heart filled with the love of God is worth more than any material possessions I could have? And finally, what would you think if I told you that by acknowledging that the price to pay to live a simple, yet authentic happy life, is to accept the violence and criminality which we face day after day?

Don Constantino turned to Andrés, who was feeling bad for having made those comments.

—I can imagine that you would think I'm crazy, right?

Andrés nodded and they both laughed.

—Andrés, after God granted me with more years to live my life, I knew I couldn't live life thinking about myself only. Even though I had to drop out of university after my mother's death, I always knew I was committed to come back for my family and also for other families in *El Diamante*.

—We are all so different; thank God —joked *don* Constantino —. To some people money is the most important thing. But it isn't for me.

Andrés felt alluded by this comment, but he knew *don* Constantino was right.

—God has provided each one of us with a blank canvas, and it is up to us to paint the drawing with which we want to be remembered in this Earthly experience. The colour, texture and shape will depend on us. Your essence will be reflected in this piece of art you paint with your life, Andrés. What do you think would be your legacy if today was your last day in this world?

These words resonated deeply in Andrés and he regained the sense of peace he had lost a few minutes back. Although it was painful to listen to these words, he was now able to appreciate them and put them into a different perspective as he was willing to start all over again. Now more than ever, he wanted to believe the lump in his testicle was not going to be critical. He then gave himself permission to dream how his life would be if he was given the gift to live more years of his life.

—Andrés, all of what you have experienced these last few days has a reason, and only you and God will know the purpose. Don't ignore these experiences. It is up to you to decide the direction you wish to take in your life from now on.

After a couple of hours on the road, they finally made it back to *El Diamante*. Before heading up to *don* Constantino's house, Andrés shook hands with him and thanked him for all he had done in the last day and a half. Andrés took his wallet out, and even though he didn't have much money, he handed eighty *quetzales* to *don* Constantino.

This wise man only smiled and grabbed Andrés' hand.

—My dear Andrés, promise me two things.

Andrés nodded, but was a bit surprised as to why he hadn't accepted the money. He thought that maybe it wasn't enough for everything *don* Constantino had done for him.

—You will give this money to someone who needs it more than I do. I know a couple here in the community with a sick baby. You will walk to their house and you will tell them that you want to help them out.

Andrés was struck by this. How could there be someone as detached and as noble as *don* Constantino? How could he not accept some help when he also needed it?

—And the second —continued *don* Constantino after pausing for a few seconds —. Promise me you'll do your best effort to listen and follow your heart.

Andrés' eyes filled with tears once again. They hugged each other and told him he would fulfil his promises.

He walked towards an even smaller house and gave the money to a family who needed it to pay for the baby's medicines. They hugged him for a long time; they cried and told him he was a true angel. It was the second time he was called an "angel", and he didn't quite understand why.

The second promise he made *don* Constantino was going to become a day to day habit though. Even if he was anxious to know what was going to happen to his body, he felt he had achieved a liberated soul.

That night they shared their last dinner together. It was filled with funny stories once again and they promised each other this would be the beginning of a special friendship. Andrés had no clue as to how he was going to be able to come back, but he promised them he would.

Before going to bed, Pedrito came to his mattress and said:

—Thank you for choosing our home. If you need any more help to see how humans live, please come back again.

Andrés hugged him with all the strength he had and told Pedrito he was definitely going to come back and that he was also welcomed to visit his "planet" any time he wanted. Pedrito was thrilled to receive this invitation and went to bed feeling very happy and excited.

CHAPTER XXIV

The next morning when Andrés woke up, the three kids had left to go to school. *Doña* Rosa who was preparing his breakfast had left the family mobile phone on top of the table, so that he could get in touch with whoever he needed to talk to. Andrés was anxious to call his parents, but he didn't know how to contact them though. He decided to call the rental car agency first, and once he was back in the city he'd find a way to meet up with them.

First, Andrés had to walk down the mountain to find the car and get a number to call the agency. *Doña* Rosa told him he could find the car in the warehouse which was located a few metres from the dirt road.

That morning Andrés woke up feeling a bit more of pain in his testicle and abdomen, but he decided not to pay too much attention to it. Not because he wanted to ignore what was happening, but because he remembered he had surrendered his life and illness and it wasn't under his control to do anything about it but to simply observe it.

He walked down to the warehouse and only hoped the car hadn't suffered too much damage. He wished he could simply start the engine and head back to the city as soon as possible. When he got to the dirt road, he asked for the warehouse, and *don* Fede —who was passing by— saw Andrés and was glad to see this young man recovered. *Don* Fede walked with him. Once they got there, they removed a blanket which was covering the car. It was until that moment that Andrés realised the serious damage of the accident. If he had stayed inside the car for one more second, he wouldn't have been able to tell the story.

He found the contact number and thanked *don* Fede for all his help during the accident. Even though, this humble man had only seen Andrés three times in his life, he was able to notice the calmness reflecting in his face.

—I hope you have a safe trip back home, Andrés. And don't forget to come visit us —said *don* Fede with affection.

Andrés got back to *doña* Rosa's house and started arranging for the car rental people to assist him. Andrés told the customer service agent he had travelled that morning to *El Diamante* and that he had experienced an accident while driving through a hill. The agent on the other side of the phone told him a crane would come and pick him and the car up. Another person from the insurance company would have to come as well, as they needed to evaluate the damage of the car. If there were no problems on the road, the crane would get to *El Diamante* in a couple of hours.

He returned the mobile phone to *doña* Rosa and told her he was going to have a last walk in the mountain before the crane got there. *Doña* Rosa could see Andrés' eyes were now shining, even though she could still sense a bit of sadness within. She suggested him to walk to the viewpoint where *don* Constantino had taken him the first night he was there, as he was going to be able to appreciate a magnificent view which would help him strengthen his energy.

Andrés left this house feeling like a member of the family, and walked towards the viewpoint. As he was walking, he was observing the green tones of the mountains, listened to the birds peeping and felt the morning sun shining through his skin. He was not only observing, but he was reflecting a lot too. The last few days of his life had unfolded in such an unusual manner and he was now starting to feel like God had talked to him directly. He relived every experience and started conceiving the idea that perhaps God uses different people, or something like an illness, the death of a beloved person, a broken heart or an economic crisis to talk to us directly.

"Why do you allow suffering to happen if you are supposed to love us?" he asked God in silence. The moment he formulated this question, his inner voice replied: "I don't want you to be suffering from an illness, Andrés. But thanks to what you're living now, you decided to talk to Me again, and I don't know if you didn't realise it before, but I have always been by your side. However, you decided to disconnect from yourself because you're always distracted with a computer, a mobile phone, Internet, the TV and your job. All of these distractions haven't allowed you to focus on your true self, in Me, in paying attention to what your heart is asking you to do. You haven't been able to dream and to think about others".

This resonated inside of him and it made sense! He smiled. He confirmed he was definitely not the same person now. Living, touching, experiencing, seeing and listening to a reality which was so different from his —in every single sense— had opened his eyes and heart. The contrast lived between his life in London with the way people lived in these communities allowed him to see the true reality of the majority of the world.

He was now willing to make big changes in his life, but he was afraid. He wasn't fearful because he was afraid of dying, but he was scared to being the same person he was before. He was afraid of not having enough courage to fulfil the promise he made to *don* Constantino about surrendering completely to the voice of his heart.

If he was lucky enough not to be suffering from cancer, or even if he was, but managed to survive, he was afraid of not having enough strength to change his lifestyle. However, he now conscious he was living a comfortable but empty life. He had enough money to do whatever he wanted, but he didn't have anyone to share it with. He had a beautiful flat in an exclusive area in London, but no one who waited for him at night. He had many investment funds and an enviable financial projection, but not even all the money in the world was going to save him from living a meaningless life.

It took him about fifteen minutes to get to the viewpoint where he had been with *don* Constantino and Pedrito a couple of nights back. As there were no trees blocking the view, the scenery under the sunlight was even more impressive. The sky was blue and decorated with a few white clouds. The green mountains surrounding this tiny town were all equal in size and magnitude. He was able to observe a small river between the two mountains in front of him.

For a moment, Andrés let the natural beauty before him penetrate his mind and soul. He felt the wind passing by his face and body. He felt each breath from his lungs all the way to his nose. Suddenly, the same voice he had heard a few minutes back, said: "Let your heart be the guide, don't be afraid, Andrés. This is the beginning of a new life for you". Hearing these words, Andrés felt peace again. The voice continued talking and said: "I have never left you, Andrés. I have always been by your side and I will always be here with you". The voice he was hearing was the voice of God which resonated inside of him.

In that moment, Andrés dropped to his knees; got his hands together close to his chest and raising his eyes to the sky he promised he would do his best to live a meaningful life. He recalled the scene from two days ago, in which after suffering the accident he was on the ground complaining to God. Two days later he received an answer: God wanted Andrés to give meaning to his life. How could he achieve this? Only his heart knew.

He'd have to first accept himself. He'd have to identify his weaknesses and strengths. He'd have to be able to dream again. And more importantly, he'd have to stop being afraid of loving and being loved. He knew he'd have to break with many chains and fight against the demons from his past which had turned him into a modern slave. The biggest challenge now was learning to unlearn that status, power and money weren't necessarily the elements to achieve true happiness. And above all, he would have to start prioritising the real important things in his life such as health, spiritual life, family, service and work.

In that mountain, Andrés realised the challenge lying in front of him was not going to be easy. First point, his illness. What was it going to be? Was he going to be able to live more? Second point, if he was able to live a bit longer, he'd have to change his lifestyle, his many years of rigid routine and open up his heart which had been stored in a trunk for many years. He knew this wasn't going to be an easy task but he was grateful with life because it wasn't late to try and be a better person. "It is never late to change", he told himself. His new goal in life wasn't to conquer New York City but to give meaning to his life. As he stood up, he smiled at the sky and shouted out loud:

—Life can change in a split of a second, right? —and winked an eye.

CHAPTER XXV

After having spent an hour and a half reflecting and meditating in that mountain, Andrés got back to say good bye to *doña* Rosa. The selfish and controlling man, who had entered *El Diamante* two days before, had died in the car accident. It was during that accident that a new man was born. This was a man who was willing to live life with a purpose and love. When he got back to the house, he walked towards *doña* Rosa and gave her a huge kiss and a hug which took her by surprise. It had been a long time since Andrés gave a kiss in the cheek to a stranger. But to him, *doña* Rosa was not a stranger anymore; she had become like a mother to him, and *don* Constantino like a father. In just 48 hours, Andrés was feeling like a new man who was eager to live life at its fullest.

—Thank you for everything, *doña* Rosa! —said Andrés with a smile from ear to ear.

—You don't have anything to thank for, son. I'm happy to see you're so full of life —replied *doña* Rosa.

—And I won't forget my promise to come and visit you soon —said Andrés, convincing himself that he was going to do so.

—We'll be waiting for you with open arms.

Doña Rosa walked towards the room Andrés had stayed in. And as she walked out, she was carrying the image of the *Moreneta de Montserrat* with her.

—Take it, son. The *Virgencita Morena* will keep you company, and you will see she'll help you through your illness.

Andrés assumed *don* Constantino had told his wife about his condition, but he didn't care. Andrés also knew this image was very special to *don* Constantino.

—I can't accept it, *doña* Rosa. That would be too much —said Andrés overwhelmed by her kindness.

—Look, Andrés, she has already helped us with a miracle. Plus, life is not about accumulating things but about sharing them. If one day you know someone who needs it, I hope you share it too, because this is what God expects from us: to share with each other —added *doña* Rosa.

Andrés didn't feel he was worth of this, but he was flattered to have received such a special gift. Ever since he came to this house, the image of the *Virgen Morena* had made him feel protected somehow. He hugged *doña* Rosa once again and asked her to greet her kids for him and especially *don* Constantino who he really wanted to say goodbye personally. He asked her for their mobile phone number and her address (if there was any) and he wrote it down a piece of paper.

As he was walking away from this humble house, Andrés felt melancholy by leaving this family, but he was happy to know they were part of his Perfect Plan and that all the lessons learned in those two days had been necessary for his awakening. He was walking with a huge smile on his face.

He got to the warehouse and *don* Constantino was removing the blanket they had used to cover the car as this would make it easier for the crane to pick it up. *Don* Constantino spotted Andrés carrying something under his arm.

—I can see you're leaving with some presents —he joked.

—Yes, *don* Constantino —answered Andrés as he blushed —. I want to thank you for... —said Andrés when he was interrupted by *don* Constantino who said:

—Andrés, I don't like farewells. Plus, the least I expect is for you to come and visit us when you`re completely healed.

It was true. *Don* Constantino really hated farewells. Even though these two men had just met, they both grew fond of each other. Andrés' eyes filled with tears but he didn't shed one. He managed to keep it all under control. They wrapped themselves in a strong hug until they saw the crane approaching the warehouse.

The car was loaded to the crane and the insurance agent asked him some detailed information about the accident. When he finished telling the story, Andrés got inside the crane. The driver started the engine and after advancing a few metres from the warehouse Andrés saw a few kids running after the crane on the rear view mirror. Two of the little ones running were Pedrito and Marina who were waving good bye to their *Jupiterian* friend. Both of them didn't realise they had saved this man's soul with their pure love and affection.

Those two days in *El Diamante* were definitely going to remain in his mind forever and ever. Not only because of the unexpected adventures he experienced, but mostly because he was aware the pact he had made with himself and with God was non-negotiable.

The crane driver was amazed by how this man had survived such a cruel car accident. Being a good and curious Guatemalan, he asked:

—Excuse me, sir, I know it isn't any of my business but, what were you doing around here?

—Don't worry —said Andrés calmly and he replied —: You see, I was coming here to visit my grandmother's graveyard, but God wanted me to stay in this community with some angels. Can you believe it?

As Andrés heard what he had said out loud, he was surprised by the words he used. He had said something neither rational nor objective, but he couldn't care less because it was the true. The driver stared at him and said:

—God sometimes talks to us in very funny ways, don't you think?

Andrés answered with a huge grin on his face:

—Tell me about it, my friend.

CHAPTER XXVI

The journey from *El Diamante* to *La Mina* developed without any inconveniences. Andrés chatted with the crane driver about the problems the country was currently facing. The number one issue in everyone's mind was the violence related to drug trafficking activity which affected all of Guatemala. Fear and paranoia were the bread and butter of the Guatemalan society. Andrés only hoped his family hadn't suffered from it.

After leaving *La Mina* behind, they drove into the more developed *Atlántico* road which would take them back to Guatemala City. Driving through this road felt as if he had been thrown a cold bucket of water to his face. Andrés felt as if he was entering the wild jungle once again. The experiences lived in *El Diamante* and *Los Manantiales* seemed as if it had been just a mere dream whilst they entered the city. He observed once again the chaotic traffic with cars, buses and lorries driving madly and honking their horns without a reason. As they got closer to the city centre, he started noticing the increasing urban poverty in the streets which could not be compared with the poverty he experienced in *El Diamante*.

"Urban poverty was more dangerous", he concluded. In the city people weren't able to survive by planting and harvesting their own food as in the communities nearby *El Diamante*. Life here was much more expensive too. The living conditions worsened as there was no nature around them which could mitigate the hopelessness of their poverty. That's why he wasn't surprised there was so much violence in the city. Andrés recognised that living in these conditions didn't allow people to dream; they simply struggled to survive.

Andrés was now seeing poverty with different eyes. With the eyes of a man who has actually experienced it. He felt vulnerable once again, as he felt like he was returning to reality, and feared all the lessons he had learnt with *don* Constantino and his family would soon be forgotten. And this was just the beginning... getting back to London was going to be even more challenging!

They finally made it to the hotel where Andrés was staying at. He got off from the crane holding the image of the *Virgen Morena* under his arm. He thanked the driver for his help and shook hands with him.

When Andrés was entering the hotel lobby, the girl from the reception —who had assisted him with the car rental a few days back— was open mouthed to see this man dressed in rags. The same guy, who only a couple of days seemed like a European aristocrat, now looked like a poor rural farmer. Behind him, she noticed a huge crane carrying the crashed car she had helped him rent. She was shocked by this scene. Her eyes and mouth were wide open. Andrés recognised this girl and walked towards her in the reception.

—If you ask me what happened and I tell you the real story, I'm sure you won't believe me —he said to María as if they were old friends.

Are you... —she wasn't able to finish the question as she was so astonished by his looks, but after taking a deep breath she continued — ... are you OK, sir?

—I am, thank God! —replied Andrés in a cheerful voice —. I need to connect to the Internet because I lost my mobile phone and I don't have a laptop and I need to get in touch with my family ASAP! —he shouted feeling excited.

Maria was still in shock, and by inertia she raised her left arm and pointed to a computer room which was a few steps from the reception. She wrote the password in a piece of paper and handed it to him. Andrés ran as fast as he could to the computer room as a kid who has just been given a new toy and can't wait to play with it.

He placed the image of the Virgin next to the computer, and as he was entering the password on the computer, he asked the *Moreneta* to help him find the number in which he could reach his family.

Andrés logged in to his personal email which he rarely checked. No one wrote to him! He started reading emails from the last ten years. He started using the search function and used words like: mom, phone number, house, dad, but no email with a phone number would come up. He kept on checking emails, from the older to the newer ones. He realised there was a high probability he had erased the few emails he received from his parents after reading them. Suddenly he spotted an email from his sister with the subject "At least one time, Andrés".

He opened the email and noticed this email had been written three years ago. In this email she was telling him about his father's health issues and about a heart surgery he had undergone. As he read this email, Andrés' heart twisted with every word he read. His sister wrote:

"Andrés I understand you are busy with your life, but you have to remember all the sacrifices mom and dad did for you, even if you never realised it. After dad came back from the anaesthesia effect —because of a heart surgery he went through— the first thing he asked was: "are you here, son?" Once he realised he had said these words and that you weren't there, he burst into tears. These tears were because of you. I was annoyed to see how dad was suffering for a selfish bastard who never thinks of anyone but himself. If you have some compassion, please call him on (502) 568900292. Regards. Mariela".

He had found his dad's mobile number! He wrote it down on the same piece of paper he was given by Maria in the reception and put it inside one of the pockets of his trousers. He recalled reading that email back in the day it was sent, but decided to get in touch a few days later. Days passed by, months and in the end, three years had gone by and he never made a phone call because he was "always busy".

In that very moment, Andrés was able to see his life retrospectively and realised how long it had been since he walked away from his family. He wanted to assimilate the bitter taste he felt for having been such a selfish bastard —as his sister had rightly referred to him— and thought about a way to make up for all the damage he caused them. Even though it was very hard for him to accept his mistakes and to ask for forgiveness, he knew this was the least he could do after showing so much indifference to them.

He approached María and told her he was heading up to his room. In a friendly way, he requested to transfer any calls from the insurance company to his room. Inside, he was feeling ashamed for having been such a selfish son of a bitch all those years. However, he spoke to María in a polite and friendly manner because he knew she had nothing to do with it. For the first time he wasn't thinking about himself only! María couldn't believe this was the same guy she had spoken to a few days before. She was curious to know what had happened during those days, but she was afraid he may be schizophrenic and decided to just let it go.

Andrés ran to his room and walked straight to where the phone was. On his way to the room he had planned to shower and then call his dad, but his conscience didn't let him waste any more time. He was very excited to call his parents, but he feared their reaction after all those years. "If I was one of my parents, I wouldn't want to talk to me", he told himself. He picked up the phone and started flirting with the keyboard. After a minute, he decided to hang up without dialling any number. He was scared to face his father and explain himself; especially because no explanation could be good enough to heal all the harm he had caused them all those years.

Suddenly he decided it was time, and dialled the number. His heart was racing so fast, and the palm of his hand started sweating. He was afraid his father wasn't going to recognise his voice anymore. But this would make it easier to hang up and for his father to ignore the call.

The first tone rang... Andrés was sweating even more than when he was in *El Diamante*... the second tone rang... Andrés' hands were shaking... the third tone rang... if his father didn't pick up after the next tone he was going to hang up... the fourth tone rang... he switched the phone to his other hand... the fifth tone rang... he finally heard a voice saying "hello?". Andrés remained silent for about ten seconds. He was petrified. From the other side of the phone he was hearing a male voice saying:

—Hello, who is this?... hello?.... hello?

He finally had the courage to open his mouth and say: "dad, is that you?" None of them could see each other's faces, but the silence between them simply showed the strong emotions and surprise both men were feeling at that very moment. At last, *don* Rafael —who had tears in his eyes and was talking with a broken voice —said:

—Andrés, where are you? —before Andrés was able to respond to this question he said —I'm so happy to hear your voice, son.

—I'm in Guatemala, dad —replied Andrés feeling shy.

—In Guatemala? —shouted *don* Rafael with excitement.

—Yes, dad. And I was thinking maybe... —Andrés paused as he was feeling embarrassed to talk to his dad after such a long time —. I could come visit you?

Don Rafael laughed out loud on the other side of the phone and responded:

—You're asking me, if you can come visit us? Please, son, seeing you would be the best thing that has happened to us in a long time —said *don* Rafael with sincerity in his voice.

Andrés told his dad he was staying at a hotel and asked for the address to his house —which he had also forgotten— so that he could order a cab. His father told him he was crazy if he was going to let him go by cab. He asked him to be ready in half an hour as he was going to pick him up himself. He wasn't going to say anything to his mother or sister so that they would surprise them. Andrés and his father were both filled with excitement. Before hanging up, *don* Rafael told him:

—I love you, son.

Hearing these words filled Andrés' eyes with tears.

The voice he had recently start hearing again told him these weren't just any tears. This time around these tears were actually a reflection of the cleansing of his soul. Andrés replied:

—I love you too, dad.

And they hung up.

Andrés got into the shower. He got naked and saw the lump on his testicle, but he didn't fear. He didn't want to focus on it, or on the million possibilities of what it could be. The only thing he wanted to do at that very moment —without getting bothered by anything else— was to live thoroughly the reunion with his family. He showered and changed clothes. He saw himself in the mirror again, with the difference that this time he was able to face his own reflection. That morning he didn't want to show off his expensive clothes or his social status. None of that mattered.

Half an hour later, he came down the reception and his father was already waiting for him. When *don* Rafael saw him, he started running towards Andrés and they both embraced each other in a hug. Andrés, who was taller than his father, managed to lay his head on his dad's shoulders and hugged him as hard as he could.

After a few minutes embracing in this hug, Andrés whispered to his ear:

—Forgive me, dad.

Don Rafael let go of him for a second, and staring straight into his eyes, he kissed him on the forehead and said:

—There's nothing to forgive, son. You're here with us and that's what matters.

Both of them stayed wrapped in a hug in the middle of the hotel lobby. So many years had passed since these two men had embraced each other, and at that moment, Andrés felt like a child again. He recalled his grandmother's face once again and wished this was the beginning of his new life. Once again, the letter left by his grandma hit his head: "true love expects nothing in return". And his father had shown him just that. Nothing else. He felt truly happy and protected around his father's arms.

CHAPTER XXVII

On the way from the hotel to Andrés' house, father and son did not stop chatting. Not even for one single second. *Don* Rafael kept telling Andrés how happy his mother was going to be when she saw him. He also tried updating him with the most important family events. For instance he told Andrés about his sister's marriage to a nice and hardworking man. They were about to be parents for the first time too. Andrés told his dad about the experience of living in London for the last ten years. He described his business trips to New York, Sidney and Hong Kong. His father listened carefully to his son, and even if he wasn't able to fully understand what his son was saying, he felt a proud father.

—It seems like my son is an important person in the world —said *don* Rafael.

—It is not like that, dad —said a humble Andrés.

—Son, I don't want to talk about the last ten years of your life; not because I don't care, but because we have missed you so much. I would love to start from scratch, and I know your mom would like that too. You and your sister are the most important people in our lives and we don't want to lose you again.

Andrés felt bad for what his dad just said. More than 3,650 days had gone by and during this time he managed to drive his family away from his life. Driven by a materialistic and selfish ambition, he was able to distance himself from the people who loved him unconditionally despite of his many mistakes and flaws. He had missed his sister's wedding, his dad's heart surgery and who knows what other relevant family events.

—I could have called more —he said feeling like a cockroach.

—Andrés, I told you already, let's leave the past behind. Today you're here by my side, and you can't imagine how happy I am to have you here and to see you're doing so well.

"If he only knew", thought Andrés in silence. He didn't want to say anything about his situation until they were all together.

—Look, Andrés —said his father in a paternal way —, sometimes we have to suffer a lot so that we can then appreciate the most important and simplest things in life. Today, I don't really care what happened in the past. You are here and I hope you can stay with us for a few days.

A tear fell from *don* Rafael's eyes and his voice broke as he was so genuinely excited to have his son next to him. He got to a point to which he thought he was not going to see his son ever again and so he wanted to enjoy each and every second of his presence.

It was Saturday and it had become a family tradition for Mariela and her husband —Alvaro— to have lunch at her parent's house. Mariela — who was the eldest child— assumed the role of son and daughter after Andrés' departure. She got to hate her brother as she was able to see the suffering her parents went through because of his absence and indifference.

Don Rafael and *doña* Margarita questioned themselves repeatedly if they had been good parents or not, as they blamed themselves for Andrés' decision to leave his home. They felt guilty about it, and that really bothered Mariela. They would never say anything bad about their son and they also didn't talk about him in public as the mere fact of listening to his name hurt them deeply. Mariela stopped contacting Andrés after their father's heart surgery, as she then realised how selfish he was. She decided not to waster her time with someone who couldn't care less about them.

Mariela had met her husband while studying her university degree. They got married a couple of years back and were now expecting their first baby. *Don* Rafael and *doña* Margarita were thrilled about being grandparents for the first time. Even if Mariela ignored it, both of her parents were aware of the sacrifice it represented for her to be the single child in that family after Andrés left them. Her parents greatly appreciated the devotion she had for them.

Mariela was so hurt by her brother that Alvaro never asked about him or brought his name to any conversation, as just hearing her brother's name would put her in a bad mood. Sometimes she wondered whether she really hated him or if the pain she felt was because she missed him immensely.

Back in the car, Saturday afternoons were the worse to drive around Guatemala City. The traffic jam they ran into was very intense. However, for these two people who had just reunited, time seemed to fly by.

Andrés smiled as his father drove past the streets which brought memories from his childhood. The last couple of weeks of his life had turned into an emotional roller coaster; but that Saturday afternoon, in the middle of the Roosevelt Avenue —which was packed with buses and cars— Andrés confirmed that God's plan —just like *don* Constantino had told him— was simply... a perfect plan! True, there were still many things to figure out, but in that precise moment he was assuming the compromise that his life required many changes, and the first step to take was to ask for forgiveness to the people who loved him the most and whom he had hurt so much.

After a forty minutes' drive, they finally made it to the de la Vega's home which was located in a residential area built in the 70s. *Don* Rafael had worked very hard to purchase this home when Mariela was a newborn baby.

When they got home, *don* Rafael, who was thrilled to have his son there, put his arm behind his son's back and said:

—They are all here, son. It seems as if they knew you were coming because they usually arrive later.

In that very moment, Andrés felt his blood running up and down his body. He was very nervous. He started sweating and thinking the worse things about himself. In a matter of a few seconds, he came up with different scenarios as to how he was going to be received by his mother and sister. His father, for being the most laid back one in the family, perhaps had taken a more flexible approach when welcoming him back; however, his mother and sister, being women as they were, it was likely they could react less affectionate as they were still hurt.

"I deserve it", thought Andrés to himself. He was feeling guilty about the damage he inflicted in them. His family stopped trying to get in touch with him as he had only shown indifference and decided to leave him alone as they didn't want to be an obstacle in his life. Even though, they knew very little about his life, they tried to convince themselves he acted like this because he was an important and busy businessman. They considered he may have been embarrassed of them and that's why they decided to stop making more attempts to reconnect with him.

While living in London, Andrés never talked about his family to anyone. He thought it could be taken for granted that he came from a well of Guatemalan family even if that wasn't the case. He wanted to believe people could only focus on the external things. He considered it was enough for people to see the fact he had been able to study in London and was a successful man. If someone asked him about his parents, he responded his father owned a business and his mother was a housewife. He would always make sure he told people his family had a maid working at his house. In Europe, these elements could easily give the image Andrés was well positioned in Guatemala. He even created a story around his last name. He used to say his ancestors from Spain had some royal blood. None of this was true though.

His father's business was a small company which didn't even generate 10% of Andrés' yearly income. His mother was a housewife because she wasn't able to complete her university degree as she decided to devote her life to taking care of her children and husband. They employed a maid who helped *doña* Margarita three times a week as she wasn't able to do all the chores herself after all those years working at home. His last name could've sounded elitist, but his great great grandfather who sailed his way from Spain to Guatemala wasn't a duke. He got to Guatemala in the XIX century and established himself as a barber. Just like his great grandfather did. It was his grandfather, who had ventured into the entrepreneurial field, but the "de la Vega" was never —at least from his side of the family— a last name related to the elite class in Guatemala, as he wanted to believe it himself.

Andrés' father opened the door to their home and called on his son who was immobile next to the car. Hearing his dad calling his name brought him back to reality. As he started walking towards the door he convinced himself the worse possible scenario he had created in his mind, was going to actually become a reality. He was walking with his head down and with his eyes fixed to the ground.

Andrés walked inside the house he had lived for 18 years of his life. Everything remained the same. His mother had an exquisite taste for decoration. It wasn't pompous or extravagant. On the contrary, it was a classic and rustic style, yet simple and elegant. Most of the furniture was made of wood and it was decorated with vintage objects. The roof and the columns which sustained the house were also made of wood. In front of the dining room there was a large window which showed *doña* Margarita's little garden in which she had roses, sunflowers and bougainvillea.

As Andrés got closer to the dining table, he heard a radio playing from the kitchen. He realised this was the same radio show they would hear each Saturday and Sunday when they visited his grandmother's home. Ever since she passed away, it became a family tradition to get together for lunch and to listen to this marimba show.

Ever since they were kids, Andrés and Mariela hated this traditional Guatemalan instrument, but as they grew older, Mariela started liking it for what it represented to her family and not because of the music per se. She was looking forward to share and pass on her traditions and costumes to her baby. Andrés, on the other hand, hadn't heard a marimba melody in so many years.

By the time they got to the dining room, the very melancholic *"Luna de Xelajú"* tune was playing on the radio. He got the goose bumps when he heard it as it brought so many memories from his childhood, his parents and his grandmother.

Doña Margarita and Mariela were upstairs, as *doña* Margarita was showing her daughter a couple of gloves and a hat she had knitted for her grandchild. Alvaro wasn't home at that time. When *don* Rafael noticed they were both upstairs, he shouted:

—Margarita! Mariela! Come down stairs. I have a surprise for you!

Andrés felt like a foreigner in his own home. He felt like a stranger and he wasn't comfortable with it. Thirty seconds after *don* Rafael called his wife and daughter to come down, they heard some steps coming down on the stairs. Both women were discussing whether the baby was going to be a boy or a girl as Mariela didn't want to know until the delivery date. *Doña* Margarita was sure it was going to be a baby boy and her daughter bet on a baby girl. As they were almost on the ground floor of the house, *doña* Margarita shouted:

—Rafa, where is my surprise then? —she asked with sarcasm as *don* Rafael was not a romantic man, and even less after forty years of marriage.

—Here in the dining room —replied *don* Rafael filled with excitement.

Doña Margarita and Mariela kept talking why the baby was going to be of either sex, when they finally got to the dining room and saw a young man standing next to *don* Rafael. This young man looked like Andrés, *doña* Margarita thought to herself. Both women stayed still for a second as if they were facing a ghost. Not far from reality though. Sadly, Andrés was now just a simple ghost in their lives.

Doña Margarita dropped her knitting needles on the floor when she finally realised this young man was actually her lost son. There he was. The son she thought she would never see again. She ran as fast as she could towards him. When they were face to face, she fixed her eyes on him and with her right hand she caressed his face with so much love in an attempt to get assurance that he was real.

—Hi, mom… I just wanted to…

Doña Margarita interrupted him —just like his dad had done earlier — and put her hand on his mouth so that he stopped talking. She smiled and hugged him as hard she could. She couldn't help it, and started crying on her son's chest. Andrés held her and caressed her hair. *Doña* Margarita burst into tears and the more she cried, the more he would embrace her. Andrés couldn't help it himself, and started shedding tears as well.

Seeing mother and son reunited was a very emotional scene to observe. *Don* Rafael who wasn't able to keep it together started crying too. He knew the love *doña* Margarita felt for Andrés was stronger than he could have ever imagined. He loved his son with all of his being, but he was aware that a mother's unconditional love could not be compared.

And there she was. *Doña* Margarita was wrapped around the arms of a person she thought she was not going to see again. She was holding him and crying on his chest.

Mariela, who felt some resentment towards her brother for all the pain he had caused her and her parents, had her eyes filled with tears and was trying to keep it together because of her pride. However, even if her baby was still inside of her womb, she could somehow understand what her mother was feeling in that very moment and decided to let tears roll down her face as well.

For five minutes, this house was filled with a monastic silence. No one moved from where they were standing. No words were spoken. It took only five minutes for all the suffering and resentment to disappear. Perhaps ten years had gone by since they were all together, but it only took five minutes for all of this to be a thing of the past.

The suffering was gone. The damage was already done, but today, things were about to start heading in a different direction. If pride and resentment had taken over *don* Rafael, *doña* Margarita and Mariela, these five minutes filled with love, forgiveness and hope would've never existed. This house, this family —even if it was for five minutes only— was complete! Something none of them imagined could happen again.

Andrés gave his mother a big kiss and with tears rolling down his face he said:

—Please forgive me, mom. I love you.

Doña Margarita saw the sincere look in her son's eyes, and trying to dry the tears from his face; she hugged him again and replied:

You don't have to ask for forgiveness, my boy. I will always be your mother and I will never, ever, stop loving you.

With these words, Andrés raised his head —which was resting on his mother's shoulders— and fixed his eyes on his sister's. He walked away from his mother's arms and walked towards Mariela. He gave her a sweet kiss on the cheek and said:

—I will be in debt with you forever in my life. You suffered this pain for the two of us. With all my heart I ask you to please forgive me.

Andrés had never asked to be forgiven. He had never expressed those words out loud to anyone. His pride had always been stronger than anything else, so accepting he had made so many mistakes in his life to the people who loved him the most was a huge step for him. Asking for forgiveness was something new to Andrés. He was aware that if his heart had remained cold and distant as to when he boarded the plane in London, he would have never have the capacity to say these words.

Having heard the words "please forgive me" coming out of Andrés' mouth wasn't what impressed them the most. It was the sincere and humble voice in which he had said it that touched their hearts so deeply. They all knew this was a new version of Andrés. And he was aware of that too. He felt liberated, complete, protected and happy. This was the return of the prodigal son.

CHAPTER XXVIII

Doña Margarita had cooked a delicious meal without knowing her own son was going to be the guest of honour. In an attempt to get things back to normality, the proud mother walked back to the kitchen to arrange the last minute details of the meal. In the meantime, *don* Rafael walked towards a little bar he had and took out a bottle of whiskey which he was saving for a special occasion. And this was definitely one special occasion! He asked Andrés if he wanted a drink, and he agreed.

—Do you want it like your old man drinks it? Whiskey with Coke? —and winked at him.

The truth was that Andrés disliked people who mixed whiskey with Coke, as he believed only ordinary people could insult whiskey in this way, but this time around he didn't give any importance to this stupid prejudice of his.

—Sure, dad, just like you drink it —and smiled.

He sat next to his sister and asked her about her pregnancy, her husband and all there was to know about her life. *Doña* Margarita and *don* Rafael were ecstatic to see their two children sharing together. This was the most beautiful gift they could have asked for. For some families, these little details were all part of a set routine, but to this family, this was something extraordinary that they were experiencing for the first time in many years.

Don Rafael whispered into his wife's ear:

—It is true the simplest moments are the ones we treasure the most, right love?

Doña Margarita agreed with her head. She didn't want to think about

164

anything else in that moment. She just wanted to absorb in the deepest part of her soul each second they were allowed to be together. *Don* Rafael took his glass up and they all cheered. *Don* Rafael and Andrés with two glasses of whiskey and Coke, and *doña* Margarita and Mariela with two glasses filled with *Rosa de Jamaica*.

—Here's to this family, for the love we have for each other and because Andrés is back —shouted *don* Rafael with excitement.

—Cheers! —shouted all together.

They waited for Alvaro to arrive so that they could eat lunch. When he entered the house, he was so surprised to see Andrés at his in-law's home as he thought he was never going to be able to meet him. He was shocked to see him so unexpectedly. Andrés thought that he seemed like a nice guy from a first impression, and even if he was a simple man — unlike most of his colleagues in the financial world— he could perceive the love he had for his sister and that was enough.

Doña Margarita and Mariela placed the different dishes on the table. As the head of the family was about to start serving the food on the plates, she served Andrés first. With this tiny detail —which for some is simply part of a routine— he was feeling loved and protected. When everyone was served, *doña* Margarita asked them all to close their eyes.

—In the name of the Father, of the Son and of the Holy Spirit — she said as they all made the sign of the cross before praying —. Our Father, I want to thank you for allowing us to be together once again. I thank you because this home is complete. I ask you to please let us forget the past and to heal any wounds we may have. And finally, I ask you to let us enjoy this gift of love which you have granted us with. Amen.

Andrés recalled the prayer at *don* Constantino's house. He remembered how this little detail made him feel part of this family. This time around, he felt even happier and more complete, because he was sharing it with his own family!

While they were eating, *doña* Margarita kept talking and talking as she wanted to update Andrés with all the events which had happened since he left. At the same time, *don* Rafael kept pouring more whiskey and Coke to his glass. Mariela and her husband remained a bit quite at the beginning, but they started sharing more and more as the minutes passed by. After an hour at the table the marimba show ended, and the show that followed was one of *don* Rafael's favourites as it was *boleros*. They laughed, sang and cheered.

Andrés recalled all those expensive and luxurious restaurants he had visited around the world, and concluded that not even the best restaurant —according to The New York Times— could give him what his home was gifting him with. "It definitely isn't the food which makes a restaurant so special but the people you share the moment with", he reflected in silence. This was a very simple, yet honest thought.

Andrés hadn't said much after three hours around the table, as different topics kept being discussed. Mariela told him how he had met Alvaro, about her wedding, and about the pregnancy. *Doña* Margarita tried to update him with the lives of his many cousins, uncles, aunts and school friends. Andrés didn't remember most of the people his mother was mentioning, but he noticed the happiness reflected in his mother's eyes so he decided not to interrupt her. He was paying close attention to each word she uttered. *Don* Rafael was a man of few words, but you could see through his eyes how joyful and happy he was to have his son next to him once again. Alvaro was just a spectator, as he was still trying to change his mind about his brother-in-law.

Don Rafael interrupted his wife and daughter —who didn't stop talking— and said:

—Now it is your turn, son. What are you doing here in Guatemala?

Andrés felt perplexed by this sudden question as he didn't want to spoil the moment for everybody. He knew he had to tell them at some point the reason why he was there but he didn't know when it was going to be a good moment to spill it out.

—The truth is that... uhmmm... —he paused and after taking a deep breath he continued —, I came here because I wanted to be close to grandma.

Everyone at the table was confused by what he had just said. It didn't make any sense to travel all the way from London after so many years of absence just because he felt like "being close to grandma". Andrés himself knew that this explanation was not good enough, and so he said:

—I didn't mean to say that I came here to be with grandma, I'm not that crazy —he joked —. A few days ago I went to see a doctor because it seems like I have a tumour in my left testicle.

Andrés imagined that after saying this, both of his parents and his sister would freak out and make a huge drama about it, but it didn't happen. They let him continue talking.

—I won't lie to you, but ever since I saw the doctor in London and he told me that there was a chance this could be cancer, I felt very scared. Maybe you don't really know me anymore, but I made a huge mistake in thinking I was invincible. I turned into a very proud man who believed that material wealth, status and power were the most important things in life.

His voice started to break a bit, and his father grabbed his hand under the table as to trying to give him enough strength so that he could continue to let it all out. His mother was looking at him with so much tenderness and just wanted to get to the other side of the table and hug him, but she felt it was time for him to express all of what his heart was feeling. Andrés continued:

—Many years passed by, and I kept on living as if I was an immortal being. And now I realise that the more material wealth I was accumulating, the more miserable I was feeling inside. I can now see all the pain that I caused you when I decided to get away from you, but believe me, the one who suffered this separation the most was me. I haven't let anyone inside my heart because I was afraid of losing control of my life. I let go of a woman who loved me for who I was. I ran away from you guys and I can now see how much I have lost in my life.

Doña Margarita couldn't keep it together and stood up from her chair and walked towards Andrés. She embraced him in what seemed like an eternal hug. Each hug he had received and each tear he had dropped those last few days were allowing him to liberate himself from so much guilt and remorse in his heart. He was now filling himself with love, peace, protection and calmness regardless of his physical illness. The barricade he had built around his heart for so many years was slowly coming down. His heart —just like his grandmother's trunk— was getting cleaned, and he was filling it with more pure and sincere feelings. Andrés continued letting out all of what he had accumulated inside his mind and soul for so long:

—However, facing my mortality because of a possible cancer made me come all the way here. During this short trip I have come to the conclusion that we're in this life only for a little while. The memory of grandma helped me break with my objective and rational mentality, and so I decided to travel in an attempt to feel closer to her. I wanted to feel protected by her.

Everyone around the table was in a state of shock. They were impressed by the sincerity he expressed with his words. They all knew how Andrés had always been extremely rigid and rational in his actions, so to hear him saying he had taken wild decisions because of his impulses and because of love, simply astonished them. "He must be very afraid and scared and that is why he has been breaking his old structures behind", they all concluded.

—A few days ago I had to do some medical tests and apparently the doctor will have the final results next week. Feeling scared and vulnerable I decided to fly here in an attempt to visit grandma's graveyard in Los Manantiales and head back.

If they were already shocked by what he was saying, this just confirmed they were actually in the presence of a new Andrés.

Andrés continued narrating his story and told them how he arrived to Guatemala and how he had rented a car and drove all the way to Los Manantiales, even if he didn't exactly know where this town was located. He told them about the car crash and how some local people helped him and took care of him after the accident.

Andrés told them about don Constantino's family and described the precarious conditions that people in *El Diamante* and in the neighbouring communities lived in. No one at that table could believe what this man —who now looked like an English aristocrat— had experienced in the last few days. He got excited when telling the story though, as listening to himself out loud allowed him to appreciate and value all the lessons he had learned those days. He also told them what had happened in the natural pool when he and *don* Constantino had surrendered their lives to God.

—It was in this place where I freed myself from the fear which had taken over me. It was in this place, with my feet in the water, that I realised I had an outstanding debt with you —said in a calm and confident tone.

No one said or asked anything. Andrés was narrating this story with so much excitement —and even with a bit of romanticism— that no one dared to interrupt him. Each reflection, each tear, each smile and each landscape he described created the sensation they were also living this life changing adventure with him.

—It was inside this turquoise water when I realised how God had used grandma as an angel so that I could get to that remote place, which otherwise I would have never ever attempted to visit. Grandma wanted me to experience this contrasting lifestyle. She wanted me to experience what it is to be a poor economic person, not only for me to appreciate what I have, but mostly to understand that the simpler life is, the greater the chances to live a happier life are. She also wanted me to see a reality in which the most used drug is faith in God, because they can't afford anything else. The majority of these people live without the opportunity to dream. On the contrary, they dream to survive.

Mariela put herself in the position of the people Andrés was describing and thought about her baby. Even though the baby wasn't born yet and in spite of how difficult things could be for her and Alvaro, she wasn't able to imagine the reality her brother was talking about. She couldn't understand how people with children could struggle like this without anyone giving them a hand.

—During this time I have come to understand that God has a plan for each one of us, but it is up to us to decide whether we allow our hearts to be the sole guide of our lives. It is up to us to flow with whatever our heart is asking us to do. I'm now happy to know that if I have to face an early death, I have been able to free myself from so many ghosts and chains which distracted me from the voice of my heart. I have now started to heal my heart by asking you to forgive me.

His mother embraced him once again and said:

—No, Andrés, you won't die soon. You are being given the opportunity to be born again. Have faith, just like the people you stayed with these days, because there is nothing more powerful than God's love.

Andrés replied:

—Mom, I'm now willing to accept whatever I am supposed to go through.

Ego, ambition and feeling superior to others were no longer part of Andrés' attitude towards life. Instead, Andrés was now filled with humbleness, calmness and with the conviction to accept whatever God had in store for him.

Don Rafael, who up to that moment had remained silent, raised his glass and feeling moved by his son's words, said:

—Here's to a new life for all of us. For this family who has been born again.

—Cheers! —shouted everyone feeling very emotional.

No one felt uncomfortable with the situation they were living in that moment. On the contrary, this family felt more united and stronger than ever before. They continued chatting, joking, cheering, and this was all being serenaded by the *boleros* music which was being played on the radio.

They didn't discuss anything about the economic crisis of the world nor did they talk about the politics of the United States or Europe. Andrés' family was never going to be able to appreciate his success in the financial world, and he didn't care. Everyone sitting around that table was happy to be together once again and nothing else mattered.

As the evening progressed, Mariela and Alvaro decided it was time to go home. Both of them gave a big hug to Andrés. Alvaro was very happy to have met him, and given they were both very relaxed thanks to the whiskeys with Coke *don* Rafael served throughout the afternoon, they remained in each other's arms for a while.

As they left, *doña* Margarita and *don* Rafael walked Andrés to his bedroom, which looked still the same way as when he had left it ten years ago. He found it a bit strange that his mother hadn't changed a thing, but he felt as if he was back to where he belonged in the first place. At that moment he realised he was always going to be able to count with his own bedroom, house and family.

They decided they were going to visit another doctor first thing Monday morning to have a second opinion about his condition.

—We would have liked you to be here under different circumstances, but regardless of this, you can't imagine how happy we're to have you with us —said *don* Rafael.

—Everything will be fine, honey —said his mother.

—You're right, mom. Everything will be just fine. And I'm so very happy to be with you guys too.

—Good night, son. Get some proper rest.

Andrés lay on his bed and realised this was the first time in a long time he actually felt like a human being again. He thanked God in a brief prayer and fell asleep.

CHAPTER XXIX

The following morning, his father walked into his room, and even though Andrés was still sleeping, he kissed him on the forehead and said:
—Andrés, breakfast is ready —and left the room.

These simple words, the beautiful gesture of kissing him in the forehead —even if he was a grown man— and feeling his parents' pure love, made Andrés feel as if he was a renewed human being. Something so simple was able to revolutionise his heart with joy, even if he felt a bit silly. These simple gestures of love and affection filled him with more happiness than his job, his bank account, his travels and any other thing he could own.

Father, mother and son shared breakfast together. This time, Andrés told them a little bit more about his life, about his flat in Richmond close to the Thames River, and extended an invitation for them to visit him any time soon. He also shared with them about his business trips around the world, about the new opportunity of moving to New York. Even if his parents weren't able to understand the magnitude of his success in the financial world, they felt very proud of his achievements. *Don* Rafael absorbed each word his son pronounced as if he was the one living the experience. He never imagined his son being such a successful man at a relative short age. He wanted to believe he was part of his success too.

Doña Margarita had no idea of what a financial house was, and she didn't understand most of the words Andrés used to describe his profession, but just like her husband, hearing about his trips to big and famous cities like New York, Paris, Sidney and Hong Kong, made her feel proud of her son. "An intelligent and travelled man", she thought to herself.

Andrés was aware his parents didn't understand half of the things he was saying, but he could still see happiness reflected in their eyes with every word he said. Andrés wanted his parents to feel proud of him, even if he had made many mistakes along the way because of many material and social distractions.

—Honey, yesterday you mentioned something about losing a girl who loved you. What happened? —asked *doña* Margarita curious to know about her son's love life.

—I let her go because I was afraid of accepting I also deserved to be loved.

—Don't even say that, Andrés —said his mother a bit annoyed by what his son had said.

—No, mom. I need to be honest with myself. I have been a selfish man all of my life and I have only looked after myself, and even if it hurts us to accept it, you know that this is true.

Of course it was true. It was a reality which was not to be manipulated by anyone. *Don* Rafael and *doña* Margarita felt touched to hear the authenticity of his son's words. They were both confident — given Andrés was able to live longer— he was now conscious about the changes he needed to make in his life. They wanted to be there to support him.

After breakfast, *don* Rafael drove him to the hotel he was staying at to pick up his luggage and the image of the *Moreneta de Montserrat*. Once at the reception of the hotel, he was told to get in touch with the insurance company to sort out the final arrangements related to the accident. He picked up his stuff and headed back home. *Doña* Margarita was waiting for them to go to church.

Ever since he graduated from high school in Guatemala, he became a rebel against all types of religions. In Europe he was feeling comfortable as many people around him shared the same attitude. His starting point to criticise the Catholic Church was: "why having so much wealth —as the Vatican had— could they not be able to feed all the people in Africa?" He also used to say that the only objective of the church was to control masses and that he didn't agree with this manipulation.

Since his graduation day, he hadn't even entered a church to attend a mass. He entered a couple of times whenever he was visiting a big city and his focus was on appreciating the architecture of the building but not on anything related to faith. However, that morning Andrés entered once again the church he had attended with his parents during his childhood and which was located in the city centre. Mariela and Alvaro were also there as they accompanied *doña* Margarita whenever *don* Rafael wasn't able to make it. As he was about to enter, he took a few minutes to contemplate the church facade first. He recalled when he was a child and every Good Tuesday of *Semana Santa*, he would come to this church early in the morning with his father and sister to see the traditional exit of the procession known in Guatemala as *La Reseña*.

This church was built in the neoclassic period between the XVIII and XIX centuries but it wasn't as architecturally impressive as *Notre Dame* in Paris or the *Sagrada Familia* in Barcelona or Saint Paul's Cathedral in London, but to Andrés this church was more meaningful than the rest. Not because his art appreciation was poor but because this church was part of his life.

They finally entered the church and Andrés felt uncomfortable. He felt like this because he was invaded by the feeling of guilt. After all that he had criticised the church, and after having lived a life in which he considered himself to be god himself, he felt ashamed. He wanted to ask God forgiveness for his arrogance.

His mother noticed there was something going on with her son. Even if they hadn't seen each other for a long time, *doña* Margarita knew more about her son than he did himself. She got closer to him and whispered in his ear:

—My prayers have been heard and that is why you're here with us. Don't be afraid, Andrés. Everything will be fine because there's nothing impossible to God. I love you, son.

Andrés smiled and felt these words penetrating into the deepest part of his heart.

During the mass, Andrés couldn't help but to keep observing his parents, his pregnant sister and his brother-in-law and kept thinking about how valuable another simple —yet transcendental— moment was for him. Sitting all together on a church bench just like they used to do many years before was now something which filled with his heart with joy.

He reflected about his life in London and the rigid routine he had lived for the last few years. He also reflected on the last days of his life. He thought about *don* Constantino and his family and all the lessons he had learnt while being with this poor family —in economic terms— but so rich in spirituality. He thought about the contrast of realities he had experienced during his time in *El Diamante*. He recalled the wonderful moment in the natural pool when he surrendered his life to God. He also recalled the memories from the day before and the happiness he felt while sharing a meal and some drinks with his family. At that moment, Andrés felt the urge to keep on living; only this time he wanted to live a life with a purpose.

He was still feeling a bit scared about his health condition, but he was grateful because this whole experience had awakened him. He had learn how to say "I'm sorry" and if he had to face an early death, he was now at ease with himself because he was on time to keep mending his many mistakes and all the damage he had caused to the people he loved the most. Marie was included in that list too.

By the end of the mass, Andrés knelt on the bench they were all sitting at, closed his eyes and lowering his head he said out loud: "God, I want you to give me enough strength to face whatever I'm supposed to go through from this moment on, enough humility to be able to hear you when you talk and enough courage to change the person I have been up to now".

They spent Sunday as a family, as they used to do in the past. Each one of them felt complete. Andrés was impressed by how different he felt. He felt in harmony for who he was, and felt comfortable with what his heart, mind and soul were experiencing.

He noticed that there was something unusual in him: he didn't feel the need to be "connected" to the world. He wasn't interested in having a BlackBerry in his hand nor did he feel the need to read any newspapers or financial magazines. He didn't want to have any shallow distractions in that moment of his life. He just wanted to enjoy each and every second he had next to his family. He wanted to feel part of this as he wasn't sure what was going to unfold in the next few days.

CHAPTER XXX

On Monday morning, *don* Rafael went back into Andrés' room to wake him up and to tell him he had managed to arrange a doctor's appointment that same day. Andrés got up from bed and showered.

Whenever he had an important meeting he was used to taking longer than usual under the shower. He would also take some time to shave and then he would get dressed to impress. During this ritual he would focus his mind on winning the deal. This time he did the same ritual, however his goal was different as he didn't want to impress or win any deals. He only wished to be able to live longer. And only that.

His father advised him not to eat anything as he may be required to have some tests done on him. The positivism and strength his parents were showing helped Andrés overcome this with more courage. As he was waving goodbye to his mother, she draw the sign of the cross just like she did when he was a little boy. She winked at him and told him that everything was going to be all right. *Doña* Margarita also told him that she was on her way to church to pray a Rosary for him. This injected Andrés with more strength.

Father and son made it to the clinic. As they were waiting to be seen by the doctor, *don* Rafael noted nervousness in his son. He was trying to chat with him but Andrés would only reply with one syllable words. He was feeling as if he was out of himself. *Don* Rafael knew what his son was going through.

—You're a bit nervous, right? —asked from friend to friend.

—A little bit, yes —answered politely as wishing to just say: "I'm actually shitting my pants right now".

— Everything is going to be all right, Andrés, you will see.

After a few minutes waiting, one of the nurses called his name and both of them stood up. Andrés was surprised to see his father coming in with him. He started walking and noticed his dad was following him. For him it was embarrassing enough talking about this lump in his testicle with a stranger, and to have his father next to him would increase that; but he didn't say a word as he didn't want to be rude to him. They both walked into the doctor's little office. "The doctor is going to think I'm a spoilt brat", Andrés thought, but in that moment he didn't give any importance to what other people thought of him.

Andrés noticed that this doctor had studied in a European university. Doctor Muñoz greeted them and asked which one was Andrés. The young man raised his hand timidly.

—Tell me, Andrés, how can I help you? —asked the doctor in a friendly voice.

Andrés wasn't sure where to begin as he was feeling embarrassed to talk about this in front of his father, but he had no other option.

—OK, doctor. A few days ago I had a medical check-up because I felt a lump in my left testicle and also an abdominal pain I have been experiencing for the last couple of weeks.

As Andrés finished saying this, *don* Rafael —who had remained silent— jumped into the conversation and said:

—The doctor who saw Andrés was in London because that's where my son lives —said the proud father.

Andrés smiled inside of him as he knew why his father had intervened like that.

—And what did the doctor in London say, Andrés? —asked the doctor.

—He said that he wasn't going to be able to give a final diagnosis until he had the results from an ultrasound and some blood tests back.

—How long have you had this lump? How long have you been feeling pain?

—I noticed the lump a few days back, about a week or so. I have been feeling pain in my abdomen for a few weeks now.

—OK. Come here, Andrés, I'll have to check you —and pointed to a tiny stretcher.

This was the routine Andrés got to hate the most from this whole experience. Having to show his genitals to a complete stranger felt like a complete humiliation to him. The ritual had been the same everywhere. First he had to walk to a stretcher, he had to remove his trousers and underwear, lay back on the stretcher and finally let a stranger touch him. He was the fourth person in the last couple of weeks who touched him.

—What do you think? —asked Andrés feeling a little bit scared.

—Get dressed and wait for me on my desk —said the doctor in a calm tone.

Andrés got dressed and walked to the doctor's desk where his father was waiting with a smile drawn on his face. They didn't say a word to each other until the doctor got back.

—OK, Andrés, this isn't a normal swelling, but as the other doctor told you, we must do some tests in order to have a final resolution on this.

—Doctor, but could this be cancer? —asked Andrés trembling.

—I don't want to lie to you, Andrés. I can't get ahead and tell you what I think it is without the results from these tests; but we have to be clear that this can indeed be a cancer.

Father and son felt the impact of these words as if they had been punched. The doctor took a sheet of paper and started drawing the structure of the testicles, its functionality and explained how this lump was located underneath the left testicle. What the ultrasound had to show was whether the lump was attached to the testicle or not. If it was attached then it was cancer —being it benign or malignant— if it wasn't then they had to see what type of swelling it was. The first impression seemed to show that it was attached to the testicle though.

—We would have to do another ultrasound and the blood tests as well. I would also like for you to get some X-rays of your lungs and a magnetic resonance of your abdomen. We will do this as long as you want to treat yourself here in Guatemala. If you're thinking of going back to London soon then it is up to you to make a choice.

—Why do you recommend doing the X-rays and the magnetic resonance? —asked *don* Rafael a little intrigued.

—I don't want to scare you, but I don't want to lie to you either. If this lump has been attached to the testicle for a long time and it is cancer, then there's a high probability that it may have spread around the body, being the lungs and the abdomen the most common areas where it spreads to. If you're here on holidays, I believe we should do a complete analysis so that we can disregard many possible options. Let me also tell you that testicular cancer is common in men between 25-35 years old, and you must also know this is the only treatable cancer in the world of urology.

—What would proceed if it is cancer? —asked Andrés expecting the worst possible answer.

—It depends, Andrés. If it was cancer and it hasn't spread around your body, then we'd have to operate and then we would have to analyse the type of cancer it is. If it was a benign cancer or a seminoma, as it is scientifically called, then the surgery would have been enough to end this nightmare. If it is a malignant cancer and it has spread, we would have to operate as well and proceed to do a radiotherapy treatment for a few months. The only risk involved in radiotherapy is that it can affect your fertility. If the results show this isn't cancer, then we would have to analyse what it is and decide whether we should operate or not.

—Even though the scenarios doctor Muñoz had described were all very difficult to accept, Andrés felt he could trust this man. In the business world, Andrés had grown accustomed to disregarding his instincts but this time he felt the need to trust them back again. He felt afraid from what he had just heard but this was the first doctor who took the time to explain him —even with drawings— what was actually happening to him. He appreciated the honesty in his words. He felt more comfortable with this doctor than with doctor Lovestone back in London. Andrés liked it when people got straight to the point, and doctor Muñoz had done that.

—OK, doctor. I appreciate you telling me things as they are —said Andrés —. Do you think we can get started with the tests today?

—The magnetic resonance requires you to be fasting as you need to take some iodinated contrast agents; but apart from that we can get started with the rest of the tests with no problem, and we would have the results in two days.

"Two days? How can a first world country like England take a week to give results back?" he wondered. He had paid fifteen times more of what he was going to pay for a doctor's appointment in Guatemala and the results would be ready in only two days. He couldn't understand this irony between these two very different countries.

—He hasn't eaten any food —said *don* Rafael in an attempt to move on with this process.

—Great! Then I'll fill in this form so that you can go downstairs to the laboratory. Come back here on Wednesday at 11am and we will see what the results show.

Doctor Muñoz filled in the form and when handing the sheet of paper to Andrés, he looked straight to his eyes and said:

—The most important thing right now is to keep on being optimistic, Andrés. I'm glad to see your dad is here with you —*don* Rafael smiled —. Now go to the laboratory and if you need anything else here's my mobile number. You can reach me here at any time.

Andrés thanked him for his sincerity and told him he was going to follow his advice. They both shook hands with doctor Muñoz and walked downstairs to the laboratory. Words weren't needed to know that even if they were both scared, they were there for each other. Andrés was grateful and fully appreciated being able to have his father next to him through this difficult moment of his life.

The probability he was suffering cancer was very high, but he felt content as he was now clearer over the potential scenarios. He was now ready to face this reality and the first step was to get over and done with these tests. He had the blood tests and then the X-rays done. For the abdominal magnetic resonance he had to drink a glass of iodinated contrast agent every fifteen minutes during a period of two hours. This would show whether the cancer had spread through the abdomen or not.

During this four hour process, *don* Rafael remained next to his son at all times. He was letting him do all he was required to do and with his simple presence he wanted to assure his son he wasn't alone in this. Andrés was feeling a bit embarrassed as he considered himself an adult, but having his dad next to him also made him feel protected and at ease.

Andrés finally stopped taking the iodinated contrast agent and after two hours waiting he walked inside the place where he was going to have the MRI. This wasn't the typical ultrasound he was used to. The MRI required him to be introduced into a machine which would "take shots" of his abdomen. Ever since he was a little kid, he always related this machine with cancer. He recalled a movie he had seen many years ago in which the main character who was facing cancer had to get inside a machine just like that one before dying.

From that moment on, this machine became a synonym of cancer, and he was now living it first-hand. He got undressed and stayed with his underwear only and a white robe. They asked him to lie on the stretcher and then his body was pulled automatically into the inside part of this machine where he was going to get photographs of his abdomen. The nurse warned Andrés he was going to feel heat on his abdomen and a need to pee, but this was just an effect of the rays and the iodinated contrast agent he had drank for two hours straight.

They asked him to take a deep breath. Then they asked him to stay still so that they could get a "good quality photograph". Andrés was very scared. He closed his eyes and as he took a deep breath he saw his life passing in the form of images.

In this parade of images which was going on inside his head, he saw his grandmother hugging him. He recalled when as a child he would play in the park with his father. He thought about the night he had made love to Marie. He also recalled the conversation he had with *don* Constantino in that magical place. He relieved each second he had spent with his family in the last couple of days. He felt alive. Once again he confirmed he wanted to live. Fear started to slowly dissipate and instead, the desire to live took over him.

Ten minutes after lying down on the stretcher, Andrés' was moved from the inside part of the machine. He dressed up again and walked to the room where his father was waiting for him.

—All good, son? —asked *don* Rafael who was affected by the vibe inside the hospital, but who at the same time never stopped showing his son he was there for him.

—All is good, dad. Can we please go home? —asked Andrés feeling tired from all of what he had just experienced.

—Of course, Andrés. Let's go home. This nightmare is coming to an end soon. Don't you worry —he said and he hugged him.

CHAPTER XXXI

That same afternoon, Andrés wanted to have some alone time. Having gone through all the tests and after making the final arrangements with the insurance company in regards to the car accident, he felt the urge to be alone. Not because he wanted to get away from his parents, but because he needed some time to let it all sink in.

He had lunch with his parents and then asked his mother if he could borrow her car as he decided to drive to Antigua Guatemala. She didn't hesitate and told him she was going to go to church in the afternoon once again to pray for everything to be fine with his health. He gave her a sweet kiss on the forehead and grabbing her hands he said:

—No, mom. I want you to ask God to give me enough strength to face whatever I need to go through.

Doña Margarita was speechless. The genuine maturity, strength and calmness his son was showing while living such a difficult moment of his life made gave her have peace inside.

—I will pray for all of us to have enough strength, Andrés; because you're definitely not on your own. We are all here with you on this.

Andrés winked at her, took the car keys and walked outside the door. His mother's car was a golden 2000 Ford Focus. It didn't look or feel like his silver 2008 Aston Martin, but to him this was now irrelevant.

During this experience he was now able to understand the basic needs of any human being: health, food and a roof to sleep under. He was now able to see the eccentricities of the Western societies. He came to the conclusion that whenever a human accumulated something, he wanted even more. "What is the price we are willing to pay in order to accumulate more and more things? How much more do we need to own to call ourselves happy people?" he reflected.

As he got into the road which would take him to Antigua, he played a classical music radio station and was able to listen to one of his favourite pieces: *Spiegel im Spiegel* by the Estonian composer Arvo Part. While listening to this peaceful musical composition in which a violin and a piano create a subtle and inspiring melody, he was able to appreciate life's beauty. Watching the blue sky, feeling the sun shining, appreciating the green trees and allowing for the wind to caress his face drew a smile on his face.

Even though he was physically ill, he had a heart full of love which could fight against anything else. The demons and chains from the past kept tormenting him once in a while, but he didn't want to give it too much importance. Instead, he decided to focus his emotions and thoughts on living his present moment. And nothing else. He just wanted to enjoy the piano, the violin, the sky, the sun. His eyes filled with tears, not because he was sad, but because he felt like a human being again. That was all that mattered in that specific moment. He wasn't afraid of seeing through his feelings and emotions. He was now able to see life like something more than a degree, a job, a house, a flashy car or a financial fortune sitting in a bank account. Life had a purpose beyond accumulating material wealth. And recognising this simple truth filled him with joy and happiness.

When he got to Antigua he realised this little colonial town hadn't changed one bit since he last visited it. This magical city filled with so much history, culture and beauty was Andrés' favourite town in Guatemala. The stone-made roads, the houses with Spanish colonial facades, the ruins which were still preserved after the devastating earthquake in the XVII century, the beautiful and classy squares and the majestic churches which decorated this city transmitted an unexplainable peace to its visitors. Andrés' grandmother used to say that a plant spread throughout Antigua called *florifundia* gave people a sense of peace.

Andrés parked his car close to the main square —or *Parque Central*— and decided to walk without a set destination. He didn't want to plan or organise anything as he didn't want to feel the need to have things under control. He just wanted to walk freely and breathe the pure air only Antigua could provide him with. He walked for a couple of minutes until he got to the *Parque Central* where he was able to observe the majestic cathedral. Just like he had experienced the day before in the church back in Guatemala City, he realised that this cathedral —which wasn't as architecturally impressive as the ones in Europe— meant a lot to him. There was a time during his adolescence when his family would attend mass in this church every Saturday. He felt a stronger connection with this cathedral compared to any other cathedral around the world as spectacular as it could be.

He sat on a bench in the main square facing the cathedral and started reflecting about his life in London. "What do I really own?" he started questioning himself. On paper, he owned his flat in Richmond, his Aston Martin, shares in many companies around the world and a university degree. But none of these material things made him feel connected to the source of life. Not that they weren't important but he didn't have anyone to share any of the things he had worked so hard to get. All of the material wealth he had accumulated throughout the years meant nothing to him. His parents' home meant more to him than his classy flat in London. All of the sudden he realised that during the last ten years of his life he had pretended to be someone he wasn't.

Andrés stood up from the bench and continued walking towards the *Arco de Santa Catalina*. For the first time in his life he was able to control the betrayal games his mind was used to play on him which made him feel scared and anxious. Whenever he felt his mind was about to generate fear in him, he recalled the moment he surrendered his life. He realised he was actually able to observe his mind and that he had the power to control it!

He walked past the *Arco de Santa Catalina* and saw the *Merced* church which was close by. The facade of this church had always given him the impression of a decorative cake. The facade and the external columns were all painted orange and were decorated with little white sculptures which gave the impression that this was a giant carrot cake.

Andrés walked in, made the sign of the cross and knelt down. He closed his eyes, lowered his head and started having a conversation with God. He didn't want to rationalise his thoughts as he only wanted to let things out.

"Dear God, here I am once again. In these last few days I have come to the sad conclusion that we only lookout for you whenever we're too damn scared and when we realise we actually don't have anything under control as we foolishly believe. Even if we rant all of our lives saying that you don't exist or that you're an image used to control masses, we all come back to you one way or another. We can call you different names like God, Buddha, Allah or Universe, but at the end we come to understand that you're just One. Today, in this church, I come to you with a content heart. I won't lie to you, I'm very scared about what can happen with my life, but I'm also grateful that during these last few days I have been able to fill my heart with love, even though I didn't actually know what this meant. I have also been able to understand the real basic things we must have in order to live a fulfilled life. I have realised that I must reach a balance in my life to be able to enjoy the beautiful gift that you have given us in the form of living our lives. Having experienced poverty first-hand with people who struggle with it each day of their lives has opened my eyes and made me understand I have so much that I can't think only about myself all the time. I have come to the beautiful conclusion that living a life without sharing is completely worthless. I want you to give me enough strength to face whatever I need to get through and for it to be your will, and not mine. Thank you for never leaving me alone even if I walked away from you a long time ago. Thank you for the angels you have put in my path as they have helped me understand that everything and everyone who comes in my life have a purpose for being there. And finally, I just want to ask you help me be a better man."

Andrés opened his eyes, raised his head and felt peace within. He was fully confident that whatever was meant to happen with his life, it was going to be for the better. He was still afraid, but accepting things as they were —in a realistic manner— gave him enough peace of mind to face anything that could come his way.

This man who for a long time had been proud, selfish and used to make things his way, detached from everything and allowed things to simply flow. He was eager to live his life now. He had come to the understanding that his arrogance wouldn't take him anywhere. On the contrary, this could only limit him from living the Perfect Plan he was supposed to live.

Andrés left this church feeling complete. He kept on walking without direction and passed through many little streets until he found a botanical garden. Here he decided to drink a cup of coffee and to enjoy a delicious chocolate cake. He didn't need his BlackBerry or a newspaper in his hands to entertain himself. He didn't want to let any distractions get on the way of the inner peace he was experiencing. He just wanted to enjoy the moment, the second, the minute. He wanted to be at peace with himself. And he was getting there. He stayed in this place for an hour and the only thing he did was to drink his coffee, eat his cake and enjoy watching people as he contemplated the magical world of plants and flowers. He had a happy and joyful heart.

CHAPTER XXXII

On Wednesday morning, Andrés woke up knowing there was a high probability that life as he knew it could change. However, deep inside he felt at ease by accepting that whichever direction his life took, it was simply part of his Perfect Plan. He even woke up in a good mood. His father had left home to go to work. His mother was still at home.

Andrés told her that he was going to prepare breakfast for her. *Doña* Margarita was thrilled about this and said to him

—We will see what you have learned all these years, darling — and smiled.

Andrés wanted to try and cook for his mother a dish Marie prepared for him many times, and so he decided to go to the supermarket and get all the required ingredients. He was very excited to cook for his mother. He was filled with joy. Doing something for someone else was a new feeling for him.

Andrés got back from the supermarket with a plastic bag full of food and his mother asked in surprise:

— Son, are you going to prepare a meal for a whole army or what? —and they both laughed.

The person standing in front of *doña* Margarita was already a grown man, but she could still see the innocent little boy he had been as a child. His mother was able to see a different look in his eyes, despite of the physical and emotional tiredness he felt. Even though she wasn't too familiar with the arrogant and big headed Andrés from London, she now knew that this arrogance, selfishness and coldness which he had felt for so many years, was starting to dissipate.

Andrés cooked some scrambled eggs with smoked salmon. *Doña* Margarita didn't quite understand the name of the dish in English, but she was happy to share this moment with her son. Andrés asked her to wait on the dining table, as he was going to serve the food to her whenever it was ready. He wanted to spoil his mother and she was excited and thankful for this beautiful gesture.

In the kitchen, Andrés thought of Marie with a smile on his face. He wanted to be able to see her and to chat with her again. However, at this very moment, he was only focusing on his family and the results he was going to receive later that day. Nothing else mattered!

The new Andrés realised how music had a positive effect on him, and so that morning he turned on the old radio his mother had in the kitchen. He played the classical music station once again. He felt peace every time he listened to classical music melodies. He was able to disconnect from his own thoughts and he let the sublime sound of the violin, piano or the whole orchestra take over him.

Andrés prepared some scrambled eggs, but he used a bit more of milk than usual, so that the eggs could taste creamier. He cut a piece of baguette bread in half and put it inside the toaster. He removed the smoked salmon from the package and cut it into slimmer slices. He turned on the coffee machine —which was just like the one he had in his flat— and cut a few oranges in half to make natural juice.

It took him fifteen minutes to prepare this delicious dish. On the plates there were two pieces of toasted bread covered with scrambled eggs and smoked salmon on top with a touch of pepper and lime. He had also brought two glasses with natural orange juice and two cups of coffee with milk. One cup of coffee with sugar was for his mother and the other one without sugar for him.

He opened the kitchen door which connected it to the dining room, and he found his mother's face glowing to see her son preparing breakfast for her. It was the first time in their lives Andrés did something like this for her and so she was very touched. She couldn't help it and got very emotional about it. When he was placing the plates on the table, his mother stood up from the chair and hugged him. She gave him a big kiss on the cheek and whispered in his ear:

—This is the most beautiful gift you have ever given me, son.

Andrés felt happy to be able to do something for someone else, and he was even happier to do so for his own mother.

—You deserve much more than this, mom —said in a tender way.

They both started eating and enjoying the food which Andrés had prepared. His mother was trying to learn how to pronounce the name of this dish in English —something which amused him— and then told him this was the most delicious breakfast she had ever tasted.

Andrés knew this wasn't true, as his cooking abilities were definitely not one of his strengths, but he understood his mother really appreciated the care and effort he had done with this simple act of kindness. Andrés could now appreciate how sitting down at a table with someone special could change the eating experience. They enjoyed their scrambled eggs with salmon, drank their orange juice and cups of coffee and enjoyed the Fourth Movement of Tchaikovsky's Violin Concerto.

When they finished eating, his mother asked Andrés —worrying for her son's reaction—:

—Andrés, who is the woman you were talking about on Saturday?

Andrés didn't really feel like talking about it because it saddened him. Now that he was aware of his selfishness it hurt him to think he had let go of a great woman; but he also didn't want to feel guilt anymore. That's why he decided to openly talk about Marie to his mother.

—She is a wonderful girl, mom —said Andrés with a smile on his face —. And there's something I still find hard to understand —his mother was intrigued by this—. I still don't know how she could love me for the person I was.

—You were not a bad person, son. Stop blaming yourself for your past. All that you lived all these years have taken you to this point in your life. And let me tell you that as a mother I couldn't feel any prouder to have a son like you.

—Thanks, mama —said Andrés feeling content.

—But tell me more about her. What's her name? Is she English? How old is she? Where does she work?

—Hold on, mom, dad is the auditor, not you, remember? —joked Andrés and continued —. Her name is Marie, she is Norwegian and she is simply gorgeous. She has reddish hair, beautiful green eyes and a face that makes everyone think she is a true angel.

His mother could perceive how her son was so in love with this girl with every word Andrés used to describe her. Andrés continued:

—And she isn't beautiful just on the outside, mom. She has a big, humble and noble heart. She loves to live her life enjoying the simple pleasures, and even if I didn't realise it in that moment, she helped me see life with different eyes. Being next to her I understood that life isn't about external appearances or about accumulating material wealth only.

Doña Margarita got excited with her son's love story and wanted to know every single detail.

—Then, why did you break up? —asked in a sad voice.

—Because of my selfishness, mom. Commitment scared me away. At that time I thought I needed to keep on living my life as I was used to and so I decided to take a job in New York.

—But love is more important than a job in New York, isn't it? — asked *doña* Margarita in an attempt to share her wisdom on true love.

—Now I know that, mom; but it is too late —responded Andrés looking down at the table.

—It is never late, Andrés. If she's the woman of your life, she will be there for you and you for her, but you can't expect her to come back to you though. If she's not the woman of your life, I want you to write down the things you can change so that you can give yourself completely the next time you're with another woman you love. I want you to keep in mind that a woman needs to be taken care of and loved with all the love you have in your heart. There will be many women in your life, or maybe not; but the most important thing is to be aware that whenever you meet the woman you wish to spend the rest of your life with, you must be willing to commit to her, to take care of her, to love her and to respect her. You have to be kind, tender and understanding —in that moment, *doña* Margarita's voice broke a little bit.

After forty years of marriage, *doña* Margarita knew her marriage hadn't been the best one, and that she had doubted her decision of getting married to *don* Rafael many times; but seeing Andrés and Mariela growing up, she gave a purpose to her daily struggle and to the love she felt for them and the love she once felt for *don* Rafael. She was conscious all of these factors helped her be the woman she was in that moment.

Perhaps things were different now, but she didn't feel loved by *don* Rafael any more. She always doubted his faithfulness and they had stopped being friends since they got married. The only thing they shared in common was their kids, and it was the love they both felt for them which helped them face each day with a positive attitude. She wanted her kids to learn from her experience and not to make the same mistakes they had done.

—But how will I know if she's the woman of my life? —asked Andrés feeling frustrated.

—You will know it because your heart will tell you. I can only tell you, son that the woman of your life will be someone you admire. She will have to be a life partner who will be there to support you through the good and the not so good times.

Andrés recalled the conversation he had with *don* Constantino as he had also used the term "life partner". At that moment, Marie's face appeared in his mind again. Her red hair and her green eyes. Marie was a girl he truly admired and who he believed would be next to him, regardless of any problems they could face in the future. She got to love him for who he was, even if he didn't even know who he really was himself.

—You have to understand that God has to be centre of any relationship —continued *doña* Margarita.

Andrés got scared by this. In the world in which he lived, atheism and other sects pushed people to live meaningless lives and to enjoy the short term pleasures without worrying about the truly spiritual connection people needed to have regardless of creed and religion. That was why the concept of "God" had even turned into a taboo topic. To Andrés it was hard to understand the difference between being a spiritual being and not necessarily a religious one.

—You're right, mom. I just hope I can live a bit longer so that I can find that woman you just described —and winked to her.

—Of course you will find her, son —said *doña* Margarita.

—OK, mom, I hope you enjoyed breakfast. I loved sharing this moment with you, but it is getting late and I need to go to the doctor.

—I know I told you this before, but I will say it again: this was the best gift I have ever received. Thanks, Andrés —said *doña* Margarita feeling genuinely happy —. And you won't be going by yourself to the doctor as your dad is going to come and pick you up.

Andrés felt liberated after being able to talk openly about Marie with his mother. He needed to let his thoughts and feelings out in the form of words.

A couple of minutes later, *don* Rafael honked his car's horn and Andrés stood up from the table. His mother walked him to the entrance door and said:

—I'm confident everything will work out just well, son. No matter what happens we will all stick together, OK? I love you and I want you to know your sister and you are the most beautiful things I have in my life —and she hugged him as hard as she could.

Andrés, who was very emotional for all the things he had experienced in the last days, felt like crying. He was so grateful that neither his mother nor anyone from his family had created a drama out of this situation. On the contrary, everyone was so optimistic and through their support and calmness he was able to face this with a more positive attitude.

—Thank you, mom. I love you too —and kissed her.

For Andrés to say "I love you" to his mother or anyone else was a rare thing to do. The coldness of his heart which was put under the light of love had completely melted. He was now able to see and accept his feelings and emotions. He felt free to express what he felt and this gave him so much peace within.

Before leaving his house, Andrés quickly ran to his room and kissed the image of the *Virgen Morena de Montserrat*. After that he got inside his father's car and knew that life as he knew it was likely to change.

CHAPTER XXXIII

The moment of truth had finally arrived. Father and son got off the car and they were both feeling a tension which didn't allow them to even share a word. Andrés was shaking as he walked and his father noticed it; but didn't want to say anything. He just put his arm around him as wanting to tell him 'I'm here you'.

They walked into the doctor's clinic and the receptionist asked them to wait for a few minutes, as the doctor was with another patient. Andrés and *don* Rafael sat down in the waiting area which could only take up to six people. The ambience —even though it was just the two of them sitting there— felt heavy.

In those moments, Andrés' strength was threatened. In his mind, the possibility of dying at a young age was real, and he was scared. He was eager to live.

Sitting in that waiting area, he thought about all the years he was away from his family and how he wanted to make so many changes in his life so that he could actually enjoy living. He remembered he was about to become an uncle. He wanted to meet his nephew or niece. He thought of Marie and all that this woman had taught him. He wanted to have a second chance to show her he was willing to love her and he was able to commit to make her a happy woman. He even thought about *don* Constantino, his family and his community. He was eager to go back to *El Diamante* and help as many people as he could who didn't have the opportunities he had had. Somehow he realised he wanted to stop living an egocentric life. But, would he have enough time? Or was it too late?

Fifteen minutes passed and the other patient wasn't leaving. Andrés and his father felt these fifteen minutes like fifteen hours instead. Each second that passed by seemed like an eternity. There was anxiety and nerves. Andrés was conscious that these results were going to be the most important news he had ever received in his life. Up to that day, the most anxious moments Andrés had experienced were related to receiving a "yes" or a "no" for an answer while negotiating a deal. If the answer was a "yes" that meant a lot of money in profits, and if it was a "no" then this would simply require preparing a second offer or looking for new clients. However, this moment could not be compared with the answer he was about to receive from the doctor. If the answer was a "yes", he would have to ask the doctor "what now?" and if it was a "no" it would mean he had the possibility to start a new life from scratch.

After half an hour they were still waiting to be seen by the doctor. Andrés was starting to get irritated by this, not only because of the lack of punctuality —which he now appreciated very much— but because he was too anxious to keep waiting. He walked to the girl in the reception and in an angry voice he said:

—We have been her for thirty minutes waiting for doctor Muñoz. How much longer will we have to wait?

—Eehhmmm… I hope… not much —she said feeling nervous.

—Come here, son. Take a sit —said *don* Rafael trying to keep his calmness mode on —. He will be with us soon.

Andrés listened to his father and walked out to the hallway outside the clinic. He took a deep breath, closed his eyes and told himself: "Please, God, don't leave me now". He went back in again and the moment he sat down, the doctor came out with the patient he was with. The doctor saw both of them sitting now and very calmly said:

—I'm very sorry for the delay, gentlemen, but we had to arrange for this patient to be operated soon. Please come in.

Through this very short walk to the doctor's little office Andrés reflected on the words the doctor had just said referring to the other patient: "Arrange a date for an operation?" Will he have to go through that too?

Andrés and his father sat down facing doctor Muñoz. The doctor took out a large size envelope from the drawer of his desk.

—We have the results we need to know what this lump you have in your testicle is, Andrés.

Father and son both took a deep and long breath. *Don* Rafael, by impulse, grabbed his son's sweaty hand. They both squeezed their hands as hard as they could. Whatever the doctor was about to say would dictate the faith of Andrés' life. The doctor continued:

—The ultrasound shows that this lump —he paused and continued —is actually attached to your testicle, and it seems to be a cancerous tumour.

As he heard these words, Andrés felt he was sleeping and he just wanted to wake up from this nightmare. However, feeling how his father squeezed his hand even harder, he realised that this was no dream. This was his reality. He felt his head heavier than usual, and started to get dizzy. Both the doctor and his father noticed how his face turned pale. Andrés didn't know what to do, what to say or how to react. The doctor offered him a glass of water to calm him down a bit.

This successful man who had travelled around the world, who was a genius in the financial world and who had achieved professional success at such an early age, never imagined listening to these words. He never conceived the idea his life could make a 180 degrees turn in a matter of weeks, days and seconds.

This man, who until a few days had been used to doing things his way and to have everything under control, was now seeing that his Perfect Plan went beyond his arrogance and egocentrism. Today he was confirming something he had been reflecting on: one proposes and God disposes and this sometimes includes events we never imagined we would have to go through.

Doctor Muñoz, who had been an urologist for a long time, was talking with ease and serenity as he was aware the words he uttered were not the news the person sitting in from of him expected. This was part of his daily routine, but he was still conscious something like this was never easy to digest for his patients. The doctor took more sheets of paper from the envelope and looking straight at Andrés' eyes said:

—But not all are bad news, Andrés.

Andrés simply nodded by inertia. He wasn't sure what the doctor considered to be good news for him in that situation. All the security and comforting peace he had managed to feel before this moment were now almost disappearing as fear was taking over.

—The other results from the X-ray and the MRI show that this cancer hasn't spread through your body, and so we will have to undergo a surgery as soon as possible to determine if this tumour is benign or not.

For a moment, Andrés became hopeful again. His father, who hadn't said a word —as usual— quickly asked:

—What does that mean, doctor? —he paused and swallowing saliva through his throat said —: My son is going to be fine, right doctor?

—The first thing we need to do now is to define when would be best to operate, and after this we will be able to know exactly what are the next steps. The good news, as I said, is that this hasn't spread anywhere else.

—But what would happen if it isn't a benign tumour? —these were the first words that came out of Andrés' mouth since his life had changed.

—Andrés, if it is a malignant cancer, then we would have to undergo a radiotherapy treatment in an attempt to remove it completely from your body.

Andrés remained silent. He was aware that a radiotherapy treatment could put an end to his fertility, but in this moment the most important thing was to survive. Everything else was a luxury.

—I want you to also understand that we will have to remove your left testicle, Andrés.

Andrés' face turned even paler and felt like fainting. The thought of having his testicle removed affected him a lot. Noticing the reaction in Andrés' face from what he had just said, made him walk Andrés to the little stretcher before he passed out. Before heading back to his desk, doctor Muñoz grabbed Andrés by his hand and said:

—I know that this is all very difficult for you, son, but we will do all we can for you to be just fine. Let's all have faith, OK?

Lying on this stretcher, Andrés was able to hear some voices coming from the desk but he wasn't able to understand what they were saying. His mind was blank. His life took a sudden turn he never expected in a matter of minutes. For a second he wanted to complain to God for what he was going through. He wanted to complain about all the things he had lived in the last few weeks. He didn't want to die. However, he didn't let those complaints materialise and remained quiet.

Instead of reproaching and complaining, Andrés shut his eyes even more and wanted to be able to see his heart once again. He moved his hands inside and out and after a few seconds he told his inner self: "Please don't leave me, God. Give me enough strength to face this. Help me understand how I can use this situation to be a better man".

He took another deep breath and stood up from the stretcher. Regaining his confidence he walked back to the doctor's desk.

—OK, doctor, now that we have almost all of the information, we need to have this surgery and then we'll know what needs to be done, right? —asked Andrés with conviction.

—That's right, Andrés —said the doctor.

—When can we have the surgery? —asked Andrés.

—We could do it in two days, if this suits you. Tomorrow we would have to do some pre-surgery tests and on Friday we could operate.

Don Rafael had turned into a mere spectator of this conversation and felt glad to see how his son was reacting after almost passing out. He thought his son was a strong man. He knew that if he was in his shoes, he wouldn't have been able to react like Andrés had, and so he admired his son's strength and calmness to accept this difficult reality. He decided to ask one last question:

—Forgive my ignorance, doctor, but if you have to remove his testicle, would he still be able to be a father or to have sex in the future?

Andrés felt ashamed about his father asking this question, but he hadn't thought about it and was eager to hear the response from the doctor.

Doctor Muñoz, who was known for his ethics and serenity, replied:

—If the tumour is benign we wouldn't have the need to do a radiotherapy treatment and this would mean Andrés could easily have kids in a future with his right testicle only.

—That's why God creates a pair of the most important things — said *don* Rafael and they all laughed.

They arranged all the details for the operation on Friday and said goodbye. As they were about to leave the doctor's office, doctor Muñoz hugged Andrés —and this wasn't something he would usually do to his patients— and told him:

—Let's have faith, Andrés. Your family is with you and we will do all that is in our hands for you to be OK.

Andrés smiled back to the doctor, raised his hand and said:

—Thank you, doctor, I know I'm in good hands with you and my family.

—See you on Friday! —shouted the doctor as they were walking away.

—See you on Friday! —shouted back father and son filled with excitement as if they were planning a beach trip.

As they both got inside the car, *don* Rafael looked straight at his son's eyes and in a very emotional voice he said:

—I'm very proud of you, son. Your strength makes us be strong too. God will help us through this, you will see.

—I know, dad. And thanks for being here with me —he also got emotional and continued —. You can't really imagine how happy I feel to have you next to me.

They both held each other in a hug, and for the first time since they reunited, father and son cried without any type of fear or without wanting to control the tears which were rolling down their faces. They didn't feel the need to show they were "strong men" anymore. The only thing they wanted was to let all their feelings and emotions out. Andrés knew his father was there for him and vice versa. After a few minutes, *don* Rafael moved away from Andrés and drying the tears from his face he put his hands on the car's steering wheel.

—Let's go home, son.

In that very moment, Andrés wondered how he would have to get through this situation all alone in London. This simple thought gave him the goose bumps. These simple words: "let's go home, son", were enough to make this tragic situation turn into a loving moment. He had everything he needed to pass this test. He counted with his family's love but moreover, he felt God was with him in his own heart.

When they got home, Andrés' mother rushed down the stairs to hug her son. Andrés wrapped her in his arms and whispered in her ear:

—I'm going through a surgery on Friday. They will have to remove my left testicle and hopefully this will be the end of this nightmare —he paused and smiling said —: But don't you worry, mom, I will still be able to make you a grandmother.

Doña Margarita smiled and hugged him even stronger. She was also proud of her son's strength to face this. He knew God had heard her prayers. Andrés had asked for strength to face anything and He had conceded it to him.

His mother still wrapped inside his arms, whispered in his ear:

—I hope this girl, Marie, doesn't mind giving me the opportunity to be a grandmother —and they both laughed.

CHAPTER XXXIV

Everything had passed by so quickly those last days that the day before the operation Andrés recalled the promise he had made to *don* Constantino about being able to listen and follow his heart. In the morning, he went to the hospital to make the last tests before the surgery, and then he went back home and enjoyed some alone time. He knew he had to write two emails. The first email was going to be written to his boss in London as he had to let him know about his situation and would also ask for a couple of months off to recover. The second email was going to be written to Marie. Even though he had no clarity as to what he wanted to say or how to say it, he felt his heart needed to let her know what he was feeling and thinking.

The email to Richard didn't require much time. It took him a few minutes to write it and in a couple of minutes he received a reply simply saying:

"Andrés,

I hope you get well soon, mate. Take the time you need and keep me posted on your plans to move to New York. We need to keep on making money, kid!"

Andrés felt disgusted after reading Richard's reply. He had been his mentor and sometimes his only friend. He was trying to convince himself that these dry words were because he was an Englishman who didn't like to intrude other people's businesses, but he was telling him he had cancer for God's sake! He didn't want Richard to pity him, but he expected more from the only person he considered a friend. However, this made Andrés realise the type of people he had been dealing with all that time. He thought it was fair for English people to also show their weak and compassionate side. He decided not to give it too much importance, but this simple email showed him he didn't want to get back to that cold and emotionless world.

In that moment Andrés was grateful for his Latino culture. He was aware Latinos were more likely to be dramatic, but his people weren't afraid of showing his true feelings and emotions. And in a difficult moment like this, Andrés needed all the support he could get from his loved ones.

He struggled with the second email though. He didn't know how to start. He didn't know what he was supposed to write to Marie, because he didn't want her to feel he was using this situation so that she could pity him. The only thing he wanted was to tell her all of what he had gone through in the last few weeks since they last saw each other. He also wanted to let her know —somehow— how important she was to him.

Andrés remained hypnotised to the computer screen. He had been in front of the computer for half an hour and all he had managed to write was "Dear Marie". He wrote ten different versions of the introduction, but he kept on deleting whatever he had written. After so many attempts to write something, he was ready to give up when he told himself out loud: "I will let my heart speak without any fear and without trying to make sense. I will let words flow just as my heart desires".

As he pronounced these words, his fingers suddenly started moving and didn't stop for about fifteen minutes. The final version read the following:

"Dear Marie,

How have you been? I hope that this email finds you well. You will wonder why am I writing to you after so many weeks of absence and more so, after it all ended between us without any type of explanation.

I had to leave London a few days back and came home to Guatemala. The man who always had to have everything under control and who was afraid of letting his heart guide him through life and show his true feelings, was moved by an impulse and decided to come all the way here.

You may ask why this sudden decision. To be honest with you, when I decided to fly here I wasn't sure what I was doing. However, as the days have passed by, I have come to understand the reason of this "crazy" move. You know what was it? The reason was that God wanted me to get reunited with myself and with Him. Due to my arrogance and selfishness, God had to be very creative so that his plan of making me question the way I was living my life could work.

In just a few days I have been in places I never imagined I would be. I have lived things I never imagined that existed. I experienced extreme poverty in a town which was located in the middle of nowhere but I learned that in material poverty there's also spiritual richness. I learned how to see through my heart, to listen to it and I'm now in a process of letting it be my only guide in life. I surrendered myself to God in front of a magical natural pool with turquoise water. I realised all the time I wasted living away from my family. I came to understand that the love they have for me and the love I have for them is unconditional even if I decided to be away from them for a long time.

But more importantly, I realised the big mistake I made by leaving the woman I have loved the most because of my stupid selfishness and my fear of committing to such a beautiful soul. I realised how coward I was by not giving you any explanation and instead opted for the easiest way out: to run away. I know the type of woman you are and let me tell you that I admire you. During the time we spent together you were able to make me be and feel like a better man. I know I made a huge mistake by letting you go just like I did with my family as you taught me the true meaning of love.

I want you to please forgive me for my actions, for not being able to treat you the way you deserve to be treated and for not being able to make you feel loved.

Tomorrow I'm facing the toughest challenge of my life. I will have a testicular surgery. The doctor says testicular cancer is the only treatable cancer there is and that it hasn't spread throughout my body. I have a lot of faith that everything will work out just fine as God has given me enough strength to face this. And also because I know my family will be with me during this adventure.

You will think that I'm a crazy man as I'm talking a lot about God; but after all I have lived and experienced I'm certain he exists and that he is talking directly to me. After all that I have been through, I have realised life as I knew it, as I was living it, was not the best way to be a genuinely happy person. I don't know if it'll be too late to learn this, but I have come to accept that this all part of a plan he has for me.

I don't know if you have given yourself the opportunity to be with someone else —and I would totally understand it if you did— but I wanted to apologise to you as I know that letting you go has been the biggest mistake in my life (and you have to consider that I have made many). I hope I can invite you to a coffee if our paths cross again.

I love you and I will love you forever.

Andrés"

Andrés clicked the "Send" button on his email account and he immediately started fearing her reaction after reading it. Would she reply? Would she think he was taking advantage of his situation? Would she think he was just being vulnerable and he would go back to being the same man he had been before? He didn't want to think too much on the possible scenarios though, because it was all out of his control. However, something inside asked him to feel at ease with himself as he had been able to express in words all of his feelings. Whatever she was going to think about the email didn't depend on him; but he felt good for apologising and for having accepted the mistake he had made by letting her go. This was something the old Andrés would have never done.

That night before going to bed Andrés chatted with God —a practice which had turned into a routine now. During this chat, he thanked him for everything he had lived in the almost 29 years of life. He thanked him for all the opportunities both from a personal and professional perspective. He thanked him for the family he had been gifted with as they had shown him how much they loved him no matter what. He also thanked him for meeting Marie, and for having been able to experience the true meaning of love with her. He didn't ask for anything. Andrés thought that maybe God gets tired of hearing so many petitions and just a few "thank you". As he ended his chat with God, Andrés closed his eyes and slept while listening to one of his favourite classical musical pieces: "Adagio for Strings" by Samuel Barber.

The day Andrés feared the most had finally arrived. After that day, Andrés would have a clearer view of where his life was heading. On that sunny Friday morning of September, Andrés woke up in a good mood. And he wasn't faking it. He felt a genuine sense of peace within. The moment of weakness he had experienced back in the doctor's clinic a couple of days before were now a mere memory.

His mother reminded him he couldn't eat anything before the surgery. Andrés was very hungry but knew this couldn't be negotiated. He was going to be able to eat and drink after the operation. His father and mother drove him to the hospital where his sister and brother-in-law were also waiting for him.

Doctor Muñoz greeted them all in a friendly way and asked them to walk towards the hospital reception to register Andrés. After this, he wouldn't see the doctor until he was taken to the operation room in a few hours' time.

Andrés filled in all the information with his personal details and the receptionist offered him the menu for the following two days he was going to stay there recovering. His stomach was roaring as he was hungry, but this wasn't just because of the food, but also the nerves he was experiencing at that moment.

After registering in the reception, Andrés walked into his room — accompanied by all of his family—, where a nurse asked him to get undressed and to put a white robe. Andrés followed the nurse's orders and in less than three minutes he was ready for the operation, even if there was still a bit of waiting to be done. An hour before the surgery, the anaesthesiologist came to Andrés' room to introduce himself and also to ask some more questions as he wanted to make sure he was going to be able to get through the general anaesthesia required for this type of procedures.

As they all waited for Andrés to be taken to the operating room, everyone kept joking, reliving moments from the past with *doña* Anita and finally, all of them decided to pray together a Rosary so that Andrés could feel protected during this procedure which would take about two hours to be performed. A few minutes after they finished praying, Andrés was put on another stretcher with wheels and they all said goodbye to him. The last thing Andrés heard before leaving his room was his mother's voice saying "I love you, son".

As they got to the operation room, the anaesthesiologist —who had come to his room a few minutes earlier— greeted him. In about five minutes after being introduced to this room, a nurse had put a mask on his face. Whist having this mask which covered his face, the nurse said:

—Please, count to three.

Before getting to two, the anaesthesia had kicked in and he was completely sedated. What happened during those two hours inside this operation room was something Andrés would forever ignore thanks to the anaesthesia effect.

CHAPTER XXXV

Six months passed by from the moment Andrés had gone through the testicular cancer surgery in Guatemala on a sunny September morning. On his sixth month "anniversary" he was back visiting his beloved London. He was sitting in a café in Portobello Road very close to where Marie and he kissed for the first time.

It was a cold Saturday afternoon. Even though it was only five o'clock in the afternoon, this majestic city was already in darkness. Andrés was sitting at a table inside the café anxiously waiting for Marie to arrive. They had agreed to meet at five that afternoon and it was already 5:15 and there was no sight of her. Andrés started wondering if she was going to make it as he feared the worst. He was so nervous his hands and forehead were all sweaty. "I need to keep it together. She can't see me like this", he kept repeating to himself.

Six months had passed since Andrés had lived the toughest experience of his life. Six months of having faced a testicular cancer. Six months which he had actually started seeing, breathing and living life through a more human and spiritual perspective. Even though it had been challenging at times —as he was starting to get used to a new way of doing things—, he didn't let ambition or egocentrism guide his life as he understood that these two things could only take him back to live a lonely and empty life.

During these six months, Andrés fought many times with his own mind, which would constantly threaten his inner peace. His mind loved to make him doubt the promise he had made to *don* Constantino about letting his heart be the sole guide of his life. There were many times when Andrés failed on his promise, but he would always stand up again with a humble attitude. A lot of people criticised and judged him during this period of time for trying to be a better person, as they would say he was a hypocrite.

It became a period of tough adjustments, but he had also experienced the benefits of feeling a better human being. He realised how the love from his family helped him heal successfully from the surgery and the recovery which followed. He acknowledged the importance of his family in recovering his essence as a human being as well. Andrés didn't fear expressing his emotions and feelings anymore. He felt a complete man now.

During this time, Andrés also applied a philosophy of life which included leaving everything in the hands of the Superior Force. Andrés experienced first-hand that every situation —being it a good or not so good experience— always happened for a reason, and so he let things simply flow. Now perfection wasn't his most important goal. This man was no longer trying to have things under control all the time. Now this man was aiming to give his life a purpose and to enjoy the time he had with his family and friends. The purpose of his life was to enjoy and be grateful for all that he had each and every day —his talents and even his money— and to share it with his family and people around him who hadn't had the same opportunities as he did.

A couple of days after the surgery, doctor Muñoz called Andrés feeling very excited and told him the pathological tests showed it was a benign cancer and that his right testicle was just perfect. This meant that the probability to be a father one day wouldn't be threatened by this operation.

Hearing these words was like taking the weight of a cathedral off his shoulders. Even though he was completely surrendered to God and had shown a strong character going through the operation, there were also moments in which his mind played tricks on him which made him fear the worse.

However, his faith was stronger than anything else, and even if all he wanted was to heal completely, he never asked God for that. He only prayed to God that he was able to endure whatever he needed to go through during this moment of his life; whether it was an early death or the opportunity to live more time. And this acceptance filled him with inner peace and drove him to live his life to the maximum day in and day out.

Andrés got this call from the doctor in the afternoon right about the time he was going to contemplate a beautiful orange coloured sunset in Guatemala City. These words from the doctor removed all the fear he had inside. His mind and soul felt liberated. He knew this was God telling him: "I'm here now and will forever be with you, son". Andrés thanked doctor Muñoz for all his support and after hanging up the phone he cried just like a little baby.

After this, Andrés had to spend three weeks fully recovering. During this time, he was looked after like a child does when he gets sick. His mother would cook any dish he could think of. His father would come home early from work so that they could watch a film together or to simply lie in bed with him as they both enjoyed a good book. At the beginning of this recovery process his sister would visit him as often as she could until she started getting closer to delivering her baby. But she still phoned him every day to check on him.

It was during this healing process that Andrés also changed his literary taste in a radical manner. He was now reading about the state of the world economy and the financial markets, but also about the lives of many saints and other world figures that had devoted their lives to living a selfless life. He was aware he needed to be inspired by people like this to be able to keep up with the promise he had made to himself.

He was impressed by the life of *Santa Teresa de Jesús* because of her detachment —just like many other inspiring saints— who had devoted their lives to God. All of her life was used to serving others despite living long ill periods. Regardless of this, she faithfully stuck to her own Perfect Plan. Andrés was greatly impressed by a phrase of hers which read: "the greatest fortune is to possess nothing".

Andrés didn't want to compete with *Santa Teresa de Jesús* and leave all of his wealth behind and become a monk just like the main character of a heroic film. However, he was now aware that he had to let the voice of his heart guide him regardless of how illogic or irrational it seemed to his mind.

He had experienced how listening to his heart was a difficult task, but if he wanted to live committed to becoming a more transcendental human being then this was his only way to achieve it. And this wasn't an easy task.

There were many times when he just wanted to go back to be the old Andrés, but once he reflected on what this involved, he always found emptiness being the outcome which awaited him. Andrés was now fully conscious that living his life driven by the desire of money or status was not an option for him anymore.

The first weekend after doctor Muñoz told him he could start living his life normally, he decided to visit *don* Constantino's family in *El Diamante* just like he had promised he would. This time his parents came with him. On this occasion he got there with a 4X4 truck which would take them all the way to this community.

Once they got to the community, Pedrito noticed his *Jupiterian* friend was arriving and started running towards him as fast as he could. They embraced each other in a strong hug. That afternoon *don* Constantino's family and the de La Vega family shared a meal together. *Doña* Rosa prepared a delicious *caldo de gallina* as having Andrés and his family there was a magnificent event! Everyone thoroughly enjoyed the *caldo de gallina* and more importantly, the company.

Before saying goodbye, *don* Constantino walked with Andrés to the viewpoint as they had done a few months back, and told him:

—I'm very proud of you, Andrés. Now your eyes reflect love and generosity. Never forget that aiming to become a better person is a daily effort and God will never leave you alone, not even if you make huge mistakes or if you get away from Him for some time. Remember your heart will always be the sole guide of your life as it'll take you to the place you are meant to be.

This visit to *El Diamante* allowed a recovered Andrés —both physically and spiritually— to plan his future plans. This process took a few weeks of reflection. The question Andrés asked himself every morning as he woke up was: "what will I do with my life now?"

He was aware any decision he took would drive him out of his comfort zone but he trusted it would be the best decision he could take. The first thing he did was to call Richard Stephens in London and tell him he was resigning from his post. He thanked him for all he had done for him, and without giving too many details —as Andrés knew he wasn't going to be able to completely understand him— told him that as a result of the operation he had realised his priorities in life were not related to work only and that he wanted to make some radical changes in his life.

When Andrés told him this, Richard offered him to double his salary and to remain in *London* if that's what he wanted. At that moment, money was the last thing on Andrés' mind so he declined his offer. He was confident that moment he had enough money to live without worrying for a good period of time. As Andrés hung up the phone, he felt completely liberated and free. Even though his professional future was uncertain, he felt happy to have broken a chain which had driven him to perdition.

The same day he called Richard, *doña* Margarita received a call from Mariela saying they were heading to the hospital as her water had broken. The birth of little Felipe brought more joy to this family which was now starting to appreciate the beauty of simple blessings in their daily lives after having suffered a long period of pain.

Andrés started enjoying his role as an uncle. He was also happy to take care of his sister, of getting to know his brother-in-law better and to share the happiness his parents were experiencing for becoming grandparents for the first time. Andrés, who wasn't keen on being around children, learned to change Felipe's nappies, bathed him and fed him whenever he required. This man who once took a child in his hands as if he was a garbage bag was now able to show love to a little creature.

He was feeling happier as the days passed by, but the memory of

Marie still saddened him. She had replied to the email he wrote the day before the surgery. In the email she told him she had cried after reading his letter and that she would have given anything to be next to him. She also thanked him for his sincere apologies and words of admiration but said that the most important thing was for him to recover. She ended the email telling him he could count with her at all times.

Andrés didn't get to read this email until a week after the surgery. Andrés replied back to her and without any planning this turned into a daily practice of writing back and forth to each other. Andrés opened up his feelings with every email he wrote to her. She was a bit more careful with what she wrote —as she didn't want to get hurt again— but thoroughly enjoyed reading about this new Andrés who wasn't afraid of expressing his feelings and who was now enjoying some of the simple things in life.

A few weeks after little Felipe's birth, Andrés sent Marie a picture of him with his nephew through the post. When she opened up the envelope and saw this nice surprise from Andrés, she felt tenderness to see this man —who she had loved with all her heart— holding a baby in his arms. She wrote him one day that she was eager to see him again. Andrés, without hesitating, emailed her back saying he was planning to fly to London in a couple of months to sort out his things there —even if he hadn't considered flying there yet— and that he'd be happy to meet up for a coffee with her. Marie once again responded and said that she would love to share a cup of coffee with him.

Christmas and New Year's Eve passed and they stopped writing to each other for a while as Marie was busy with work and he was busy taking care of his nephew.

A sunny Thursday afternoon in early February, Andrés decided to buy a ticket to London leaving on the next day. His heart told him to do so and he embraced it. With no agenda or without thinking things through   —knowing that he could get his heart broken— he decided to fly back to London town.

He wrote an email to Marie and told her he was flying there and that he wanted to meet up with her in the café —which they both knew— on Portobello Road on Saturday at five in the afternoon. She immediately replied back saying that she was going to be there. And just like that, Andrés flew to London because he wanted to see the woman of his life.

He told his parents he was simply going to travel to arrange some of his personal things; but everyone knew that the sole reason for going there was to see this woman he was in love with. Everyone in his family felt happy for him.

His plan was to leave Guatemala on a Friday morning and land in Heathrow by Friday night. When he arrived he'd take a cab to his flat and on Saturday he would meet up with Marie. He didn't want to plan what could happen next. His mother drove him to the airport and as they were saying goodbye, she said:

—Please let me know when you come back so I can come and pick you up —and smiling she continued —. And if she comes with you, I wouldn't be bothered at all.

—I hope that's what happens, mom —said Andrés giving her a big kiss on her forehead.

Just as he had planned, Andrés landed in London by night and went straight to his flat which was a complete mess. The mixture of the jet lag and nerves didn't let him sleep so he made the best use of his time by cleaning up the mess in his flat and hoping that this would make time fly.

The day Andrés had dreamt for a long time had finally arrived. He was waiting to see the woman he loved. Marie rushed through the main door of this tiny café as she knew she was late. Andrés' heart started racing when he saw her. She was looking for him because she didn't see him at first. Andrés —feeling very nervous— raised his hand to show her where he was.

When Marie got closer to the table, Andrés couldn't control himself any longer and he stood up from the chair, and wrapped his arms around her. She felt his heart beating and he felt hers. They remained like that without saying a word, without thinking about the outside world and without caring what other people might think of them.

Andrés kept his eyes shut as he just wanted to be able to enjoy every second he was close to Marie. There was no need for words or a kiss to confirm that Marie was the woman of his life. He didn't want to let her go ever again. He wanted to be her life partner and make her happy.

They finally sat down, ordered a cup of coffee and chatted for hours. Andrés knew this wasn't going to be an easy task, but he was sure he wanted to show this woman, who had taught him what true love was, that he was committed and ready to devote his life to love her and to walk a path together.

ABOUT THE AUTHOR

Fernando Grajeda is a Guatemalan author who enjoys being a citizen of the world. He has a degree in Economics and Finance from London Metropolitan University but has found in writing a platform which allows him to express and share his feelings and emotions with readers around the globe. He is a strong believer in the principle that we can all be the change we wish to see in the world and he aims to achieve this through his writings. This book is a self-translation of his first published novel called *"Un plan... sencillamente perfecto"* (Eride Ediciones, Madrid, 2012). More recently he published a second book in Spanish called *"Una vida sin hubiera"* (Eride Ediciones, Madrid, 2014). Fernando also volunteers as an article journalist with www.ServiceSpace.org

Made in the USA
Charleston, SC
01 September 2014